BOY FRIENDS

BOY FRIENDS

KAI SPELLMEIER

BLOOMSBURY
LONDON OXFORD NEW YORK NEW DELHI SYDNEY

BLOOMSBURY YA
Bloomsbury Publishing Plc
50 Bedford Square, London WC1B 3DP, UK
Bloomsbury Publishing Ireland Limited
29 Earlsfort Terrace, Dublin 2, D02 AY28, Ireland

First published in Great Britain in 2026 by Bloomsbury Publishing Plc

A catalogue record for this book is available from the British Library

ISBN: PB: 978-1-5266-9354-9; eBook: 978-1-5266-9685-4

2 4 6 8 10 9 7 5 3 1

Typeset by Six Red Marbles India
Printed and bound in Great Britain by Clays Ltd, Elcograf S.p.A.

Ben,
asking from boyfriend to boyfriend:
will you marry me?

‘To burn with desire and keep quiet about it is the greatest punishment we can bring on ourselves.’

Federico García Lorca, *Blood Wedding* (1932)

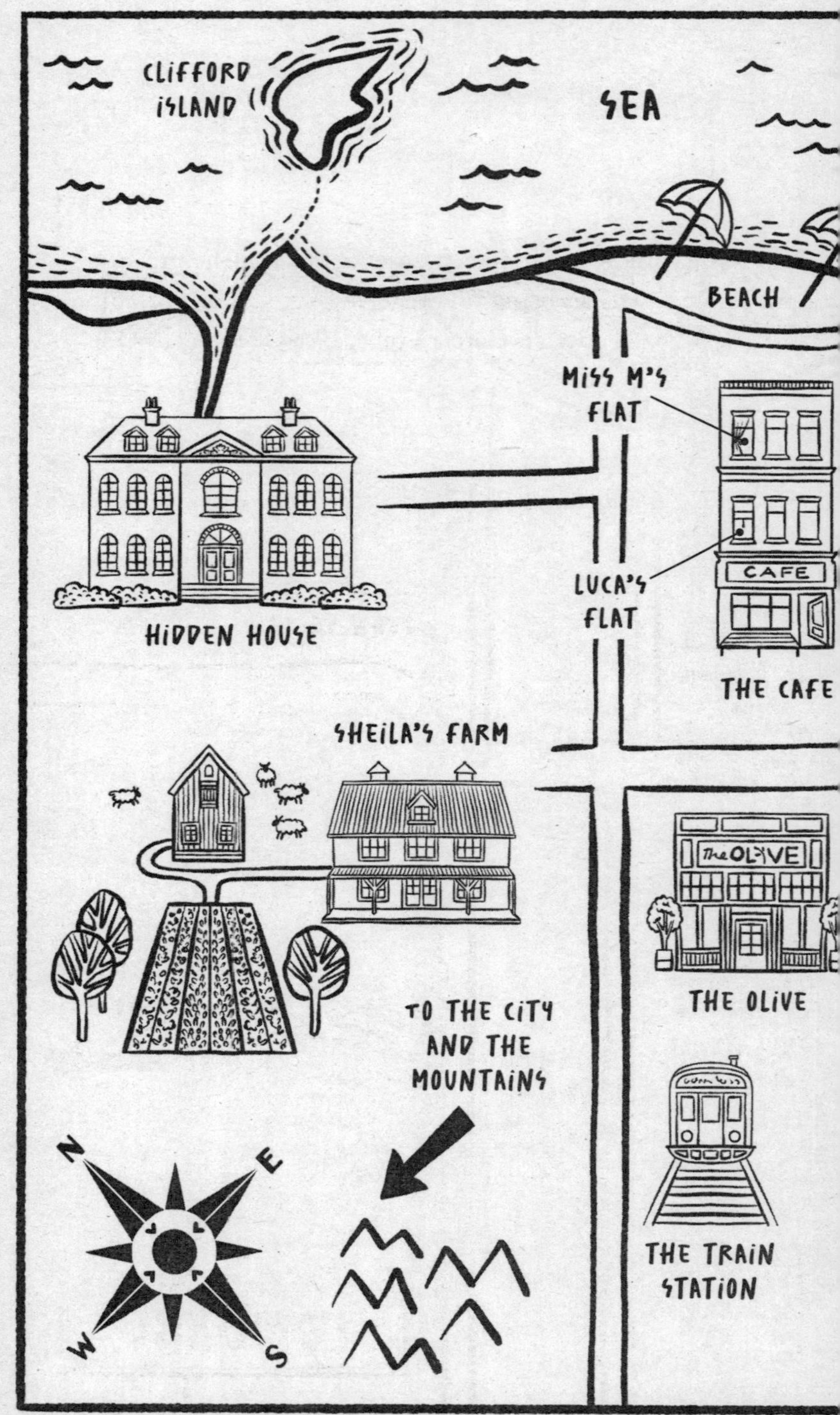
CLIFFORD ISLAND
SEA
BEACH
MISS M'S FLAT
HIDDEN HOUSE
CAFE
LUCA'S FLAT
THE CAFE
SHEILA'S FARM
The OLIVE
THE OLIVE
TO THE CITY AND THE MOUNTAINS
N
E
W
S
THE TRAIN STATION

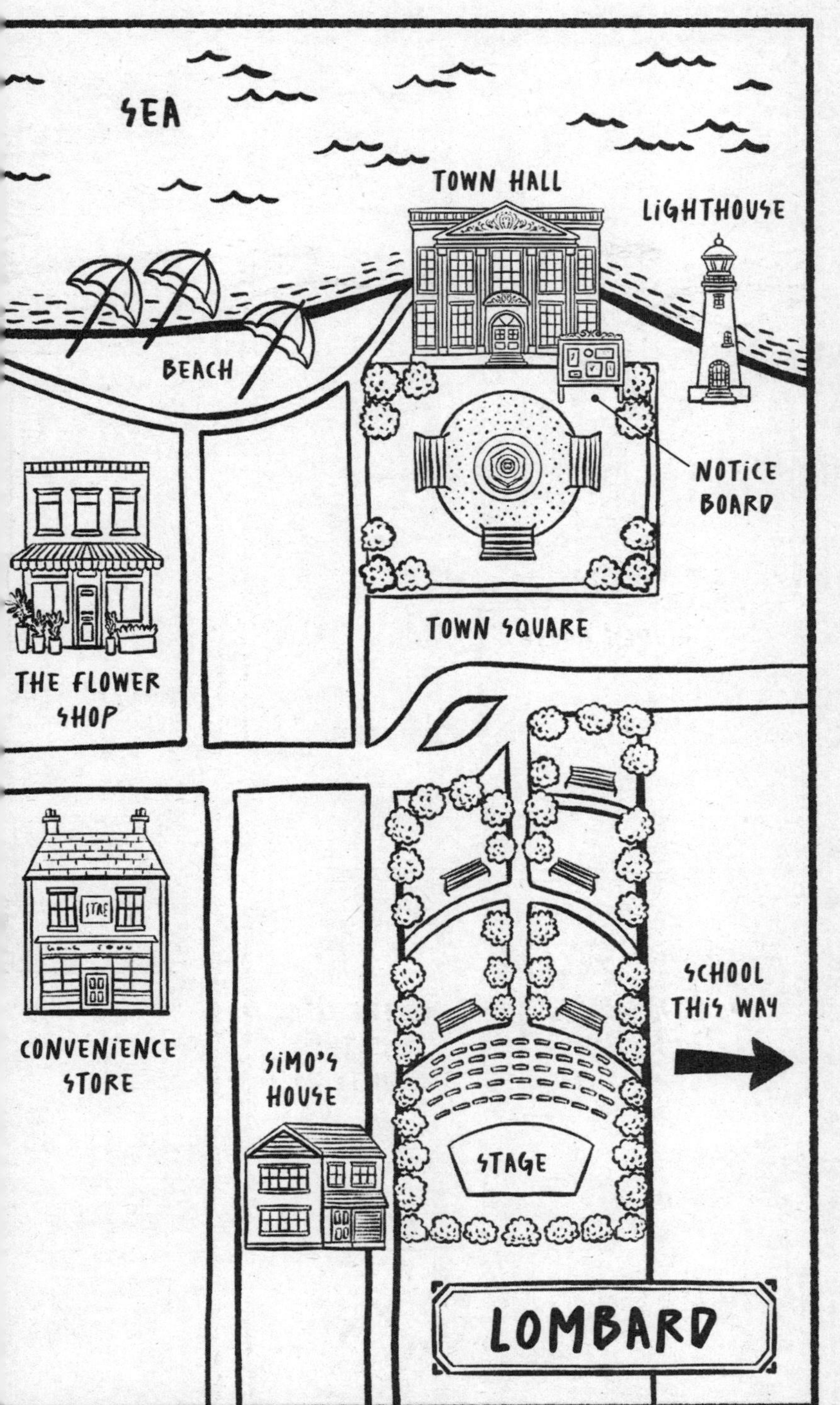
SEA
TOWN HALL
LIGHTHOUSE
BEACH
NOTICE BOARD
THE FLOWER SHOP
TOWN SQUARE
CONVENIENCE STORE
SIMO'S HOUSE
SCHOOL THIS WAY
STAGE
LOMBARD

PROLOGUE

It's twelve minutes past five on a Sunday morning, when I realise I'm in love with Simo Lorca. The thought that I love my best friend arrives fully formed in my head, like it's always been there. A piece of knowledge I've held for so long, yet always chosen to ignore. There's no denying it. I am in love with him. And suddenly the truth isn't scary at all. It's just fact.

Next to me on the sofa, Simo sighs in his sleep. His warmth seeps into my skin, his breath the only sound. We're sprawled out on the L-shaped couch, my legs facing one wall, his legs another; our heads meet in the middle. From where I lie propped up on a bunch of cushions, my gaze falls across his sleeping form.

His chest lifts and breath escapes through his parted lips. And maybe it's the first rays of the rising sun that press against the curtains and fill the lounge with a cool glow, or it's ten years of soaking up his features, but Simo's lips are what a Renaissance painter's wet dreams are made of. The bottom lip is full and soft, while the upper lip is two sharp lines arcing into a Cupid's bow.

I have never allowed myself to think about kissing

them. To imagine their weight on mine. That's asking for heartbreak, and I don't have a single masochistic bone in my body. But in the early morning, with the world still caught in a dream and Simo dreaming next to me, I see clearly. For the first time, loving him comes easy.

Even in his sleep, Simo remains calm and put together. He rests on his back, duvet tucked in, no slobber in the corner of his mouth, his hair perfectly tousled. His lashes form two dark curves against the rise of his cheeks, and I almost – almost – reach out to trace them. The half-light softens his edges, steals his imperfections. I miss the pockmarks on his temples, even though they make him feel self-conscious. I like the spattering of scars on his skin, though I have never told him this. In my eyes, they make him even more beautiful. The vein above his eyebrow has faded into shadow too, the one that appears whenever he's deep in thought, or when he gets annoyed with me. Sometimes I provoke him just to see it pop.

He doesn't stir when I pull the TV remote out from under his shoulder, careful not to disturb his dreams. We stayed up late, celebrating his birthday, only for midnight to strike and mine to begin. We were born on consecutive days, hours apart. We always spend our birthdays together, as they blend into each other, making sure we remain the exact same age.

With a deep breath, I sink back into the sofa. My body grows heavy and my eyes flutter shut.

I know that when I wake up again, this moment of clarity will appear to me like a dream. I'll turn to him, seconds away from telling him every fuzzy detail I recall – *Simo, I had the strangest dream; I was in love with you, would you believe it?* – but I'll stay silent. Because I'm not ready to say it in bright daylight. So right now, in this moment with him close to me, I savour the peace. I am filled by the knowledge that I love the boy lying next to me. With one heavy blink, consciousness slips away. The last thing I see is the shape of him filling my vision, following me into slumber.

SUMMER

CHAPTER 1 – LUCA

September is a controversial month. Nobody questions August's summer status, and October annually turns into a cult-like festival where the average person obsesses over knit jumpers and pumpkin spice. But September remains stuck in an identity crisis so severe that even the Christmas crowd tries to claim it through the strategic distribution of chocolate Santas. When I was eleven, I started a petition to ban the sale of Christmas-related goods before November, but I only collected three signatures – Dad, Simo and Miss M – and had to admit defeat.

I make my way up to the second floor of our building, a mug in one hand filled to the brim with coffee – black, three sugars – minding every step I take in my sliders. Like every Monday, the lady of the house awaits my attendance. I can feel her impatience simmer before I've reached her door. I knock and walk into the flat, incense lingering in the air. She sits by the window, glancing out on to the street, like a queen observing her kingdom. Her curls are a deep silver, a stark contrast against her umber skin. She taps the tabletop, every finger adorned with rings. She's unchanged from how I remember her from when I was a toddler.

Loyalty and love make my chest swell, and as if she senses the shift, she turns. A grin splits her face.

'How dare you expose your toes to an old lady, and before I've had my coffee!'

I smirk back and set the mug down in front of her. Miss M opens her arms wide and wraps me into a hug, bony but strong. Then she orders me into a chair without releasing my hand. Her eyes fall on the necklace that rests on my chest, but she doesn't comment. It's a fine golden chain with a pearl pendant, shaped into a round disk no bigger than a thumbprint, its surface uneven, like crests on a wave. '*I know pearls are passé or something*,' Simo had said when it struck midnight and he'd placed the gift box in my hands, '*but I saw this and thought of you*.'

The memory, barely a day old, gives me goosebumps.

'Now, tell me about the bonfire last night. It all but smoked up my apartment!'

Miss M has a taste for dramatics. While it may be true that the wind carried wisps of bonfire smoke all the way up the street from the beach and through her top-floor window, I know she still welcomes every source that keeps her informed of the goings-on in town.

'It was perfect,' I say, and I mean it. It's one of my favourite birthday traditions. There's something magical about a fire by the sea. Flames tickling the sky as it turns purple. Stars popping up by the millions. Dad to my left, Simo to my right, as we hold sticks towards the flames, the dough wrapped around them gaining a golden crust within minutes. Then we slather the still-warm bread in sour cream and cheese and herbs and olives. The latter is a new development. I used to detest olives, but eating them feels very adult. It's what I like to think of as character growth.

I tell Miss M all this and she nods and hums, her eyes half closed. 'Paul shut the kiosk and joined us with ciders,' I tell her. 'Librarian Joni brought her dog and her guitar and had Dad choking on his food with some of her bawdier sea shanties. And even Simo's parents came by to say hi, though they didn't stick around.'

'Don't like sea shanties, do they?'

'Not exactly,' I say. Simo's parents are complicated, to say the least, but they have their reasons. 'You should have joined us, Miss M. We missed you.'

Miss M effectively adopted us when Dad showed up in Lombard one day, with my heavily pregnant mum and a broken-down car. Seventeen years later, Miss M is the most constant person in my life, apart from Dad. And Simo, though Miss M has been around for longer. She is the only grandparent I have ever had.

Miss M gently presses the palm of my hand. 'I'm not one for beach outings. I prefer the comfort of my home to any other place on earth, you know that.'

I also know she hasn't left her flat in months. I know she's happy in her own home. She loves few things more than people flocking to her doorstep like carrier pigeons to feed her gossip. When I was a child, she used to be the epicentre of Lombard social life, but after a couple of ugly falls, she withdrew to her flat. Now she observes everything in the town below her from her perch up high.

'And what about my favourite explorer? My very own Jane Goodall?'

She always asks this question, but I rarely have anything new to tell her. 'Mum is Mum. She's probably crouching in the dirt right now with a pair of binoculars, watching a rare bird pick a worm out of the mud.'

Miss M grunts, satisfied by the image I've drawn.

'She says she'll be back in the country when I turn eighteen next summer.' Mum is often the first person I speak to on my birthday. But sometimes, like last night, Simo beats her to it. He's usually right there when Mum phones from half a planet away.

'She can't miss her baby becoming a man,' Miss M confirms.

I nod, but then I think, Mum's missing so many other things. She tries to keep up and makes me tell her everything that's going on in my honestly not that exciting life. But it means she only hears about things after they've happened, rather than being a part of them. I don't think she regrets moving away, but I can tell that she misses Lombard – and Dad and me – more than she lets on.

'School's calling,' I tell Miss M, then let go of her hand.

'Ah, a new year. Are you excited, Luca?'

I shrug. 'Just like every other year, isn't it?' Change means chaos, and I like the way things are.

'We'll see,' says Miss M with the authority of someone decades older than me. 'Don't forget to send me today's message on the noticeboard!' she calls in lieu of a goodbye.

'I'd never forget!' I shout back, the familiar words rolling off my tongue before the door to her flat falls shut behind me.

We do this every Monday morning; I bring her coffee

and updates from the cafe, and she gets to inquire about my life and give me advice that I generally ignore. In my defence, Miss M gives awful advice for someone so old. I'm not going to start eating liquorice because it allegedly 'makes ashy elbows moist again'. Body lotion exists for a reason, and besides, liquorice is rank.

I descend the stairs to the first floor, where I've lived all my life. I change into more sensible footwear, grab my school bag from my room and make my way down to the cafe on the ground floor. There's chatter in the air and the smell of freshly ground coffee.

'Miss M all good?' Dad asks from behind the counter, busily filling pots of tea with steaming hot water.

'Chirpy as ever,' I respond. I grab a sourdough sandwich and a chocolate cookie, the latter earning me a stern look. Dad disapproves of sweets for breakfast but doesn't get the chance to tell me off. A group of half a dozen tourists enter the already crammed place, and so I use the opportunity to escape.

Out on the street, I'm hit by a wave of salty air and the familiar cries of seagulls as they circle the town from above. A quick jog takes me to the promenade. The ocean glimmers silver in the sunlight, as I go to greet Paul in his kiosk. Instead of waving back, Paul turns towards the radio and frantically begins working its buttons. I don't think much of his strange behaviour, until a pack of primary-school kids walking the other way spots me and instantly stops chatting. They giggle as I pass, and I make sure that I'm zipped up. I go to check if there's something on my face with my phone camera and see several missed calls from Simo. I hit the call button.

The boulevard begins to slope up, taking me above sea level. If you pluck Piccadilly Circus out of London, then swap the mega-screens for a big slab of wood fixed between two poles and stick the whole thing bang on the coast of our little town, you basically get Lombard town square. It's way cuter though, I think as I step on to the cobbled square from one side, with the town hall and a lighthouse offering shelter from the sea wind and rowan trees dotted all around, their branches loaded with red berries.

'Have you seen it?' Simo says, picking up after just one ring.

'Seen what?'

'You haven't seen it.' His voice is oddly toneless. 'Where are you?'

'Almost at the noticeboard,' I reply, rounding the square so I can read the announcement.

The thing about the noticeboard is that its message changes weekly. Most of the time, it'll be birthday wishes for residents reaching a significant age, or a massive storm warning, or holiday greetings. But now and then we get something hilarious or unexpectedly raunchy, like the time when Linda, the mailwoman, announced a split from her husband after she caught him cheating with the pet-shop owner. For a week, all of Lombard saw the words *HARRY HICKS SLEEPS WITH FLEAS* blasted across the town square. Suffice it to say that nobody's seen Harry since, and the pet shop shut down a few weeks later.

Heloise, the mayor's right hand, is watering the plants in front of the lighthouse, but freezes when she sees me, as if

I caught her in the middle of committing a crime. 'Why is everyone acting so weird today?'

'Luca, I need you to—'

'Wait,' I interrupt Simo. 'Let me take a picture of the message and send it to Miss M.'

I open my phone's camera, stride towards the noticeboard – and stop short. My heart drops out of my chest and my phone clatters to the ground. I don't hear it fall, don't hear Simo calling my name. Paralysed, I stare up at the board, each letter the size of a loaf of bread.

The words are absolutely, terrifyingly impossible to miss.

There in black and white, my best-hidden feelings turned inside out for all the world to see.

SIMO AND LUCA ARE
IN LOVE

'I ship it!'

'Congrats, you guys!'

'This is so cute I could die!'

Students I've never even spoken to shout at me from across the school hallway. Others pat my back, and a group of guys holler and clap in a weirdly non-offensive way. One girl shrieks so loudly I almost run into a locker to escape her, and I swear there are tears in her eyes.

I walked to school in a state of shock, skipped registration by hiding behind the bike shed in a state of shock, then sat through design and technology in a state of shock. So far, I've successfully avoided Simo; avoided thinking about what this means for him, for me, for us. But as I'm headed to English, I know he'll be there. We'll be sharing a table for the next two hours. I've never been so scared to face him. Usually his presence fills me with a sense of calm that no other person can induce, but today just the thought of him has the opposite effect. I want to run.

It's like I'm experiencing my worst nightmare, the embarrassing sort, where you end up naked in front of your entire school. Except I'd prefer that humiliation to everyone knowing that I'm in love with Simo. To *Simo* knowing I'm in love with him. But I'm painfully awake and about to be sick in a school bin.

I stop in front of the classroom. I *could* run. If your gut tells you to do something, why would you ignore it? But the only thing worse than facing Simo would be to avoid him forever. Not just a logistical impossibility in a town this small, it would also, quite possibly, break my actual heart. So I do what I've been doing for the past ten years: pretend I'm not in love with my best friend. I've lied so well I even had myself fooled.

I try not to trip over my feet as I walk in and slide on to the chair next to him. I take a notebook out of my bag, a pen, a bottle of water that's as good as empty, a pack of tissues I don't need, anything to keep me busy. Simo doesn't interrupt, but I can feel his eyes bore into me. When there's nothing left in my bag I could possibly require, I send him a sideways glance.

Simo is looking right at me, and to everyone else he might appear mildly amused. But I can tell by the most gradual raise of his brows – his flawless, ever so sorrowful brows – and the stark vein between them, that he's annoyed. It's a look that topples my defences, which pretty much applies to every look he sends me. But in this awkward, excruciating mess we're in, I realise that I need him and that he needs me. I'm about to launch into an explanation, or an apology, just to say something, but I'm cut off before I get the chance.

Mrs Leppla enters with a stack of books and plonks them on her desk. 'Students, meet your required reading for the year.'

A choir of groans rises, and I want to join in. For the next two hours I'll be unable to focus on anything but Simo's presence beside me. I prepare for 120 minutes of intrusive thoughts, but when Simo shifts his weight, and our arms touch, my mind hushes. Despite everything, he never fails to have this effect on me. And, truth be told, there are far worse things to think about than Simo Lorca.

When class is over and the room empties, we stay in our seats, compelled by an unspoken agreement. I do my best to ignore the curious glances and all-but-quiet whispers around us, but I can't help squirming. Simo musters an unbothered expression, but the vein remains. The last student leaves the room, and we're alone.

Silence spreads. I don't want to prolong this any more, and so I square my shoulders and face him. The problem is, I can't put my thoughts into words, and for once it's not because the sight of his soft brown eyes makes me forget my own name. Though it's not helping either.

Simo also seems at a loss. He starts, then closes his mouth again. I watch him do this four times, his expression darkening. It'd be cute if I wasn't shaking in my trainers. At the fifth attempt, he succeeds.

'Someone told me we're their Bella and Edward, but less toxic.'

We stare at each other for several beats. I might break out in tears or panicked laughter, but my body can't decide which emotion to give into.

'Someone told me we're *almost* as cute as Nick and Charlie,' I say instead, trying to gauge his reaction.

'My psychology teacher said she'd like us cast in *Red, White & Royal Blue*.' Simo's face slips into a grimace and I make a gagging sound, and that's when we finally break. Simo wheezes, his entire body rocking with silent laughter. Tears pour down my face and I slide to the floor, unable to stay upright on my chair. This delirious episode lasts several minutes, until we have caught our breath again.

Simo's head appears beneath the table. His eyes are red-rimmed and when he speaks, it sounds as if he's caught a cold.

'You staying down there or … ?'

'I haven't decided. I'm not sure I can take more of this.' I wave towards the door and what lies beyond.

'OK, fine,' Simo replies and slips off his chair to join me on the floor. He sits cross-legged and gives me the look. The one that says, I've done my bit; now it's your turn.

He did break the tension. And I know it wasn't easy. Simo and I aren't exactly used to discussing my sexuality. In fact, we never talk about it. Not because he's narrow-minded – we wouldn't be best friends if he was – but because it's never come up. Because I've never brought it up. At first, I feared his reaction to my coming out, but as the years passed, I assumed he just knew. It's not exactly an open secret, it's just … open.

People say best friends talk about everything, but people are naive. We all have things we keep from even the closest people in our lives. Simo and I are no exception.

Still, thanks to him there's air in the room again. I'm equal parts grateful and relieved that we're still on speaking terms. That things might not be normal, obviously they're anything but, but at least we're here together. I prop myself up. We still have a problem, one the exact shape and size of the town noticeboard, and I'm still scared to address it. There's just no way around it.

'I don't …' I begin, but I'm unable to finish the sentence. 'I'm not sure … I'm not prepared for this situation.'

'One boat and we're both sitting in it,' Simo replies.

'We need to let people know that we're not … that it's not true.' My throat is dry as chalk as I force out the words. Simo holds my gaze, like he's searching for something in my expression. I tell myself to keep a straight face, to not feel any of the things I'm feeling – like the paralysing fear of getting caught in my lies and losing my friend.

After several heartbeats, he finally nods. 'And we need to find out who put it up there.'

The relief from a minute ago is gone. Because no one could possibly know. I've not told anyone about him. About Simo and the secret I'm so good at hiding, even from myself.

I shove it down deep. And most of the time, I don't think about the way he makes me feel. I don't keep a diary, and if I did, it certainly wouldn't mention Simo in a way that describes him as anything but my best friend.

'Any suspects?' I ask tensely, and receive a shake of his head. Simo doesn't feel the way I feel, so the blame is on me, that much is clear. I'm the one who slipped up and let my feelings show. I was too obvious, not careful enough.

People know that I'm gay. And they also know that Simo and I have been best friends since forever. What they don't know is that I'm particularly gay for Simo. Or at least they didn't until the noticeboard shouted it across town. Now I feel seen in the worst way. Everyone knows I like him more than a best friend would, and denying it is pointless. And yet, it's my only option.

'We have to ask the town council. They're in charge of the noticeboard,' Simo decides. He scrambles out from under the table and gets up. I follow his example, solely because I can't stay on the dirty school floor forever. Simo shoulders his bag with the expression of a man on a mission.

'Let's ask the town council,' I agree with a lump in my throat, wishing I could pretend this hadn't happened. Bury it and never mention it again.

Together we return to hallways filled with loud students. Some try to high-five us, some hum a wedding march. It's so over the top that I can't take them seriously, but there's a knot of dread in my stomach that won't let me relax. I can tell Simo is uncomfortable too. His steps are robotic, his shoulders stiff.

'Don't you think it's weird?' he mumbles in my direction.

‘Obviously I do. All of this is weird.’

‘No, I mean, why does it specifically say, “Simo and Luca are in love”? It could’ve said …’ He clears his throat and lowers his voice. ‘It could’ve said “Luca loves Simo” or “Simo loves Luca” or any other variation. It’s so specific.’

‘Well,’ I begin, trying to get my thoughts in order, ‘someone wants to –’ I almost say ‘expose’ but opt for something else – ‘to target us both. Make us uncomfortable. Make us act.’

‘Act how?’

I don’t have an answer to that. The last thing I know how to do is act. And so I take cover in my own head and hope for the best. That’s when I remember.

‘Shit,’ I say.

‘What?’ Simo asks.

‘I forgot to send Miss M the message on the noticeboard.’

CHAPTER 2 – SIMO

I have never felt more grateful for the emptiness of my home. Most times I find it suffocating, being here on my own, and so I escape to find Luca. Then again, even with my parents around, I also escape to find Luca. But today marks the worst Monday of all Mondays, so I drop my bag as soon as the front door slams behind me and collapse on to the staircase.

Mum has a teacher's conference, and Dad will be showcasing seaside homes to buyers with dreams of the sweet small-town life. I recommend staying far away if they want their business to remain private. Because sooner or later someone will take their laundry and hang it up in the town square.

I groan and press my palms against my eyelids. My mind is a maelstrom, relentlessly replaying the day's events. It started with a text from Louise – a picture of the town noticeboard plus an endless string of heart-eye emojis – and ended with a near-attempted break-in, when Luca and I stood in front of the town hall's firmly locked doors. Clearly neither Mayor Pickering nor Heloise wants to answer our questions.

Whenever one of us has had a shitty day at school, we hole up in Luca's room or slink away to Clifford Island and watch the light fade from the sky. But today I needed to be far away from anyone, including Luca. All day long I've been faking it; Simo on the outside, mess on the inside. Now I feel like there's nothing left of me. Just a Simo-shaped husk sprawled across a staircase.

It's a new feeling, and not one I like. Not the faking being myself thing; I can never fully shake that. When you've lost someone so close to you, a piece of yourself is lost too. You're never whole, but have to pretend to be, so as not to alienate people with your grief, or worse, earn their pity. What's new is that I don't want Luca around. He's the only one who makes me feel like my real self. He's never pushed me to talk about it, that lost piece that I don't have words for.

The message on the noticeboard hit me like a storm without the kindness of preceding thunder, entirely without warning. I was still floating on a cloud of summer memories from our time in Granada: the honey-sweet taste of sangria on my lips mixing with the aroma of Abuela's home-made empanadas, Luca's toes grazing the moss at the bottom of a centuries-old fountain, the city's heat pressing against my skin. But when the realisation struck that the whole town would read these words and think them true, the bliss I felt evaporated in an instant. For hours now the message has been stuck on loop in my head, a tuneless song that won't leave me alone.

SIMO AND LUCA ARE IN LOVE

I'm desperate for a run, just to calm my thoughts, but I can't leave the house for obvious reasons. Plus I haven't eaten. Couldn't get a thing down all day. I force myself up and into the kitchen, where I fill a bowl with honey puffs and milk. I stand while I eat – mechanically, without tasting the food – and watch the street out front.

We live on a tight lane of terraced houses that tourists like to call 'quaint' or 'a pain in the arse' depending on the number of times they've reversed up and down to find parking. Rows of stone cottages, front yards crowded with flower beds, ivy snaking up to the rooftops, the occasional gnome, and our house fits right in with its abundance of daisies.

Dad is obsessed with them. The thing about daisies is that they bloom pretty much all year. It should be a soothing thought, that there is beauty that never dies. But it's the opposite. Daisies last forever; you pick one, and another takes its place, like a botanical hydra. Human lives don't work that way. They're far more fragile.

Since the day we moved here, our garden hasn't been daisy-less once. You won't find a window in this house that doesn't look out on them. Seas of daisies, in varying colours. They're low maintenance, a little sun and water and they're good, though Dad doesn't make it look that way. Sometimes I think he spends more time with his flowers than with us, his family. It's silly to resent a plant, but I can't help thinking that those flowers are shameless attention-seekers.

Dad's battered Chevy appears on the street, and the milk in my stomach sours at the thought of facing him. I place the empty bowl in the sink, grab my school bag and disappear up into my room, where I sink on to my bed and grab a book off the nightstand. Tío Andrés handed it to me when he dropped us off at the airport at the end of our stay. Federico García Lorca, *Obras selectas*, it reads – selected works of Federico García Lorca. I told him my Spanish wasn't good enough to understand it, but Andrés laughed and took me by the shoulders.

'*Federico García Lorca is your brother and not just because you share a name*,' he had said. '*You're both sons of Granada. Your heart will know the meaning of his words, even if your head won't.*'

I didn't point out that I had been born in another city, in another country, more than a century later than Lorca the poet. Dad's side of the family, all born and bred in the Andalusian city of Granada, have a very different sense of the word 'family' than the one I've grown up with. Mum long ago lost touch with her parents, for reasons she has certainly never shared with me. And though I met her sisters once, I don't think a sole meeting at my brother's funeral counts as close family ties.

Dad, on the other hand, has several group chats with family members going, but because of work, and money, and Mum, we don't see much of them. She'd never admit it, but I suspect it's because Mum doesn't speak Spanish and feels uncomfortable around Dad's boisterous relatives. The only reason I got to go to Granada this summer is because Abuela guilt-tripped Dad into sending me, by painting dramatic scenes of her own death without being able to embrace her faraway grandson one last time. I didn't mind my parents staying behind, because I got a holiday with Luca out of it. The flights were early birthday gifts.

It was overwhelming in the best way, when the family I barely remembered took me into their midst, Luca too, and treated us like they'd known us all our lives. And when Tío Andrés handed me the poetry book, I thanked him and savoured his words.

I pull a slim notebook from beneath my pillow, because that's where secrets are meant to be kept. It's no bigger than my hand, with a mud-brown cover, thick pages and a severely broken spine. It holds my thoughts, fragmented and unfiltered as they come. When I say 'thoughts', I mean flashes of memories or dreams I don't want to forget, quotes from *Obras selectas* and *A Monster Calls.* Words like lost puzzle pieces that will never fit to make a poem. It's messy feelings turned into messy scribbles where words become too rigid to hold them. It's ~~SIMO AND LUCA ARE IN LOVE~~ crossed out so many times it resembles a ragged scar.

It's not a new thought, but always a perplexing one, the possibility that Luca could be in love with me. When you're a boy, and your best friend likes boys, it's not outside the realm of possibility. As if, out of all the boys in the world to fall for, Luca would pick me. As if I wouldn't notice if he suddenly started treating me differently. But he's still the same loyal and genuine boy I met at seven years old.

'Simo?' Dad calls from downstairs, his voice muffled by the closed door. I don't respond, and soon I hear his heavy steps rising to the first floor. The closer he comes, the bigger the urge to jump out of the window. Instead, all I do is slide the notebook beneath the pillow and pick up Lorca's poems again. He knocks twice, and when I remain silent, he sticks his head in. 'Ah, lost in a book, are you?'

Dad is the oldest of his siblings, and though he shares Andrés' dark beard, his cheeks are fuller, and his skin shows lines far too deep for someone in his forties. But I know what grief does to a person, and I wonder if I'll inherit the grey beard or the lines, or both.

I can't detect anything in his eyes that says he knows about the noticeboard. But if he only speaks to his siblings in another country and newcomers looking for seaside homes, he might not know.

'Yes, sorry, lost in a book,' I say.

'That's OK, Simo. Just don't forget your homework, yes?'

I never forget my homework. But that doesn't stop him from reminding me every day. He means well; after all, even though Mum is the primary-school teacher, he's the one who has always helped me at school.

'No Luca today?' he asks, catching me off guard.

'I – no. Maybe later.'

'OK, just let me know when you leave. I'll be in the garden.'

I'm certain he doesn't know. It's not like he'd confront me. He'd take the opposite approach, avoiding a conversation until the situation either resolves itself or is overshadowed by a more urgent problem that must itself be ignored.

I see the way my parents treat Luca. They're polite, but they use this politeness to keep him at a distance. They wouldn't utter a bad word about my best friend, but that doesn't mean they don't hold prejudice against him – and his dad. It's like they suddenly forget to act like normal people whenever they come face to face with someone who's gay. I'm not sure if it's because they're scared they'll say the wrong thing or whether they disagree with homosexuality as a whole. And I don't know that I want to find out.

The thought stirs something in me, a slow burning in my gut that makes me feel fiercely protective of Luca, despite everything that's going on. I'm not my parents. I would never judge a person because of who they are.

I take out my phone and open the chat with him. A second later, I lock the screen, drop the phone in my lap, only to sigh and reopen it. My fingers hover inches from the keyboard, caught between the desire to pull Luca close and to push him away. That's when the call comes in. The vibration sinks into my bones, shakes me out of my stupor. I pick up on the second ring.

'I know where they'll leave us alone.' Luca's voice in my ear fills me with relief.

'The island?'

'Better. Meet me in five? Bring your bike.'

I race past the coffee shop without stopping. It takes Luca only seconds to pull up next to me. We head up Main Street, past the last bus stop in town, before we're surrounded by fields of green and gold. I have an inkling where we're going, but for now I want to drink up the freedom that comes with leaving Lombard.

Luca's shirt flutters in the breeze, melds itself to his ribcage. The wind plays with the pearl pendant I gave him, like it wants to steal it off his body, but the chain holds fast. We ride in silence, and neither the cows nor the sheep grazing in the fields pay us any attention. Now that I'm gaining distance, it's almost possible to believe that today didn't happen. That's how absurd this whole scenario feels.

We take a turn on to a gravel path and arrive at a huddle of barns nestled around a well. Anton, the town mascot, is grazing in his paddock and watches us as we stack the bikes against a wall. He's a Highland bull, with a thick orange coat, and a crown of two lopsided horns, one short and thick, the other curving upwards. For some reason he was abandoned by his herd, so the town adopted him.

We skip past the antiques shop and enter a building in the shadow of an oak tree. In an instant, I'm enveloped by the scent of paper and dust. I meet Luca's gaze, his eyes so blue they glow in the half-light, and a smile lifts my face. He knows me better than I know myself. Knows what I need when I don't.

'I brought the new reading list,' Luca says, and unfolds it.

'I've memorised it,' I tell him.

'Of course you have.'

I make my way deeper into the bookshop. It's three floors, divided into fiction and non-fiction only, and organised by surname. Mostly. Random stacks are found in almost every corner, piled beneath armchairs, crammed on the top of the shelves and scraping the ceiling.

Sheila, the owner of the farm and its shops, only stocks second-hand books, but she'll order in new copies where there are gaps. I swiftly track down Shakespeare and Austen, but it takes me longer to unearth the translated works and poetry collections. Not that I mind. I pick up random books and check for handwritten dedications or forgotten bookmarks. If they grab my attention, make me wonder about the people who left a part of themselves imprinted on the pages, I take them home, even copy them into my notebook. They're like stories within stories, these traces of people who once held the book I'm holding now. Dreaming up strangers' lives keeps me from thinking about my own.

I don't know how much time passes, but when I emerge again, Luca is folded into a wicker chair with a cat in his lap, both of them dozing. I don't make myself known, instead I take the moment to look at him. At first glance, he seems at ease, deep breaths stretching his shirt as his chest expands, front teeth peeking through the gap of his lips. I don't let my attention linger there and soon discover the telltale sign of stress: the raw edges of his nails, bitten down to the flesh. If it hurts me to see it, it must hurt him twice as much.

I almost wake him to tell him that I love him, right there and then. I want it to be a casual affirmation, a promise that I'll always have his back. I see other guys do it, exchange *I-love-you-bros!* like the most natural of goodbyes in the school car park. But it wouldn't land right, the meaning twisted by the insinuation on the noticeboard. Now it's a three-word landmine at the base of our friendship. It makes me regret that I've never said it before. It makes me wonder why I never did.

Luca opens his eyes, halfway at first, then they widen with astonishment.

'That's … a lot of books, Simo.'

I look down at the stack in my arms. 'I got copies for you too.'

'I don't need any.'

'Yes, you do.'

'It's not like I'm going to read them.'

'You'll have to if you plan to pass English.'

'You know I'm not going to open these.'

Luca has plenty of flaws, but this aversion to books is surely his biggest. My attempts at converting him have been fruitless, but I'm determined. Constant dripping wears the stone and all that.

'You can just tell me the plot.'

'Fat chance.'

'Fine, I'll get the audiobooks.'

'You'll have to have copies for class. To quote passages for essays, to underline stuff.'

'I can borrow yours.'

'And copy the notes I write in the margins? No, you can't.'

'Then I'll get them from the library. I don't understand why you need to buy them all when you could borrow them.'

This isn't the first time we're having this debate. Its familiarity fills me with the hope that nothing's changed, that we're still the same people we were before the noticeboard.

'I hate having to return books. I can't enjoy them with a deadline,' I tell him. I need to be able to mark them or open them at any given point to reread favourite passages.

I glance at the door and realise that it's started to rain. That in itself isn't a rarity. You learn to expect the weather's ever-changing moods when living on the coast. The world outside is blurry, daylight dimmed by clouds. Only now do I hear the lazy patter of a thousand little drops hitting the roof. It's my favourite sound in the world. I think of our bikes getting wet, of my parents at home.

'Let's stay for a bit,' Luca says, eyes half closed again. 'You can start reading now. And tell me what happens.'

I huff but set the books down and give the cat in Luca's lap a good back rub. Then I make myself comfortable on the floor by Luca's chair with my back against the shelves. The air in the shop remains warm, and all I hear is the rain and the cat's gentle purr. I open *Twelfth Night*, but only get past the list of characters before Luca speaks up.

'I'd read your book,' he says, his voice low. 'If you wrote one, I mean. I'd read it.'

CHAPTER 3 – LUCA

Dad hands me a mop and points to the bucket of steaming water on the shop floor. The sunlight that spills into the room turns his dark hair to amber and sets his irises alight. Sometimes I wish I looked more like him, less gangly more manly. People never believe that we're father and son when they first find out. Though that might just be the small age gap.

I start sweeping the floor of all the dirt that customers traipsed into the cafe. I've done this a million times and I'm still amazed by how quickly the water turns to grey soup. Humans are messy, that much I've learned from cleaning a cafe floor day after day.

'When you're done, you can order in food. Your pick.'

I perk up. Dad never lets me order takeout. He says stuff like, 'We literally own a diner,' and, 'I can cook you anything,' and, 'Don't you like my cooking?' which is completely beside the point. It's the indulgence that counts. It doesn't matter what you order; the fact that it's brought to your doorstep and you don't have to clean any pots makes it special.

'Just don't order burgers, please. Or chips. Might as well order off our menu.'

'So it's not my pick,' I retort. Dad sends me a look that tells me not to test him when he's being generous, and I quickly get to finishing the floors.

All week long, I've avoided the cafe. Even if nobody comes up to me wanting to discuss the noticeboard, I see the curiosity in their faces. It's a curse, growing up in a small town where everyone knows you and thinks they're entitled to meddle and ask questions.

Only Dad has been giving me space. 'You know where to find me if you want to talk,' he said on the first day, and left it at that. Which is why I've barely left my room. It's amazing how many seasons of *Elite* you can watch if you put your mind to it. But I know I'm not off the hook forever. Now that I think about it, I'm pretty sure the whole takeaway offer is a strategy to get me talking. So I best make it the most indulgent vegetarian food order I can.

Half an hour later, Dad and I sit on the Persian-blue couch in our lounge. The air smells of honey and garlic, chilli and lime. A tower of boxes waits on the coffee table while we select a film.

'How about that Italian comedy with the gay brothers who own a pasta business?' Dad suggests.

'Not while eating pad thai. How about the one with the miners at gay Pride?' I suggest.

'I don't want to be sobbing into my food, thanks. How about the gay romance with the farm and the actor with the stick-out ears?'

'*God's Own Country* it is,' I say, finding the film and pressing play.

I seriously love hanging out with Dad. I know not every

teenager wants to spend time with their parents, but if there was such a thing as a Dad Award, mine would win it, and I'm not ashamed to boast. It might be the fact that he was a teen dad. Or that he's gay, and I'm gay, and that bond is special. With Mum so far away, it's me and Dad against the world. Though, in fairness, the world has given me little reason to fight it so far.

'Don't get me wrong, this is great, but I wish this town had more than three fish-and-chip shops and one Thai place to pick from. I'd give a lot for a good pizza.' Dad full-on munches and talks at the same time, something he'd never do with anyone else present, except maybe Simo. But right now, I'm glad Simo isn't here, even if I feel like a bad friend for thinking it. If he was, we would not be watching a film in which two men make out.

I realised something this week. Bingeing TV shows only takes up so much of your brain power, which means the rest has a lot of time to think. I'm not sure I like the conclusion I came to, but I can't ignore it: I always thought I was fully myself around Simo. No barriers or filters to hold me back. But I censor what I say around him all the time. How weird is it, that I can talk about cute guys with my dad but not my best friend? Around Simo, I avoid mentioning my sexuality so much that I'm scared I lose a piece of myself. And now, after the noticeboard, I don't know how to be all of me with him. I don't want Simo questioning my feelings, can't bear to have him find out there's stuff I'm holding back. It never felt painful until I started thinking about it.

A flying chopstick hits my head and I meet Dad's eyes.

'I've asked you three times if you wanted to swap your

spring rolls for my green curry, but you are miles away. Can't believe Gheorghe isn't working his magic on you.' He nods to the dark-haired love interest with the sorrowful gaze, not unlike Simo's.

'Yes, curry, please,' I say, and hand over my food.

Instead of returning to the film, Dad keeps his attention on me.

'Luca,' he says.

'Maz,' I reply, and I know we've reached the point where We Talk. Dad thinks voicing your fears makes them smaller, but I don't trust the science behind that.

'I'm worried about you.'

Four little words and I already want to fall apart. 'I'd rather not talk about it,' I say, and sound like I have a cold. I hate my voice for betraying me like that.

'And I get that. But it's my job to check in with you now and then. Just following the steps in the parent manual here.' He sets his food down before lowering the film's volume. I keep my focus on the screen, where the two actors are pulling a lamb out of its mother's womb. When I don't respond, he speaks up again. 'You can talk to Miss M instead, if that's what you want.'

That gets my attention. 'What did you tell her?'

'Nothing she doesn't already know. But you know how she is.'

She's relentless. She'd offer useless advice until it's coming out of my ears.

'Luca ...' Dad starts, and scoots closer. He wraps me in a hug, and because it's physically impossible to resist his hugs, I give in. Even though I'm no less of a mess, I instantly feel better. 'I don't want you to shut yourself off. Don't push away the people you care about. Talk to me. And talk to Simo. Don't let a little gossip ruin your friendship. You boys need to stick together.'

'OK,' I say after a while, once I'm sure I'm not going to cry. 'But I want to point out that it's not "a little gossip". It's a ton of gossip. It almost couldn't be more gossip.'

Dad sets his chin on my head, and it's scratchy, but not in a bad way. 'I know how you feel.'

I snort.

'Oh boy, you forget that I was only sixteen years old when I had you. I know that noticeboard got you good, but it won't beat the scandal your mum and I caused when news of you got around.'

'Whoops. Sorry for that,' I say. He's not wrong; my sticky situation pales compared to theirs. Imagine you'd just finished Year 11 and next thing you're a parent. Neither Mum nor Dad had supportive families, so they left everything behind and landed here. And although I'm not super fond of Lombard right now, there are definitely worse places to wash up in.

'Not your fault,' Dad reassures me. 'And anyway, you're the best thing that ever happened to me. Never forget that, OK?'

'OK,' I reply, and I do feel a little lighter.

'But promise not to shut yourself off.'

'I promise,' I say, but not without a groan.

'That's all I wanted to hear.' He lets me out of his embrace, and we return to demolishing the mountain of food while watching two men making out in the mud. By the time the credits roll, Dad is falling asleep, so I bin the empty cartons and send him off to bed.

'Hey,' he says, halfway out of the lounge, 'if you want, you're off cafe duty tomorrow.'

Other kids might jump around for joy if they found out they didn't have to get up at five in the morning to start work. And usually sleep is priority number one, but I love Sunday mornings with Dad. He switches on the lights in the cafe, brews the first coffee, removes the chairs from the tables, until I join him, hair still damp from the shower. He grunts a hello and hands me a steaming mug of chai. I don't drink coffee because I hate it. The irony of working in a coffee shop while despising the stuff isn't lost on me, but I can't stand its bitterness. It's like drinking dirt. Sweet dirt, once you add caramel syrup to it.

So instead of pouring coffee, I bake. I preheat the oven and prep the sourdough loaves that have risen overnight. I whip up unholy amounts of pancake batter, I set the banana bread out to cool, I add the chocolate chips to the muffin mix and watch the tops turn crisp and golden. Then I stack them all into pyramids in the glass display out front, except I keep one back. They run out faster than anything else we sell and cause queues and, sometimes, arguments.

I don't save the spare muffin for myself. At some point around 10 a.m., the bell above the door announces Simo with a happy jingle. I swear it doesn't sound so chipper when anyone else enters. And even though he arrives a good hour, sometimes two, after we've run out of chocolate-chip muffins, I place one in front of him, dusted with a snowy sprinkling of icing sugar.

'No, it's all right,' I tell Dad. 'Like you said, I can't keep hiding. Besides, you need me. I'm the better baker between the two of us.'

Dad makes a show of clutching his breaking heart. 'I taught you everything you know!'

'That's a lie. Miss M taught me how to bake.'

'A little advice: never have children. They will grow up to stab you in the back, repeatedly, with a dull knife.'

'Goodnight, Dad!'

'Goodnight, son.'

He disappears into the bathroom, and I fall on to my bed. My phone shows a text from Simo.

Simo: Morning run tomorrow?

It's true that I like the frenzy of the cafe and baking alongside Dad, but I might have ulterior motives about working tomorrow. It gives me space – space I wouldn't have with Simo right next to me. I'm not shutting him out; all I need is a couple more days. To recover and rebuild the thick skin that has served me so well as a safety layer between Simo and my feelings for him. And yet, I could never turn him down.

Luca: I'm on cafe duty, but I'll save you a muffin?

With me in the kitchen and him by a window seat, there'll be several tables and a counter between us. Perhaps that's all the space I need.

CHAPTER 4 – SIMO

It's Monday, 6.40 a.m. and I'm considering the best way to wake up Luca. He's the type of person who can sleep anywhere, any time of day, no matter the noise level. On our flight back from Spain this summer, he spent all of it snoring away, despite the two crying children and seriously hostile plane seats. It's a skill I envy. The only disadvantage is that waking him up takes real effort. For a second, I even consider a bucket of cold water.

Since last week, I've been hyper-conscious of myself around him. The noticeboard rumours follow me wherever I go, and trying to get rid of them is about as simple as cutting off my own shadow. Instead, I weigh my words and swallow them more often than not. I take note of every time we touch. I watch him constantly but pretend not to. I go to all these lengths and act like nothing's changed. It's exhausting, mostly because I fear the cracks will start to show.

I decide to drop my whole body on to his sleeping self. It's what I would normally do without thinking twice. I'm faking thoughtlessness like my life depends on it, and maybe it does. Luca is all bones and sharp lines, but the duvet softens the fall. He barely shifts below me, so I begin to poke his ribs, and when that doesn't do it, I crawl on top of his back. It's an act devoid of tenderness, of that I make sure.

'Monster,' he groans into his pillow.

'Get up, get up, we're going for a run!'

'Can't get up,' he huffs, 'with you on top.'

If there's one thing I've learned about Luca in our years of friendship, it's that it takes a village, nay, an army to get this boy out of bed. Mostly I'm happy to tag along and go wherever Luca takes me. The only time I have to take the lead is in the mornings. Especially today. We're on a mission.

I move off the bed and rip away the duvet, revealing a very ruffled Luca. In the dim room, the hills and dips of his spine catch the light like waves on a dark ocean, the moon fracturing on a crest.

'Give a boy a minute, will you?' Luca grumbles, and I realise that I'm staring.

'I'll give you three, but if you're still not up …' I leave the room, glad to no longer be confronted with so much exposed skin.

Luca shuffles into the lounge, sleep still clinging to his every move, but he's managed to throw on running gear. A few minutes later, he's brushed his teeth, and we find ourselves on the promenade. The sun hasn't yet broken through the fog, and the shutters of Paul's kiosk remain shut, but the first dog walkers are making their way up the beach. We fall into a jog, then slowly pick up speed.

Running is the only thing that's been keeping me sane.

When Lombard hasn't yet woken up, and all I can hear are the waves and the steady rhythm of our feet hitting the tarmac, I can relax. Tall Victorian seafront homes give way to squat brick cottages, smoke rising from chimneys the only sign of life. The cottages are soon replaced by beach huts in varying shades of pastel, until we reach the edge of town and break free. Running reminds me to breathe. It's a paradox, because Luca is right beside me and he's kind of the root of my problems.

It's not like it's his fault. A whole week has passed and we still don't know who put the notice up. At the risk of stating the obvious, it's been a miserable one. Seven days of pointing fingers, of being avoided by my parents, of flinching away from my best friend, of full-blown denial. No, I'm not in love with Luca. No, we're not together.

The town council has been ghosting us. When we asked for an appointment, every councillor's schedule was full until the end of the month. When we turned up to open meetings, they were cancelled at the last minute. But today, they can't evade us. Because every Monday at 7.15 a.m., they meet to pick that week's message to go on the noticeboard. It's an unshakeable tradition, as old as Lombard itself. I'll get my answers and make sure that this week's board makes no mention of us.

We head north, and while I'd usually loop us back through town, I keep going until we reach the causeway. The tide is in, cutting off access to Clifford Island. I spot the manor's turrets in the distance, slicing through the fog and the crowns of the surrounding trees. Usually I try to avoid the old estate, with its many dark windows, half-hidden beneath layers of ivy and steeped in ghost stories, but today I want to run till I reach it and keep running on. But I've already pushed Luca further than usual, and he's not uttered a word of complaint. I won't get away with it much longer. Also, I don't want to miss our one chance to ambush the town council.

We turn back, our feet running hot. The first rays of sun pierce the mist and make the waves shine as we reach town. On a different day, in a different mood, we might throw off our shoes and run straight into the ocean. But there's none of that playfulness today.

In front of the noticeboard, we come to a stop. I ignore the message that's still there as much as possible, but I can feel the words looming above me. The initial shock has passed, replaced by slow-bubbling anger. That I don't know where to direct that anger only makes it worse, and so everyone gets a taste of it. Luca, because as mean as it is, I wouldn't be in this mess without him. Mum for ignoring what's happened, and ignoring me in the process. Dad for his inability to even broach the subject, when I can tell that there are things he wants to say. Every single person throwing looks and comments my way when they should be minding their own business. And the town council.

Luca is bent over, hands on his knees and breathing hard. His skin is flushed, his neck glistens. I watch a bead of sweat trace its way from a spot behind his ear down to his Adam's apple. It clings to him until it detaches and drops to the ground. I tear my gaze away and march to the door of the town hall. Inside, a corridor takes me to the assembly room. Luca calls after me, but I barge in without waiting for him.

Voices halt mid-conversation, and six pairs of eyes stare at me, mouths agape.

'Simo Lorca,' Mayor Pickering observes, the first to catch himself. 'And Luca Dean, naturally,' he adds, when Luca appears at my side. He's a little man with a loud voice who wears turtlenecks pretty much every day of the year. 'That's an unexpectedly sweaty sight for my sore eyes.'

'Are you quite all right? You seem upset,' Heloise asks. She leans against a blackboard that's seen better days, a piece of chalk between her fingers.

'I am upset,' I say, taking in the rest of the room. Curtained windows frame a view of the ocean, but my attention is on the members of council huddled in its centre. Besides Mayor Pickering and Heloise, there's Betsy, the owner of Pott's flower shop where Dad gets his plants, Linda, the mailwoman, and Justine Ribbons, whose daughter shares some of my classes. Maybe it's just me, but they all have a sheepish look about them. 'I have good reason to be upset.'

'And we totally understand,' Betsy says, but the apologetic smile doesn't help.

'I don't think you do,' Luca joins in, and I'm glad to hear the heat in his voice. I feel more united with him now than I've felt all week. 'I thought you were a political body, not a gossip column. Since when are you in the business of spreading lies about people?'

Heloise tuts, clearly affronted by the accusation.

'Just to be clear,' the mayor begins, 'you're not in love, then?'

'No,' Luca and I reply, one syllable like a hammer to a wall.

'Then we owe you an apology,' he says, and sounds surprisingly sincere. 'We had no intention of spreading misinformation. We merely sought to declare our support, share the joy, but it seems the gesture was … rushed.'

'What I don't understand is how you even came to think … ?' I can't bring myself to finish the sentence.

'You've been inseparable since primary school,' Linda pipes up. 'And when you returned from Spain this summer, you seemed very … together.'

'That's a little too much speculation for us to end up on the noticeboard,' I retort. 'Who made the decision?'

'We all did,' Betsy replies.

'But who came up with the idea?'

'None of us,' she says.

'I don't understand.'

'It was a submission. Online. On the council web portal,' Mayor Pickering explains. I look to Luca, who shakes his head. 'Anyone can submit a message for the noticeboard. We take all suggestions into account, weed out everything that's irrelevant or rude – you can't imagine the number of flagrantly vulgar entries – and take it to a vote. The winning submission then goes up for the week.'

He points to the blackboard, on which Heloise has written out this week's options. The top one – *WELCOME HOME, DANIEL!* – is circled.

'And these submissions, they're completely anonymous?' Luca asks.

'Correct.'

His shoulders sag, and I share in his disappointment. There's no way we can trace it back to the culprit. I'm not exactly a tech geek, and Luca's hacking skills are equally non-existent.

'It was a genuine mistake. We were happy for you and your, erm, supposed attachment. And we meant no harm,' Justine offers, speaking up for the first time. She's one of Lombard's biggest volunteers and organises most town festivals, but she never lords her charity over people. Still, I can't muster any warmth towards her today. The intention is pointless when it results in harm.

Luca looks like he's run out of steam, but I'm still fuming, and judging by the worried look on her face, Betsy can tell. 'We could set things straight for you? Use the noticeboard to say something like "Simo and Luca are not in love!"'

'Absolutely not,' Luca shoots back.

'That's the worst thing you could do,' I add. 'I suggest you keep our names off that board from now on.' With nothing left to say and zero patience for any more empty apologies, I turn my back.

'You know, boys,' Mayor Pickering calls after us, 'council meetings are open to the public. You're welcome to join any time, not just to complain.'

There are few moments in life when I'm tempted to flip someone off, but now my hand trembles with the urge. Only the respect for my elders that my parents have drilled into me holds me back – that and Luca, who pushes me out of the building and on to the square.

'Who is Daniel, anyway?' he mutters.

'What?'

'Daniel. The next poor guy on the noticeboard.'

'I almost couldn't care less.' Now Luca looks sheepish

too, and I feel worse. 'Sorry. I don't know – somehow you and I have switched roles. Usually you're the impulsive one.'

'Thanks for the assessment,' he replies drily. 'Not that I disagree.'

'Why aren't you more bothered? There's no way we'll find out who did this now.'

Heloise shuffles out behind us, with a huge box on a trolley that makes a loud noise as it clatters over the cobblestones. She propels the trolley towards the noticeboard to switch out the letters. Having seen enough of her and anything to do with the council, I direct Luca back to the promenade.

'It's not that I'm *not* bothered. I've just accepted that the mess is made, and we have to muddle through it. Doesn't mean I like it.' A sandy tennis ball lands by his feet, quickly followed by a delighted terrier. Luca throws the ball back towards the beach and the dog zooms after it. 'It's like bombing your final exams. Or crashing your car. It's happened, and it's awful, but you can't change it.'

'Except that we didn't cause this! That changes the situation, surely?'

'Does it? And what if we found out? You might get the satisfaction, but it's too late to stop the rumour mill.'

I ponder his words and come to the annoying conclusion that he's right. We have to deal. And I can't even explain how much it pisses me off. Not just that someone turned us into fodder for their tea party, but the general expectation that because Luca and I are close, we'll inevitably turn into a couple. Like people have nothing better to do than talk about us. The stupid noticeboard is only a symptom of a much bigger problem.

Suddenly, Luca's hands cup my face. The second he touches me, my eyelids flutter, and I want to fall into him. I want to pour all of myself into his gentle hands, let him brush away my worries. But that's not how it works. I force my eyes open and try not to let my thoughts show.

'Relax,' he says, 'stop grinding your teeth to dust.'

He holds my gaze, and with it my entire body. Luca fills my vision, eyes bright as the morning and familiar as the pillow that lulls me to sleep at night. Beneath his touch the tension begins to melt. I breathe in and out until only a dull ache remains.

When I realise what we're doing, standing so close where everyone can see, I step back. Luca's arms fall to his sides. A corner of his mouth lifts, but I detect concern in the slant of his smile. The ocean rushes in my ears along with my own beating heart, pierced only by the shriek of seagulls.

'We could skip school. Just for a day.'

I shake my head at Luca's suggestion. The temptation is real, but so is Mum's wrath if she found out. 'We have to muddle through, right?'

'Doesn't mean we can't cheat now and then. Exceptional circumstances allow for unusual measures,' Luca replies.

'Did you read that somewhere?'

He laughs, and his eyes are framed by a dozen little lines. 'Nope. I'm a big boy who knows big words.' He skips ahead, in the direction of his home. 'See you in school, then?' He strips off his shirt as he walks away, his back coated in a sheen of sweat. Light ripples across his spine and fractures with every step, each lift of a bare shoulder.

Even hours later, it's still on my mind, hushing every

other thought. The shoulder lift and the sunrays flitting across his skin like a swarm of honey-coloured butterflies.

If you could catch light, I write into my notebook that night, *how would you do it? Trap it in a butterfly net or gather it like dew from a leaf?*

And if you could drink light, what would it taste of? What would it feel like?

CHAPTER 5 – LUCA

'There's the new guy in our year, Jacob. He ended things with his boyfriend before he moved here. He's cute, don't you think?'

Louise looks up at me with her big hazel eyes framed by a heart-shaped face and strawberry-blonde curls. She's an unapologetic gossip, not unlike a certain elderly lady who lives in the flat above ours. But where Miss M collects rumours like a magpie does shiny things, Louise shares what she's gathered with anyone who will listen.

My plan to sound her out was purely strategic. I was quietly hoping for fresh scandal. Not that I wish other people harm, but the best way to bury a rumour is with a bigger, juicier one. Somewhere in her monologue I forgot that I wasn't listening to a podcast, so it takes me a moment to register the direct question.

'Wha— Jacob? He's in my photography class but, this is the first time I'm hearing about a boyfriend.' Or that he's gay. A tingling feeling rushes through my body, and I rock back and forth on my feet to release the restlessness. It's strange knowing I'm no longer the only gay boy in town. Good strange, I think. I'm just not used to the idea.

'Bit preoccupied, huh?'

'You could say that.' I force a smile that convinces nobody. 'So, Simo and I, we're still … ?'

'The talk of town, yes,' she confirms soberly.

'Great.' I sigh.

'What's great?' a new voice chimes in.

I freeze. And of course, Simo joins us. His hair is ruffled, the way it always is at the end of a school day; brown curls reaching up into the sky. When he's deep in thought, he twirls them without even noticing. I want to reach out and unwind them, but I control the impulse.

'The manor,' I blurt out, 'Louise was just telling me that the old manor house outside of town finally sold. And that's great because, well, it's a historic building that was falling into disrepair and now it's … not.'

Simo hates gossip. Recent events haven't exactly changed that. As much as I would like to share his position, I'm far less noble. I admit that I'm morally corrupt and that gossip is fun, as long as my name stays out of the conversation. Simo frowns, and the freckles on his forehead shift. They're a product of ten cloudless days under the Spanish sun. It'll be sad to see them fade.

'Hidden House? The one near the causeway?'

'Yeah, the buyers are this really posh couple, apparently. Moguls of some sort.'

I don't know how Louise knows this, but I'm glad she does. Simo doesn't need to hear that we're still Lombard's Number One Topic. He's subdued enough as it is.

'Must be loaded to afford it. It's basically a castle. No wonder it's stood empty for decades,' I say to steer the conversation further into safe waters.

'There's that. And people think it's haunted ever since the last owner's son drowned because he got lost in the fog.'

I watch Simo's expression turn to stone in an instant. My heart sinks. So much for safe waters.

'Louise, it's been great talking to you, but we have to run!'

I reach out to take Simo's shoulder and navigate him away from Louise and more talk of dead sons, but he turns before I get the chance. Someone wolf-whistles after us, and Simo stops abruptly. Even with his back turned, I know that the vein on his forehead is pulsing angrily.

'Ignore them,' I mutter when I catch up, but he doesn't acknowledge me. Without a word, he shakes me off and rushes past the school gate. I follow in his shadow, knowing that in this moment there is little I can say to calm him. Usually I know instinctively how to ease his anger, but I can't cut through the grief. And when one feeds into the other, I don't stand a chance.

He was like this all the time when I first met him in primary school. Withdrawn. Quiet. The new kid who kept everybody at a safe distance. He was mourning, though I didn't realise it then. The expression he wears now, every trace of emotion banished, is the same one his parents wore when they used to pick him up from school each day.

It was Dad who told me, and he probably heard from Miss M, who has a way of knowing everything about everyone in Lombard. He said that Simo had had a brother, but that he had died in an accident. He said I shouldn't ask Simo about it unless he brought it up first. To this day, Simo hasn't mentioned his brother once. One more thing to add to the list of things we don't talk about.

Our feet carry us to the street where Simo lives, but instead of passing it like we usually do after school, he stops beneath an apple tree on the corner. When he speaks, he barely looks at me.

'See you tomorrow.'

He's down the street before I get the chance to nod. I watch him retreat, and try to convince myself that this is not a dismissal. I continue to the town's main junction alone, where the cafe is waiting.

I drop my bag in the flat, which feels quieter than I'm used to. Normally, when Simo needs time to think, he'll disappear into my room, into one of his books for an hour or two, until he's back to his old self. I like knowing he's in there. Dad and Simo are like hands on a clock; they set my rhythm, give structure to my days. It's only recent events that have thrown things.

To drown out the silence, I turn on the radio and climb on to the wide window sill. Tove Lo's voice spills from the open-plan kitchen into the lounge, but I'm too caught up to follow the lyrics. From where I sit, I get a view of the junction: the awning of our cafe right below me, the empty pet shop on the next corner, a convenience store diagonally across, and Betsy's flower shop to our left. Townsfolk and tourists shuffle along the main road, and I observe their comings and goings, until I realise what I'm doing. I'm waiting for Simo to appear and I tell myself to stop. I need a distraction, and I'll find it downstairs, in chit-chat with customers and wiping up spilt coffee.

My toes graze the floorboards when my gaze snags on

the windows of the pet shop. The place has been boarded up for a year, causing much debate in town. Mayor Pickering thinks it looks like a drug den at the very heart of Lombard, but there's no point in taking the boards down until a new owner has been found. So now people, mostly kids, glue posters and stickers to the slats, which, in Pickering's defence, does look sketchy.

I wonder what it is that's pulled my attention, until I spot a new addition, a drawing of something in black marker. It's hard to decipher the writing at the centre of what I believe is a heart, so I use my phone camera to zoom in – and almost fall off the window sill. Once I've recovered my balance, I find the heart again. As I try to keep my hands from shaking, I stare at the picture on my phone. It's grainy and out of focus, but the letters are clear.

Heat travels up my spine and covers my back in little pinpricks. I sit, motionless except for the beating in my chest, and stare at the initials enclosed by the heart. A couple of random letters, a basic outline – it could mean anything and be about anyone.

But it's impossible to miss, and I'm terrified. I've barely recovered from the trauma of the noticeboard, and now this. I'm not naive enough to believe that my and Simo's initials have coincidentally appeared in a place that's visible from almost every angle of my home. The method might differ, but the effect is worse. The noticeboard might pass as a prank blown out of proportion, an innocent mistake by the town council, but the heart is no accident. It's intentional. Shame pulses through my body, knowing that my feelings have been splashed across town, not once, but twice.

'What are you doing?'

I nearly jump out of my skin. Dad is inches away, like he's appeared out of nowhere.

'Don't sneak up on people like that! It's not cool!' I shout, and lock my phone screen, hoping he hasn't spotted the picture.

'Sneak? I called your name twice. And these floorboards, they creak like a haunted house. There's no point in sneaking.' He sweeps a strand of hair out of my eyes, and from the way his hand lingers, I can tell he's picked up on my mood.

'Sorry, I was … thinking,' I say.

''Bout what?'

'About coming down to the cafe to help out,' I reply, trying to keep my tone light.

'Did you finish your homework?'

'No,' I say, instantly wishing I'd gone for a little white lie instead. But there aren't many rules in this household, and one is that we tell each other the truth.

'Then you're not helping out.'

My eyes return to the boarded-up windows opposite. Every time someone walks past, I expect them to spot the heart, but nobody pays it any mind. I can only hope that it doesn't stand out for anyone else like it does for me, because as desperate as I am to cover it up, it'll have to wait till tonight. I'd pull too much attention otherwise.

'You sure there's nothing on your mind?' Dad asks. He grabs two cartons of oat milk from the cupboard, which means the cafe's run out again.

'There's loads on my mind,' I mutter, because there's no point denying it when he reads me so well.

Dad leans against the fridge and waits until I've put my thoughts in order. I remember the promise I made him, that Simo and I would stick together.

'You said that I shouldn't push people away. But what if it's not up to me?'

'You mean, what if you're not the one doing the pushing?'

If it was anyone else, I'd be frightened to be such an open book, but with Dad, it's soothing to be understood, to know that I don't have to hide. I shuffle into the kitchen and slump against him.

'Mm-hmm,' I hum into his chest.

'Tell me what you did last week, after the message appeared on the noticeboard.'

'School,' I reply, unsure what he's getting at.

'And after that?'

I take a second to think. After school, I went home and so did Simo. But I hated the feeling of being alone with the mess in my head. Knowing that Simo would feel similarly rubbish, I thought it was wiser to stick things out together.

'We ended up going to Sheila's, to the bookstore. But that was last week.'

Now, following days of hoots and wolf whistles whenever we're seen together in the school hallways, it looks like he prefers being alone. And I can't blame him. I'm the reason our names appear on boarded-up windows. The lid I used to keep my feelings bottled up wasn't screwed tight enough. They spilt out when I wasn't paying attention. I'm the reason our friendship is starting to fracture. But I will do anything in my power to ensure that we stay together.

'You're his best friend. That hasn't changed. If he needs space, that's only natural.'

I frown, because the whole needing-space thing has never applied to me and Simo. I do my best thinking with Simo around. And when my thoughts are too scattered, Dad is there to put them back in order.

'But it can't hurt to remind Simo that you're here if he needs you. It's easy to forget that you're not alone when you're lost in your feelings.'

'So, I should remind him?' I ask.

'Gently,' Dad says.

I set the paper bag on the doormat and return to my bike. Dad let me bake a cheesecake, and I did my homework while it was in the oven. Before I left with a huge piece, he also handed me a takeaway bag of diner food. Call me delivery boy, because here I am, texting Simo that he should check the front door.

I swing myself on to the bike just as the door opens. Simo looks from me to the bag by his feet. He's in shorts and a T-shirt so faded I can see every line of his torso if I stare for too long, which is hard not to do. He looks disgruntled, but I can't tell whether he's mad or if he's just woken from a nap. Like a puppy, he only gets cuter when he's moody.

'What's this?' he asks, and takes a sniff inside the bag. His expression brightens.

'Emotional support food,' I explain.

'Who says I need emotional support food?' he retorts.

'If you don't want it, I'll take it ba—'

'Is that cheesecake? Did you bake me a cheesecake?'

'It was leftover,' I lie, feeling self-conscious and stupid. No better way to disprove the rumours than to bake a cake for the boy I'm allegedly in love with. Well done, Luca.

'It's still warm,' Simo notes. I shrug and push myself off the kerb. 'Am I meant to eat it all by myself?'

'I've seen you eat, Simo. I know you can do it.'

'That's not the question, is it?'

With the bag in his arms, he retreats, leaving the door open. I'm still puzzling over the meaning of his words when he taps his knuckles against the kitchen window from the inside. I roll my eyes, but only because I'm trying to hide a smile. By the time I've placed the bike against the fence and closed the door behind me, Simo is back in the hallway. He hands me the cheesecake on a plate with two forks. He's so close now I can see the pillow imprint on his cheek. I grip the plate tighter, fighting the urge to smooth the wrinkles away.

So much for 'allegedly'. I'm fooling no one, least of all myself. But I don't need Simo to be my boyfriend. I don't need Simo to be in love with me, ever. I only need him to need me a little. I need him to want me in his life, the way I want him in mine. Which means he can't find out about the heart. We laughed it off the first time, on the classroom floor under the tables, but we're past the point of pretending it's a joke. He'll keep shutting himself away until he's completely out of reach.

'You look like you could use emotional support food too,' Simo says, and heads up the stairs.

'When don't I?' I mutter, and follow him to his room.

CHAPTER 6 – SIMO

'Simo, did you know that our supply closet is haunted?' Maz asks from behind the coffee machine. He hands Joni her takeaway Americano, and she grunts a goodbye and walks out of the cafe, back to the library.

'You don't say,' I reply with a grin. On the counter in front of me sits an empty plate, with only crumbs remaining from yesterday's cheesecake.

'Someone ought to call Lockwood & Co.,' Maz says and shakes his head with fake concern. 'While they're on the case, they can sort out the poltergeist nesting in my sock drawer.'

'Don't forget the demon in the toaster,' I add.

'Or the soot sprites in the attic.'

'Are you done?' Luca asks, watching the exchange between Maz and me with his arms crossed over his work apron.

'Not yet,' Maz says to him. 'The opportunity to mock you for thinking there's an evil spirit in the supply closet is too good to pass up.'

Luca pouts. 'Says the man who checks his astrology app daily and greets every magpie he sees.'

‘That’s different!’ Maz insists.

‘Is it?’ I ask.

‘I feed you, Simo, so it’s unwise to turn on me,’ Maz grumbles.

‘I’m not going in there alone,’ Luca reiterates. ‘I don’t trust that door, and the light has stopped working. Again. And there’s no phone signal either. And every time I enter, something falls off a shelf and nearly decapitates me. No amount of coffee beans is worth me losing my head. And the window is too tiny to climb out if I get stuck in there on my own. And I’m not even afraid of spiders, but I swear they’re not meant to be that big. And I will keep complaining until you stop me.’

Maz cocks his head. ‘I was just curious to see how long it would take you to run out of breath.’

‘I’m coming with you,’ I say. It’s not Luca’s first supply-closet rant and I want to see what’s really behind this ‘haunting’. It’s my way of returning the emotional support cheesecake. Not that I keep a tally, but whenever I’m slipping into a bad place, Luca always manages to pull me back from the brink. I don’t think he realises how often he stands between me and a shit day. He’s my emotional support human.

‘Finally,’ he says, and stomps away. When I join him by the door beneath the staircase, he instructs me to keep it open and use my phone torch to light up the dingy room. There’s not an inch of available space, with shelves and boxes stacked in every corner. I watch Luca climb over sacks of potatoes to reach the coffee beans, mesmerised by the way the muscles in his arms strain whenever he shifts his balance. 'I changed that bulb last week, you know. The one before that flickered even when it was off.'

I grin to myself but stop when I spot a stack of pots and pans sliding off a wonky shelf.

'Watch out!' I shout, but Luca is crouching in a corner with no chance to make it out.

'No!' he shouts, when I launch myself into the cupboard. I make it just in time to shield him from the avalanche. He was a second away from being pulp. The door falls shut with a malicious-sounding click. 'I told you to keep it open at all costs!'

'It was either that or a trip to the hospital, you knob,' I retort, lying halfway across him with a bunch of rusty cookware in my arms. His breath tickles my neck. He smells of sugar and coffee, and for a moment I forget the sorry situation we're in. Until the bulb flickers and launches us back into half-light. 'OK, that's creepy. I give you that.'

It takes several minutes until we're untangled, not helped by the fact that Luca is getting increasingly flustered and I'm trying to keep from laughing. This feels too silly to be happening. I stop when I end up with my nose in his armpit, which would be cosier than it sounds, if it wasn't also for Luca's knee in my gut. When we're finally up, I'm sweaty and a dozen bruises richer.

'You don't have your phone, do you?' Luca whispers hoarsely.

'Nope,' I chuckle, realising I must have dropped it.

His breath keeps grazing my skin, which does nothing to cool me down. I'd step back, but I'm pressed between a shelf and Luca's body.

'You're finding this a little too amusing, considering we're trapped,' he huffs, but I can tell he's not mad from the smile in his voice.

'Would you like me to get annoyed instead? This is at least partly your fault. And you're squashing my toe.'

He shifts and his hip pokes into mine. It's no less painful than a squashed toe, so I move his body, my hands on his ribcage. Now his full weight is on me, but at least he's no longer cutting off vital blood circulation. Luca's chest expands, and in my fascination that I can feel the air moving in and out of his lungs, I forget to let go. I should be weirded out by the shape of his bones beneath my touch, but it's real and beautiful.

'I can't believe you're blaming me, when you left your designated spot by the door,' Luca says, pulling my wandering mind back into the supply closet.

'This is a prime example of a self-fulfilling prophecy. You're convinced something is going to happen and so it does,' I say.

He snorts. 'If I had that power, then—'

'Then … ?' I ask. A pearl of sweat runs down my neck, and the palms of my hands begin to tingle where we're touching. Luca's gaze is downcast, almost like he's purposely avoiding my eyes. The thing is, we are so close that his forehead rests against my temple. There's no avoiding me.

'Nothing,' he says after several breaths. His voice is low, more vibration than sound.

Impatience hums in my chest, but I remain still.

'No, tell me.'

I don't know why, but I'm dying to hear what he was

about to say. When he finally faces me, his pupils are dilated, something like apprehension glimmering in their depths. These past couple of weeks, I feel like we've been walking a tight line, skirting around things unspoken. Now I sense a shift coming.

His lips part. I can taste the lemonade on his breath, down to the mint leaves he likes to add. On my part, I've stopped breathing altogether. I don't know what's next, only that I must not miss it.

'Simo,' he whispers, and I tilt forward, compelled by my name in his mouth.

Something builds between us, a silence so intense that I'm seized by a sudden panic. My foot connects with something on the ground. Metal clatters with a violence that makes Luca jump. His shoulder hits my jaw, and a second later I taste blood on my tongue.

'Ow,' I whimper.

'Sorry. You OK?' he asks, and grabs my shoulders, trying to regain his balance in the dark. 'I hate this cupboard.'

'I think the feeling is mutual,' I mumble through my already swollen cheek. As the pain ebbs away, so does the tension in the packed space. I watch Luca stumble to the door, and I'm left with shortness of breath and a bitter feeling of disappointment. I don't know what I was expecting. The mood in the room changed so quickly I'm sure I made it all up.

Luca hits the door with his open palm and shouts for his dad.

'I thought I heard the door shut,' Maz notes when he arrives and props it open.

I sigh at the cool breeze that enters the room. My T-shirt is soaked, sticking to my back and constricting my chest.

'And you didn't come to check?' Luca complains.

Maz looks from me to Luca with an unreadable expression, shrugs and walks away.

Luca bends down and pulls my phone from beneath a potato sack. 'Here,' he says, handing it back. Sweat glistens on his brow. When he glances up at me, his lips twitch with amusement. He starts to pull spiderwebs from my hair, every brush of skin intense as a burn.

'I'm gonna get some air,' I say, and step away, forcing myself not to run. Because everything is normal, and I'm normal, and it's not normal to flee from your best friend. Once outside, I inhale deeply and try to get rid of the mix of dust and blood in my mouth. On wobbly legs, I cross over to the abandoned pet shop and perch on the window ledge.

Two figures step out of the cafe, iced coffees in their hands. Mairi is easy to recognise, long blue braids falling down her back. In all the years we've shared classes, there's not a single colour she hasn't tried.

She sees me and crosses the street, the guy following behind. I wish they'd stay away, but because everything is normal, and I'm normal, I stay where I am. Mairi's friend is tall with ginger waves falling into his eyes. Though he seems the tiniest bit familiar, I fail to place him.

'You look like something attacked you,' Mairi greets me.

'You could say that.'

'Either that, or things got a little rough with—'

'I got stuck in the supply closet and couldn't get out,' I

explain, to stifle whatever insinuation Mairi was going to make. I don't feel like adding that Luca was with me the entire time.

The guy makes a noise that could be a chuckle or a snort.

'Sorry, I don't think I caught your name,' I say.

'I'm Jacob. I just moved here.' He has a nice voice, much deeper than I'd expect from someone our age, and there's a shadow of an accent. 'We share a few classes,' he adds, and somehow it sounds like a dig. Like I should've noticed him in the two weeks since school started. But even when Luca and I aren't caught up in town drama, we tend to focus on ourselves. I don't need anyone but him. But I never expected this closeness to blow up in my face.

'I'm Simo,' I say, trying to sound friendlier than I feel.

'I figured. You're hard to miss, what with the noticeboard.'

I grit my teeth, almost biting my cheek again.

'Sorry, I didn't mean to put you on the spot. It was just sweet to see. I'm from a small town too, and they'd never be this supportive of two –' He stops when he sees my expression. 'Anyway, I spotted a cute shop over there that I'm gonna check out before I dig myself a deeper hole.'

'Forgive him. He's French,' Mairi says, and watches Jacob stride off towards Betsy's flower shop with a bemused smile.

'OK … ?' I say, puzzled.

'He can be very direct. But he's a nice guy.'

I remain quiet, holding back the snide comeback. Mairi hasn't done anything to deserve my ire. Despite her vibrant exterior, she's more introspective in person. An observer rather than an instigator; I've always felt we're alike in that way.

'Did you go a little sticker-mad?' She interrupts my thoughts and nods to the window behind me. Someone's plastered a whole section with recent additions. I recognise the trans and intersex flags that Librarian Joni always hands out, as well as the logo of Dad's estate agency and a cartoon drawing of Anton the Highland bull, all shiny and new.

'Uh, no. I hate stickers.' They cling to your skin and make that foul sound when you pull them off. Worse than Velcro. But I don't divulge any of that to Mairi. Instead, I suppress a shudder and inch away.

Mairi watches me with raised eyebrows.

'I'm not weird,' I mutter.

'I never said you were,' she laughs. It's a pretty sound, husky.

'So, are you guys a thing?' I ask.

'Me and Jacob? Oh, no, he's not –' She clears her throat. 'No, we're not.' Mairi fiddles with one of her braids, suddenly self-conscious. I'd feel bad, but for once it's refreshing not to be on the receiving end of that question. 'But I'd better catch up with him. I promised to show him around town.'

'Don't forget to introduce him to Anton,' I say, and point to the sticker. 'They've got the same hair.'

'Be nice to him, Simo,' she says instead of a goodbye, but I spot the grin before she turns. When she reaches Pott's Flowers, she waves over her shoulder without looking back, then disappears inside.

A sudden coldness against my chest makes me look down, and I see a hand holding out a cup of lemonade – Luca's hand. He sips from a second cup that's dripping with condensation. He's lost the apron and changed into a blue T-shirt that only intensifies the colour of his eyes. The necklace I gave him glints golden on his skin. He looks like the personification of the summer sky.

I take the cup and search his face for a sign that I didn't imagine the sudden intensity in the supply closet. He scans the stickers on the window, then his gaze lands back on me. I could be wrong, but for a second something cuts through the expression of ease, a flicker of raw emotion. It's gone before I can make sense of it. It plants a seed of doubt, whether I know him as well as I thought I did. Whether I know myself at all.

'Dad kicked me out. Says if I want to chew someone's ear off about ghosts, he'd rather I pick someone else.' He slurps on the straw, and his throat jumps with every swallow. 'And I pick you.'

I let his words wash over me, let them steal away the doubt, at least momentarily. Then I set my lips to the straw and drink, ice cubes clinking. My teeth hurt from the cold, and I'm on the brink of a brain freeze, but I keep sipping. Flavour bursts on my tongue. Sugar, lemon, mint.

'Go on then,' I say. 'Chew my ear off.'

CHAPTER 7 – LUCA

When I enter the cafe, an older couple are on their way out, so I say a goodbye and take their mugs to the kitchen. For a Friday afternoon, it's quiet. Normally students would be rushing in and out of the shop, iced drinks melting in their hands, while adults finish work early and drop in for a cheeky pastry at the end of a long week. Now the place is deserted. Everyone's down at the beach, soaking up the last of the summer before autumn arrives in earnest.

I return to the counter, where Dad is poring over a list of orders and invoices, a fresh cup of coffee by his side. He's humming an old Sugababes song, which means he's in a good mood despite the lull.

It's nice to see him happy, because, despite his best efforts to shield me from pain and ugliness, I know that life hasn't always been easy on him. He had to grow up quickly and make decisions no teenager should be faced with. Miss M and this cafe were his saving grace. To cover the rent and the running costs of a newborn, he started as Miss M's kitchen hand. Mum went back to school while Dad worked the cafe, always keeping an eye on me. And he basically became a full-time single dad when Mum's job swept her half a world away. When Miss M retired, he took over from her. He seems happy, though sometimes I wonder if he feels lonely without Mum.

'Do you want to hear something funny?' Dad says into the silence.

'I don't know, do I?' I say tentatively. I'm starting to think karma is paying attention every time I listen to gossip.

'I solved the Daniel mystery,' Dad declares, and the decision is made.

'Proceed,' I tell him.

'He came in here today.'

'So you didn't solve it. The mystery walked into the cafe and solved itself.'

'Do you want to know about him or not?'

'He came in and … ?'

'Said hi and he'd like a decaf latte to go, please. So I asked his name, and when he told me, I was like "Ah, the famous Daniel!" And he blushed.'

'You think he's cute!'

'I didn't say that.'

'You didn't need to.'

Far as I know, Dad hasn't dated anyone since I was born. Though there was that morning when I woke and found a stranger sleeping in his bed. A slightly frazzled Dad explained to my smirking thirteen-year-old self that they'd got drunk the night before. Dad let him crash at ours but then slept through the alarm that should have given him time to sneak his guest out. His name was Henry. He looked like a golden retriever and snored like an elephant.

'I asked decaf Daniel if he's related to anyone in town,

and he said I might know his mum, Joni.'

My jaw drops. 'Librarian Joni has a son? How old is this guy?'

'My age, maybe a little older.'

'I can't believe Joni never said anything about having a son. And a cute one of marriageable age. Do you think he's the one who's bought the manor house?'

'You watch too many period films. And no, Miss M mentioned that he's living with Joni for the time being.'

'No such thing as too many period films,' I say. Watching Maggie Smith roasting people is peak entertainment no matter what century she finds herself in.

'He brought his dog too,' Dad adds.

'Why does everyone get a dog except me?' I've been campaigning for a puppy since I was four, but Dad says they make him sneeze, which is the laziest excuse ever. 'We should start selling puppuccinos.'

'We are not selling puppuccinos,' Dad says firmly, and I don't argue. I can fill out an order form and fake his signature without him knowing. 'I then asked how long he was staying and he said he might stick around for a while.'

'And … ?'

'And what?'

'Well, what did you say?'

'I handed him his decaf latte and said the first one was on the house. So he got a little cocky and said thanks, if the coffee is decent he'll come back. And *I* said that even if the coffee sucks, he doesn't have a choice because this is the only coffee shop in town. He laughed and left without another word.'

'Smooth, Dad. But you need to work on your investigative skills.'

'I regret telling you anything.' He turns back to the lists and his Sugababes song.

Out of a job and a sparring partner, I decide to make myself a chai latte. To my great disappointment, we're low on cinnamon, which means a trip to the storage cupboard. Weirdly, it's less scary since yesterday's incident. I'd still prefer cutting onions or cleaning the dishwasher drain over entering that room, but now I have at least one memory linked to it that doesn't make me want to call both an exterminator and a priest. Sure, I can add another near-death experience to my tally, but it also resulted in a heroic act from Simo. The boy saved my life.

Of course, my mind had to turn that into a whole thing. Maybe the pots that fell off the shelf truly did hit me, because that would explain what happened next. In the gloom of that cramped room, with Simo's arms around my chest and his lips an inch away from mine, I nearly let myself believe that he would … kiss me. That was stupid of me, because now that the thought has formed, it's impossible to erase it from my mind. I broke my own rules and let myself believe something that couldn't be further from reality.

I return with a fresh bag of cinnamon and, naturally, a splinter in my thumb, so I make a stop by the first aid box in the hall. It takes a minute, but with a hiss I pull the splinter from the flesh. As I look at the nasty little thing, I resolve that this is where it stops. No more thoughts about kissing in the cupboard. Simo is upstairs in my room, innocently reading a book, while I've turned him into a dirty fantasy.

Not only am I hurting myself, I'm also risking my friendship. And nothing is worth that, least of all a fantasy with zero chance of ever coming to pass.

In the cafe, the bell above the door announces a new customer. Dad's humming stops, replaced by silence.

'Matthew,' a woman's voice says, which is strange. No one ever calls him Matthew. He's Maz, or Mr Dean if he dislikes you, but never Matthew. A mug crashes to the floor. The sound splits my eardrums, and I jump on the spot. I rush towards the noise, but Dad's next words stop me in my tracks.

'Mother,' he says, and I barely recognise his voice. 'What are you doing here?'

Dad doesn't have a mother. Not any more. He told me his parents passed away soon after he left home with me and Mum. I always assumed they died of old age, which, now that I think about it, makes no sense. They'd only be in their fifties. Still, Dad wouldn't lie to me. Especially not about having dead grandparents.

My feet carry me into the cafe of their own accord. In the afternoon light streaming through the large shop windows stands the most elegant woman I have ever seen. I'm blinded by her appearance, all in whites and creams, with a sharp blazer casually thrown over her shoulders. An immaculate blonde fringe falls into a pair of deep-set, strikingly blue eyes. She looks effortless and expensive. And Dad – Dad is the picture of shock. The front of his shirt is soaked, and coffee is dripping into a puddle on the floor where the mug lies shattered.

'And you must be Luca.'

The woman tilts her head by a fraction, and I get the sense that I'm being scrutinised. If she's surprised to see me, she knows how to hide it. The look she gives me is, at best, one of mild curiosity, like we're nothing but strangers standing in the same cafe, which, I guess, we are. She turns back to Dad, but he only stares at her. 'Fine, I'll introduce myself. Luca, I'm Anna, your grandmother. It's a pleasure to meet you after all this time.'

I'm unable to form a coherent response, but Dad snaps out of his daze. 'What,' he forces through gritted teeth, 'are you doing here?'

The lift of her eyebrow is as good as imperceptible, but the effect is one of refrained disdain at Dad's rudeness.

'Your father and I have moved here.'

'You moved to Lombard?'

'We've bought a house in the area.'

'What kind of house?' Dad asks with narrowed eyes.

'Excuse me?'

'I know you didn't buy a *house*. You've never lived in a house! You've lived in villas and mansions and – Jesus, don't tell me you bought the manor!'

'Hidden House?' I blurt out, because I can't help myself.

'I believe that's what it's called,' she says with a hint of disapproval. 'We might change the name.'

'You cannot change the name. You can't rock up here and go around changing things,' Dad insists. It sounds pretty pointed.

'I didn't come here to argue,' she responds, brushing away the sideswipe with ease. 'I've had enough of that for a lifetime. I am here to extend an invitation. Or an olive branch, if you wish.'

'I'll tell you what I wish. I wish for you to—'

But she doesn't let him finish. 'Your father and I are having a barbecue, in two weeks on Sunday. That ought to be enough time to recover from the surprise. We'd like you to come.'

'No, thank you,' Dad replies without missing a beat.

'Another time, then?' she suggests with a shrug.

'We won't be free at another time, sadly. In the near or distant future.'

I have never seen Dad throw a tantrum before. His temper, usually mild, is boiling over. In her shoes, I would have fled the room, but she faces him with aloofness.

'We're not going anywhere, Matthew. This is our home now, and it would be silly to avoid one's own family when we live in the same town. But –' she lifts her hands in a gesture of acceptance, and I spot a vintage designer bag dangling from her wrist – the kind that you'd need a mortgage for – 'it's up to you. There will be enough food for four, and we'll eat whether or not you decide to grace us with your presence.'

Then, for the second time, she turns to me. 'Luca?'

It's odd to hear her say my name, so odd that I'm still scrambling for an answer. A yes feels far too plain for her. I want to add a formal title, but she's my grandmother, not the Queen, though there is a resemblance. In spirit, more than in actual appearance. I settle for a nod instead.

'I believe it was your birthday a few days ago. I'm sorry to have missed it.'

For the first time since she stepped into the shop, her poise buckles. Her shoulders seem to wobble as she watches me.

'You've literally missed every single one of them,' Maz points out.

'And whose fault is that?' Anna claps back, straightening her shoulders. Every trace of vulnerability has disappeared, and she's once again the proud woman who dominates the room.

'I'll see you both in two weeks.'

She steps out of the shop. The bell above the door jingles, like she is nothing but a customer with a takeaway coffee rather than my believed-to-be-dead grandmother.

CHAPTER 8 – SIMO

At first, I'm certain the shouting is in my head. Ambience that my mind creates to go with the events on the page, a soundtrack that only I can hear while reading. It takes the violent thunder of a door slamming and Maz shouting Luca's name to crumple the fictional world around me like a hand scrunching paper.

I glance out of the window and see Luca half running, half stumbling down the street towards the beach. The anxiety is instant. Every nerve in my body flares up, and I rush out of the flat that isn't mine but still feels so much more like a home than the one I live in.

Downstairs in the cafe, Maz is crouched behind the counter, head in his hands, feet in a puddle of what looks like coffee. His body ripples, from anger or pain, I can't tell. The sight of him hits me; a man so solid and familiar he never fails to make me feel safe, now shattered in the midst of broken porcelain.

I must have made a sound, because he looks up. His eyes are red-rimmed, but they harden with resolve.

'Find Luca for me. Please.'

All I can do is nod. I head out the door, follow Luca's trail to the beach and even though I don't have the faintest idea what went down at the cafe, I instantly know Luca won't be here. The crowd is too big, too carefree for someone wanting to escape company.

'He went that way,' someone grunts, and I turn to see Paul. He leans out of the kiosk, plucks the cigar from his bushy moustache and points it north. 'Looked so livid I thought his head was gonna burst.'

I thank him wordlessly and follow his directions. Luca might have a head start, but my feet will carry me to him regardless. My heart steadies, its frantic beats mellowed by the reassurance that he isn't lost, that he'll wait where I can find him.

Still, my head is in uproar, thoughts bouncing off the walls of my skull, chasing one another. Luca and his dad don't fight. They tell each other off and regularly get into heated debates about which Florence and the Machine album is the best or how to correctly pronounce 'bruschetta', and then bully me into picking a side. They disagree and quarrel and bicker, but they don't have shouting matches.

When it comes to dysfunctional family dynamics, I win hands down. Though you won't hear any raised voices in my house. The Lorcas fight with silence. I know I'm in trouble when both my parents ignore me as best as they possibly can, and recently the dead air between us is deafening.

Sandy beaches turn into rocks, swiftly replaced by cliffs and stretches of sea wall. Clifford Island draws closer and, not for the first time, I think that it looks like the belly of a sleeping giant poking out of the sea. When I reach the causeway, I consult the info chart to reassure myself that

I won't be surprised by the incoming tide. Like a spine, the path connects the island to the mainland, mudflats flanking both sides like wings. The blues and ambers of the fading afternoon reflect in the shallow pools left behind by the tide. To my right, a row of stone pylons taller than me reminds me of the fact that this is no safe walk. When the tide is high, only their very tips remain visible, like the crowns of teeth. The thought makes me queasy and I hurry on, glad to feel packed dry earth beneath my feet when I reach the other side.

A trodden path leads me through low shrubbery and grass so tall it brushes my thighs. After a minute or so, I veer off, making my way to the heart of the island.

When I spot him, a sense of calm washes over me. His outline is set off against the endless horizon. He sits and stares across the waves, almost motionless, except for the breeze that tugs at his hair. Granada burned white streaks into the gold, and though it needs a cut, the scruffiness adds a rough edge to his sweetness. Summer looks good on Luca.

He doesn't stir when I take my place by his side. We've sat like this a thousand times, salt in the air and on our skin, on overgrown slabs of stone, a crumbling wall at our backs – a remnant of war or faith from times before there was a town. We don't talk, but that doesn't mean it's quiet. Sea and wind melt into their own kind of melody and a choir of chirps rises from the underbrush. Faint laughter tickles my ears, but for all I know it might be birdsong. When he finally speaks, his voice is steady, but I detect a wistfulness that usually isn't there.

'The day we met, I was scared of you. I don't think I

ever told you that. You were so quiet. Not your voice – you spoke so politely – but you didn't speak often. The way you looked at people though, or maybe just at me, I don't know, it was unsettling. You didn't look away. You took me in, and I had no idea what you were thinking, but you were clearly thinking something. I didn't like to be noticed, not by the other kids. Because being noticed meant getting chased around the playground when the teachers weren't looking.'

I close my eyes. Heat flickers in my gut, so I take a deep breath to extinguish it. I remember it too, the way the children at school stalked Luca, the way he shrank away from them, and me, at first.

'And then, on that first day, we were meant to go outside during the break. I was always the last kid to leave the classroom, cos if I stayed behind while everyone rushed out, they might forget me and forget to call me names. Except this time, the boy, the pack leader, he stayed behind too. And so did you.'

The memories of that day rise to the surface, and they're so strong that I open my eyes again and try to focus on something that takes their edge off. But I can't shake the images completely; the hallway with rows and rows of benches and coat hooks, the short flight of steps leading down to the main door, and seven-year-old Luca, fear written on his face.

'I don't remember what he said exactly, only that he was too close and too loud and that he spat when he talked. He pushed me. You were there, and I thought you'd hurt me too. But instead you pushed him, pushed him straight down the stairs. I heard his head smash against the tiles. Still makes me feel sick, that sound. Then he screamed and people came running. They saw him crying at the foot of the stairs and us standing above him, and, well, you remember the rest.'

There's no way I'd forget. The only other time I heard someone scream like that was when Mum found out about my brother. Both screams haunt my worst nightmares, but it's been a while since I had dreams like that. I try not to dwell on the thought, try to focus on the fact that I met Luca that day. We were taken to the head teacher's office, and he watched over us as the ambulance arrived first, and our parents second. They asked us, over and over again, who did it, who pushed him. But I was too shaken by what I'd done, scared by the destruction my own anger could cause. And anyway, Luca had witnessed it all. He would tell them.

'But we never said a word. And because the boy couldn't remember anything, and we wouldn't budge, they gave us a week of detention, and then another, and another, to make us talk. To this day, they still don't know. And honestly, it was worth it. Not one of those kids touched me again. Because of you.'

Our eyes meet for the first time since I found him. His are deep pools of blue, and I see gratitude in them, a hint of sadness, and other emotions that float too far beneath the surface. I'm unable to look away.

'I mean, who knew what else you could do?' he whispers, and his breath grazes my skin, which immediately breaks out into shivers. Only then he turns his gaze back to the sea, and I'm released.

'All the kids were afraid of you after that, me included. But the longer you and I spent time together in detention, the more my fear disappeared. I realised that you didn't want to be noticed either. By that point I couldn't help it, I noticed you all the time. And whenever you looked at me, I didn't mind so much any more. I started to like you, even if we barely spoke.'

And here we have it, the answer to why we don't exchange casual *I-love-you*s. The beginning of our friendship was forged in mutual silence. We kept our feelings to ourselves, to avoid a target on our backs, one that would lead to us getting called gay in a voice that made it clear it wasn't a good thing. I guess we never learned to shake that habit. And now they call us gay anyway.

'After that first month, the day the detentions finally ended, Dad picked us both up after school. He took us for ice cream, like a proper bad parent. I think he had his suspicions about who had really done it, but he didn't say. Two scoops each, he said, and you went first. You chose chocolate chip, not once, but twice. And I honestly remember the moment so well because that was my standard order. I looked at you standing next to my dad, and I felt so … complete. I didn't need anyone else, because I had the two of you.'

His voice gives out at the end. Breaks and falls apart. His lashes flutter, quick like a hummingbird. I spot the tears before he wipes them away with the back of his hand. 'And now … now I have grandparents.'

The words float between us, meaningless at first. The conversation has taken such a turn that it takes me several seconds to catch up. When the realisation hits, my head rocks up so fast that my neck cracks.

'But they're dead,' I exclaim. 'You said they're dead.' I can't help that it sounds like an accusation. When we first became friends, there was little that connected us. Luca had lived a sheltered life, still does. He's never known the weight of grief, how it drags your body down, rids you of reasons to get back up. I try not to resent him for it, and I truly hope he never finds out how it hurts, because 'hurt' can't begin to describe it. But I always thought the gaps in his family resembled mine. His grandparents were irrefutably absent, and nothing could bring them back.

'I don't know,' Luca says. 'My grandmother seemed very alive when she strolled into the cafe earlier. That's what they should put on the noticeboard: "Luca's grandparents rise from the grave!" Or "Maz Dean is a rotten liar!" Both would be accurate.'

Understanding dawns on me, slowly at first, until I grasp the true extent of what he's telling me.

'He lied to you? For your whole life?'

When I met Maz for the first time, I wasn't sure what to make of him. I had only ever known parents as pillars of authority – caring, yes, but voices of reason and enactors of rules that stood firmly apart from children. There was no such distance between Luca and Maz. They talked like brothers and joked like friends. Maz rarely played the dad card, and he told the truth even when it was uncomfortable or embarrassing. To keep up a lie of such nauseating proportions isn't like him.

'Makes you wonder what else he's hiding,' Luca says grimly, voicing my thoughts. 'But here's something else: my formerly deceased grandparents have moved into Hidden

House. They've bought it. It's theirs now.'

There's an entirely fake smile stretched across his face. And I get it, there's only so many shock reactions you can have before the revelations start sounding too ridiculous to be real.

I point over my shoulder towards the mainland, unable to form the question.

'Yup, the manor,' Luca confirms with an empty laugh. 'The one with the turrets and the tennis court and the private sea access and the ballroom bigger than our flat.' He turns sober. 'I can't go home, Simo. I don't want to see him. I'd rather camp out here.'

I know things are dire when Luca considers camping. He may be a small-town boy, but he's not exactly the nature type. Seeing the way he buries his fingernails in his own palms, I swallow my words. I take his hands and gently force his fists open. Red half-moons cover his palms, and I trace the shape of them, carefully, so as not to hurt him more. His skin is cold, despite the heat of the day.

'You're staying with me,' I say without thinking twice. I might not be on speaking terms with my parents, and Luca is half the reason why, but his home has been my safe haven for years. There's no universe in which I wouldn't offer him shelter in mine. It'll force my parents to talk, because they might be mad at me and out of their comfort zone around Luca, but they would never dare to be impolite. Also, in light of Maz's lies, they currently don't seem so bad.

With the horizon turning scarlet and the sea mirroring its burning hues, we make our way back across the island. The sight of Hidden House halts us in our tracks. From this vantage point, the trees part to reveal a centuries-old stone building that dominates the landscape. Two turrets point sharply into the sky, and the many dark windows appear like eyes.

Luca bites his lower lip, eyes on the manor. He shakes his head and descends to the walkway. I follow close, and we make it to the mainland minutes before the tide starts to claim back the causeway. We take the quiet route through town, which is deserted, as people are gathered on the beach to watch the sunset.

Less than two weeks ago, we were part of that crowd, blissfully oblivious to the brewing storm. Now there's a tremor, a coil of fear nestled tight in my chest that won't dissipate, regardless of how many deep breaths I take. It tells me that the worst hasn't hit us yet.

Luca is so deep in thought, I can almost hear him ponder. Instinctively I want to reach out, take his hand. I crave the physical reassurance that he's beside me. So I lift my hands and shove them in my pockets.

Braving a storm is one thing. Tempting it, quite another.

CHAPTER 9 – LUCA

There's a photo album that sits on Simo's bookshelf. Regardless of how often he reorganises, the album never leaves its spot in the top-left corner. Kids' books go, classics move in, poetry collections push novels off the shelves, but the black leather album remains. Dust never settles on it, so I know that Simo pulls it out regularly, but he's never done so when I'm around.

The spine is embossed with five golden letters that form canyons in the thick leather. The only reason I know Simo's brother's name is because these letters spell it out. They're the sole evidence that he ever existed. The rest of the house holds no signs of him, no pictures, nothing.

I've been lying on Simo's bed like this all night, facing the wall with the bookshelf, the desk, the corkboard decked out in Simo's memories. My eyes dart from the selfie of us on a class trip to a couple of ripped tickets from the play we saw in Granada. I didn't understand a thing, but the costumes were pretty and so was Simo, his face glowing, captivated by the stage actors.

I haven't slept, only pretended to when Simo climbed off the bed and shuffled out of the room an hour ago. My phone lies in a bundle of clothes, but I haven't touched it since I turned it off last night. I didn't want to hear from Dad. And when I saw that Mum had tried to call, I realised that she must have *known* about my not-dead grandparents, that she'd helped Dad keep up the lie. I wasn't going to speak to her either.

It's not like I haven't thought about it. Opening the album, I mean. Whenever I'm in here, there's a third boy in the room, one whose presence we can't deny but don't acknowledge. The mere thought of prying into parts of Simo's life he doesn't offer willingly feels like betrayal. And as it stands, I've got plenty of things to keep me up at night; I can do without adding more guilt to the mix.

A soft knock pulls my attention from the album to the door. Simo pops his head in. Only he would knock before entering his own room.

'Hungry? My parents made breakfast,' he says. I lift my eyebrows, which prompts him to enter fully and close the door behind him. 'They've gone all out,' he explains. 'I'm not sure who they're trying to fool with the pretend family harmony, but I'm not about to say no to the food.'

My stomach rumbles, and I get a whiff of fried eggs in the air that must have snuck into the room with Simo. It's my body's way of telling me I skipped dinner and need to eat, though I'd rather stay here, tucked away in Simo's room, in Simo's bed.

Hunger isn't the only thing upsetting my belly. I haven't seen Simo's parents since the noticeboard message. There's always something distant and sad about his dad, but it's his mum who intimidates me.

'Get up, lazy fart,' Simo says, and throws an old soft toy at my head. He hovers by the door, and judging by the prominent vein on his brow, I'd say I'm not the only one who's worried.

'Can I borrow a clean T-shirt? And trousers? Mine have grass stains all over.'

'This isn't Sunday church,' Simo replies, grabbing something from his dresser. He throws it my way and a second later I'm holding a pair of grey joggers in my hands. 'You don't need to try and impress my parents.'

I don't know if that's a good or a bad thing and decide not to ask. All my concentration goes into pretending it's perfectly normal that I'm standing in Simo's room wearing nothing but underwear. Which it sort of is. We've had more sleepovers than I can count. Since I was a kid, Simo has woken up in my bed at least once every other week, more so recently, which also means he sees me undressed on a regular basis. And I him.

With forced composure I pull the joggers on, while Simo searches for a T-shirt. I shrug into it, and the soft white fabric envelopes me in his scent. The vein is proof of his impatience, but there's something else in his mellow brown eyes that I can't discern.

'I'm allowed to wash my face though, right?' I ask, to break the weird tension that's rising between us. 'And brush my teeth? Or do you think your parents will like me more with morning breath?'

'You never have morning breath. It's unnerving,' Simo mutters, but he leads me to the bathroom and searches the cabinets for a spare toothbrush. He hands it over and leaves me to myself, which is for the best. Not just because I can drop the fake coolness, but because my bladder has realised that we're vertical again.

When I enter the dining room, I'm greeted by an array of foods so gorgeous that it belongs in a painting. Pancake towers so fluffy you want to sleep on them, bowls overflowing with berries, their blues and reds bursting on my tongue in anticipation. A golden masterpiece of a tortilla topped with pomegranate seeds that sparkle like rubies, next to a saucepan filled to the rim with a rich tomato stew, eggs swimming on the surface. Someone even added an arrangement of purple daisies to the table. A broad man with a round, bearded face walks in from the kitchen, carrying a loaf of sourdough. I can see the steam rising from the freshly cut slices.

'There you are!' Simo's dad exclaims. Simo clearly inherited his eyes, brown and light like wildflower honey.

'Good morning, Luca,' a woman's voice says, and I turn to Simo's mum. She holds a jug of freshly made lemonade, and when she places it on the table, the ice clinks against the glass.

'Morning,' I repeat, and smile. I don't have to fake it. It's hard not to smile with food like this in front of me.

'Now don't you think this is a breakfast that would make your father's customers green with envy? He's not the only one who can cook, you know,' Pedro says.

'Dad!' Simo scolds him.

Pedro wears a look of remorse and I realise that Simo has filled them in on everything that's happened.

'It looks incredible,' I admit, and try not to let my face slip.

We take our seats and for a minute we're all busy loading our plates with more food than they can fit.

'Have some shakshuka.' Safa fills a small bowl with the tomato egg stew, then places it next to me. I pick up the spoon, thinking that she can't harbour any grudges against me if she's trying to stuff me with food. 'My mother used to make this regularly.'

Simo stops chewing and stares at his mum like he's hearing this for the first time.

'Thank you,' I say, remembering my manners. Safa is a slight woman, her frame much narrower than her husband's and son's. Despite her size, there's a hardness in the way she holds herself, chin raised and back straight. She's tough because the softness has been whittled away. I often forget that she's a primary-school teacher. I can't quite imagine the strict woman in front of me around a bunch of small kids.

I do as I'm told, take a mouthful of the shakshuka and barely manage to hold in a moan. If red was a dish, this is how it would taste: succulent, earthy, and with a hint of heat.

'And you're right, I think my dad would fear for his customers if you decided to open a restaurant.' The compliment prompts a brief smile from Safa.

'We don't get to cook for guests every day,' Pedro says, sounding pleased.

'You have me,' Simo points out. 'You never cook like this for me.'

'There's no point, is there? Dinnertime comes around and you're nowhere to be found.' Safa slices open an egg with a single stab of her knife, and the yolk erupts like lava.

Simo takes a furiously big bite of pancake. He has a habit of making his parents sound worse than they are, though he wouldn't catch me voicing that particular thought. I mean, they're not all hugs and love exclamations, but they're not bad either. Then again, I think we're all biased when it comes to our families. We see them in a light much better or worse than an outsider would. Not entirely without reason; after all, an outsider has no idea what it's like to grow up with them. But our impression of family is warped because we look at them through lenses we've worn for years. And sometimes we forget to take them off and see them not as a parent or child or sibling, but as themselves. Maybe that's an impossible thing to do, anyway. Which is why Simo won't give them the credit they deserve for raising my favourite person in the world. Which is why I've put my dad on a pedestal and can't cope with the fact that he's fallen off.

Thankfully Pedro pulls me away from the edge I'm teetering on. 'You enjoyed Granada, did you? Simo didn't tell us much about it.'

'It's the best holiday I've ever had,' I reply truthfully. It's also the only holiday I've ever been on, not that I'm complaining. Despite the stupid noticeboard and family secrets, I never wanted to be anywhere but here. 'And Simo loved it too,' I add.

He chews longer than any pancake needs chewing, but with his parents' eyes on him, expecting an answer, he swallows reluctantly. 'I did like it,' he confesses, clearly underselling it. 'In fact, I want to go back. For a gap year.'

He wants what? I almost drop the spoon on its way to my mouth, barely avoiding a shakshuka disaster.

Pedro nods with happy interest, but Safa puts her knife down with a decisive clink. 'A gap year? That's news to me.'

Same here, Safa. I'm convinced Simo just made it up to annoy her. Prompted by the disapproval in her voice, he digs in deeper. 'I need to live there at least for a bit if I want to be fluent. And I do want to be fluent. It's embarrassing that I could barely talk with my own cousins. So, yeah, I'm doing a gap year.'

He's riling her up. And it seems to be working, because now I know where he has that forehead vein from. Its twin is appearing on Safa's brow. Simo doesn't usually talk back at them, at least not when I'm around. Also, he's stretching the truth more than a bit. He soaked up his dad's language like a sponge, and by the end of the holiday he held entire conversations with his family. Not to mention that his cousins' English was so flawless I never dared to use the Spanish sentences I'd prepared in order not to look completely ignorant. I failed at that, obviously. But my Duolingo streak is uninterrupted ever since.

'We didn't save money for university only for you to waste it on a party trip to Spain. Gap years are for rich kids.' Her words are sharp and precise. I see her glance my way for a second, but her anger overrides her sense of propriety. I try to disappear behind the vase of daisies, uncomfortably aware of my presence in this home that isn't mine.

Simo keeps quiet for the rest of the meal, which doesn't last long. The Lorcas have lost their appetites, and as soon as we've cleared the table, Simo pulls me back into his room. I decide it's better to keep quiet than to appear like I'm agreeing with his mum. Best to resent our parents together than resent each other.

Simo straddles his desk chair and disappears into his phone, and since I prefer mine in its dead state, I fall back on to the bed and stare at the ceiling. I could make a start on the assigned reading, but books never take my mind off things. When my thoughts become too loud, I bake, but I can't exactly do that in the Lorcas' kitchen and my own is currently enemy territory. It's easy to empty my head when I focus on following the steps of a recipe. There's something calming about throwing ingredients together, mixing them with my own two hands. It's hard to feel bad about life when you've created something that's pretty to look at and makes your mouth water.

'Would you be mad at me if I brought up your grandmother?' Simo says, bursting the daydream. He lifts his shoulders, as if he's trying to brace himself for my reaction. But the truth is, he would have to commit a serious crime for me to get angry with him. And even then, I'd still help him cover it up. 'It's just, I have intel on her that you might want to hear.'

'But you don't even know her.' I prop myself up, confusion rushing through my veins.

'No, but it turns out Dad does. When I mentioned your, um, falling-out, he kind of connected the dots. He's one of only two estate agents in town, and when a property like Hidden House sells, it doesn't go unnoticed.'

I'm trying to digest the fact that he's sat on this information all through breakfast. I know he's only trying to protect me, but I'm starting to feel stupid for being left in the dark while Simo, his dad and likely his mum too know more about my grandmother than I do.

'Don't make me drag it out of you!'

'I'm sorry! I'm trying to help, even if I'm doing a bad job at it. I'm hardly an expert at diffusing family drama.' He gets up and sits next to me on the bed. 'Ready?'

I close my eyes and focus on his leg touching mine. When the nagging impatience has subsided, I face him again. He is serious and beautiful. The confident arcs of his eyebrows, the way his freckles mingle with the pockmarks, the soft upswing of his nose. If baking offers moments of escape, Simo anchors me in the present.

'OK. Tell me.'

He hesitates, then he holds out his phone. I take it, but he doesn't let go. We're both holding on to it, and maybe to each other.

Several versions of her look up at me; photographs from galas and functions. 'Secret CEO: The Female Face of the Brandenburg Brand' beneath a picture that shows her cutting a ribbon with oversized scissors, 'Thirteen Women in Power Suits' reads another, next to 'Brandenburg Christmas Gala Turns Twenty'. There are a whole bunch more, on fiscal years, business growth, and bagels, of all things. She's younger in most of them, but the haircut is the same, the long fringe framing a heart-shaped face. And always by her side a man who, at first sight, I believe to be Dad. It's the same face, down to the dip in the chin and wavy hair. The real difference lies in his expression. Where Dad's eyes hold warmth, this older version of him looks on to the world with cold calculation.

CHAPTER 10 – SIMO

'How much money can you make from *bread*?'

'Enough to buy an ancient mansion,' Mairi tells Louise, and bites off the tip of her carrot. They're scrolling through articles and Wikipedia entries on their phones, researching Lombard's newest residents.

Louise is doing what she does best, spreading gossip and adding a trickle of fuel to keep the fire going. People are already losing their minds over the mere presence of multimillionaires in Lombard, I can't imagine their reaction when they find out whose grandparents they are.

'The mansion isn't that ancient, only three or four centuries,' she says, and twirls a strawberry-blonde curl around her finger.

'You try and make it to three hundred years and then we'll talk about what is and isn't ancient,' Mairi deadpans.

Louise stares at her phone, mouth agape. 'If these sources are correct, the Brandenburgs are so rich they could buy the whole town,' she tells us. 'All because they somehow turned a single bakery into a multimillion-pound bread empire.'

'I get it,' Jacob chirps up. 'I love bread.'

A group of us have swapped the packed lunch hall for the park. We're huddled on the stage of the open-air theatre, which is shaped like a giant oyster, its curved roof offering shelter from the constant drizzle. Despite that, everyone's in shorts and T-shirts, trying to make the summer last.

My gaze sweeps across the tended lawns and flower beds and keeps snagging on the town square – and the noticeboard – just beyond the park, separated only by a concrete patch of street. My chest flares with anxiety every time I read the words, even though the message has long changed.

JOIN THE HARVEST
FESTIVAL
THIS WEEKEND!

Next to me, Luca is biting his fingernails. I elbow him, because there is no sound I find more revolting, and he knows it. When I nod towards the steps, silently asking if he wants to leave, he shakes his head.

I'm surprised we're still here, listening to gossip about his grandparents, after we spent the weekend scouring the internet for information, and even watched a documentary on the bread empire in question. It was Luca's grandfather who turned the ailing family bakery around, buying up other bakeries that were close to ruin and, over the next four decades, amassing hundreds of stores all over the country. Nowadays, Brandenburg bread is sold in every supermarket and cafe. All these years we've been munching on Brandenburg toast without knowing that it's Luca's grandparents' name on the packaging. He stares at his half-eaten sandwich as if he just had the same thought.

It's Wednesday, and he still hasn't talked to his dad. I don't mind him bunking with me, but I had to find a new home for the notebook. I'd never be able to look him in the eyes if he found the many half-written poems, the thinly veiled allusions to his name. But the house doesn't feel so depressingly quiet with him in it, and my parents are on their best behaviour. That's coming to an end, though I haven't found a good moment to tell him.

'Why do you think they moved here?' Louise ponders. 'Famous people don't come to Lombard. Nothing ever happens here.'

'Now, that isn't true,' Jacob throws in. 'If you can believe what that massive noticeboard says, the harvest festival is definitely happening.'

He throws me a nervous glance from behind his ginger curtains, and I'm reminded of our first meeting outside the cafe. I've still not made up my mind about him.

'It's not that exciting,' Luca says, speaking up for the first time. He's been different these past few days, his usual chattiness replaced with something more withdrawn. 'It means you'll find hay bales and seasonal flower arrangements all over town. There'll be a big potluck, and a band playing the same five songs over and over, and some dancing around a firepit if you've had one too many.'

'Sounds nice to me,' Curtains says, and smiles at Luca.

'I didn't say it wasn't nice,' Luca replies, returning the smile, 'just not exciting.'

I've not seen him smile since the fight with his dad. Then this guy turns up and suddenly the clouds part.

'What's the story there anyway? With the noticeboard, I mean.'

It bothers me, the way Curtains directs his question at Luca like no one else is around.

'It's a Celtic tradition,' I reply gruffly, to stop him eyeing up Luca, 'a way to mark important holidays.'

'Huh,' Mairi says and swallows her food. 'My mum told me that Pickering put it up for May Day a few years ago and refused to pay for having it removed again.'

'You're both wrong,' Luca says. 'It was built by the same people who owned the manor. A way to mark the border of their land or something.'

'So, you're not going for May Couple, then?' Louise prompts, changing the topic at breakneck speed. Her expression of gleeful curiosity gets my blood boiling. Mairi stills mid-chew. Everyone's eyes are on us, awaiting our reaction.

'Why would we go for May Couple if we're not a couple, Louise?' I ask, trying to hide the thunder I feel inside. I don't know which one of us moved, but now there's a space between Luca and me that wasn't there a minute ago.

'What's a May Couple?' Jacob speaks up, confusion drawing lines on to his forehead.

'People in Lombard go a little crazy for the summer,' Mairi explains. 'The harvest festival this week marks the autumn equinox, so the end of summer, as opposed to May

Day which celebrates the summer to come. Part of the festival is the tradition of crowning a couple of lovers, who will then light this huge bonfire to symbolise a season of abundance.'

'It's very *Midsommar*,' Louise adds, 'but, like, actually kind of cute and romantic and completely without violent murder.'

Heat rises from my neck and sets my face alight. The idea of Luca and me standing in front of the entire town as we're pronounced lovers to the sound of drums and trumpets makes me want to be sick.

'I get it, Lombard loves a romance. But like Simo said, we're friends.' Luca brushes them off with a lightness that I envy him for.

'You should come, Jacob. Sunday is when they sell all the good food. We should all go, as a group,' Mairi suggests, but I'm still stuck on that pointed little question.

'Why would Luca and I go for May Couple, Louise?' I repeat. Luca sends me a look, telling me to let it go, but if this is another rumour making the rounds, I need to know.

Louise shrugs. 'We can't crown Sheila and her fiancé a third year in a row, so your names were thrown in the ring.'

I'm not happy to have my suspicion confirmed. Luca and I pulled ourselves back together after that first week, but I don't know how our friendship would cope with a second hit when I'm not sure we're fully recovered from the first one. It shouldn't be this complicated. When did we go from being Simo and Luca to becoming other people's property?

'If you could just not mention our names like that, I'd

really appreciate it,' Luca says. He addresses the group but avoids looking in my direction.

Something about Luca's nature inspires trust in others. His presence is comfortable to a degree of being addictive. It's so reassuring when you have it that you can't help but miss it when it's gone. He acts as a welcome buffer between me and the rest of the world. I tend to keep to myself more, not because I dislike people, but it's easier to exist in my own head. Trying to translate my feelings to someone else doesn't come easily.

A tap on my shoulder pops the bubble I've disappeared into. Luca fills my field of vision. I try not to stare at the birthmarks that dot his long arms or the sliver of chest peeking from beneath his vest. That's my clothes on his body, borrowed from my wardrobe this morning. My skin begins to tingle in a way I can't explain.

'Where did you go?' Luca asks, almost tenderly. It's a familiar question and, like always, I shake my head, unable to let him into my thoughts.

Behind him, Mairi is zipping up her boots, and Louise is hiding her hair beneath a cardigan, pouting at the drizzle that separates us from the school grounds. I didn't realise we were leaving.

'Ready?' Louise asks.

'You go ahead,' I say, without giving them a reason for staying behind. Even if I had an explanation, I wouldn't be able to tell them. I barely know how to soften the blow for Luca.

Jacob and Louise shuffle out, but Mairi lingers at the edge of the stage. Angular and statuesque, she looms a head taller than us, especially in platform boots.

'Let us know about Sunday, yeah?' she says, and follows the others into the mist. Now there's only me and Luca huddled beneath the somewhat derelict roof, and I've still not managed to come up with the right words.

A flicker of worry dashes across his face and settles in the strained tilt of his neck. He reminds me of a fawn watching its surroundings for a reason to bolt. Ever since the noticeboard announcement, it's a reaction I've seen more often in him than I'd like.

This morning, Mum cornered me in the kitchen when Luca was in the shower. She said she didn't mind having him around – which was less stretching the truth and more like twisting it completely – but he couldn't camp out with us forever. He has a dad that worries about him, and also my trousers are too short for his legs. She wasn't wrong about the latter. Luca's ankles are on full display, but he makes it look intentional.

'What is it?' he asks, searching my face for a sign. I'm nervous he'll find something he shouldn't see.

I've always suspected that my parents don't approve of the fact that Luca is gay, that his dad is gay and, most of all, that I spend so much time with them. They've never said anything hostile, but kids are more perceptive than parents like to admit.

I saw the reaction when Mum asked about Maz's wife once, and Maz clarified he'd never been married to Luca's mum, and that he's gay. When Maz sent Luca to ballet lessons and asked me to join, I declined, knowing my parents wouldn't approve, even at eight years old. And then, right before the trip to Granada, Dad gave me a few euro notes for a night out, but warned me, with a look I could hardly misinterpret, to stay away from 'those' bars. It made me feel gross, like I'd been accused of a crime I hadn't committed. Adding up these moments paints a grim picture, one I hope Luca never lays eyes on.

I open my mouth, still unsure how to begin, but Luca sees through my hesitation.

'I've outstayed my welcome,' he deduces.

'That's not true,' I lie. He hasn't, not with me. Luca raises his eyebrows, both of them, cos he's never mastered the art of moving just one. 'All right. My parents complained that they can't keep cooking for four.'

Luca frowns. 'Is that what they said?'

'Not in those words. But the message was clear.'

'They've seemed to enjoy cooking for us.'

'To show off.'

'They made nice conversation.'

'To pry, nothing more.'

'They didn't ask once about the fight with Maz.'

'Because they don't care.'

Luca waits a beat. He wears a serious expression, but there's something gentle in those ocean eyes. 'I don't think you give them enough credit,' he says.

'I think you give them too much,' I reply.

He only shakes his head. 'It's OK, honestly. I have a home, and a dad, and it's not like I'd planned to stay forever. I needed a timeout and that's come to an end.'

'You sure?' I ask, relieved that he's not hurt.

He smiles, softly, and at last I know he's going to be all

right. 'You've been sharing your room and your clothes with me. You must miss not having anything to yourself.'

I don't know why he's consoling me when he's the one leaving. The only thing I'll be missing is the little moments when he talks in his sleep. I've heard my name in there once or twice. I always hold my breath when it happens, hoping he'll say more.

It's confusing, knowing I'm on his mind but being left in the dark as to why. I want him to let me into his dreams. Our bodies are so used to each other that sometimes I can't sleep without the sound of his breath in my ears. But that doesn't erase the barrier between what's on his mind and what he tells me.

Ever since the noticeboard message, we're on unfamiliar ground. And ever since the moment in the cupboard, I've started seeing him in a different light. I have always been sure of our friendship, and having him around tells me that we're still Luca and Simo. But I've yet to find the line where friendship ends and turns into something else. Whatever is happening with my feelings for Luca, they're taking on a different shape, one that I can't interpret. I want to know if he feels the same, but I'm not sure I can muster the courage to ask.

I want to tell him that no, I don't mind sharing. He can have my food, my room, my bed, my clothes. He can have it all and I'd be happier for it. But the words don't make it past my lips. Because as Luca said himself, we're not a couple. Lombard wants to make us something we're not. So perhaps it's best that we sleep in separate beds again.

We head out into a rain so gentle it's like walking

through spiderwebs. Immediately we're covered in a thin layer of mist. By the time we reach the edge of the school grounds, Luca is wearing a crown of dewdrops, hundreds of diamonds caught in his hair.

I don't know who I'm fooling. If we were ever to break apart, of course I wouldn't cope. I've lost my favourite person once before. There's no way I'd survive another hit.

There's no way I'd survive without Luca. And that scares me.

CHAPTER 11 – LUCA

I never thought I'd say it, but Maz Dean is a coward. He'd say he's giving me 'space' to process, but this time it doesn't feel generous, but selfish. By avoiding me, he avoids having to face up to any mistakes he's made. He may pretend his mother never walked into the cafe and upended our lives, but I won't play along. Yes, he's got the stubbornness of a mule, but guess who inherited that character trait along with a whole bunch of other charming attributes? The boy in question is currently stuffing blocks of Parmesan into a food blender.

Instead of working in the cafe, I'm processing my feelings by making a mess of the upstairs kitchen. A Lorde album blasts from the speakers, her sound perfectly capturing my rage-infused melancholy. I've already prepared a fresh batch of chilli jam and enough apple crisps to feed all of Lombard. If Dad needs my help, he only has to ask, but since he's not speaking, I make no move to either. He can't call me petulant, because what would that make him, being twice my age?

Once I've added basil, garlic, olive oil and roasted pine nuts to the Parmesan, I hit the 'BLEND' button with more force than necessary. While the blender does its thing, I step over to by the window and check the empty pet shop across the street. The stickers remain where I put them up to cover the S x L heart, secretly and in the middle of the night, like one of those vandals that Mayor Pickering fears will spoil the town's spotless image. But I'd rather be found vandalising Lombard than be accused of having a crush on Simo. Again.

We often turn Friday evenings into film nights, but I haven't mentioned anything about it to him. Things aren't weird exactly, but they're not normal either. It's been more than two days since Louise's lunchtime inquisition and he's made no move to hang out after school. Neither have I, mostly because I'm scared he'll say no. If it was up to me, I'd rather bear the gossip than keep my distance to make them go away. But I can't speak for Simo. I'm used to the other students commenting on me liking boys, but it's a new thing for him. And whether someone's gay or not, having people question who you are day in, day out starts to wear on you.

I realise far too late that the blender is still going, and what was meant to be a textured pesto with small chunks of cheese and nuts has turned into a smooth paste the colour of a swamp. Still tastes good though. Maybe if I promise Simo fresh pesto if he comes over, he'll be unable to say no. Bribing people with food is a special talent of mine, but I'm reluctant to make use of it now. If it was up to me, Simo would already be on the couch, waiting for the film to start. It makes me miss the time when planning film nights didn't send me into an emotional crisis.

As I set water to boil in a pot, my thoughts return to Dad. He's never given me a reason to be truly angry at him before. I'm sure I've given him loads, but if so, he kept his frustration hidden. Occasionally teachers would question how a dad so young could raise a child, but being closer in age made us closer in life. He hasn't had enough time to forget what it's like being a teenager. He relates, and I've always known I could come to him with anything and he wouldn't freak out. The grandparent revelation has knocked that trust. It's made me realise that Dad isn't just Dad. He's sixteen years of a life before I existed, sixteen years he's shut away. It's no surprise I'm stress-cooking.

Dad walks into the lounge as I'm draining the linguine. I divide it between two plates and add the fresh pesto and cocktail tomatoes. The only reason he gets a plate is because I suck at measuring enough pasta for one. And maybe also because he worked hard all day, without my help, but mainly because of the measuring thing.

He spots the dinner arrangement and, for a second, he looks as if he wants to say something. Whatever it is, he keeps it to himself and joins me at the table, bringing a stale taste to my mouth that I quickly drown in pesto. The food is a tiny peace offering. I'm giving him a chance to speak. But after several silent bites I'm tempted to drop my fork and walk out. What holds me back is the refusal to turn my back on pasta. I clear my plate, then hit the stop button on Lorde.

'Care to explain?' I ask.

'I'd rather not, no,' he replies, wiping his mouth with a serviette.

'Right.' I shove the chair back and make sure the legs scrape the floor hard enough to produce the screeching sound he hates.

'Luca, please.' Dad raises his hands in defeat. 'I know I owe you answers, but it's hard. You can't imagine how hard. Look, could you sit?'

Despite the anger filling me up, I struggle to direct it towards him. I've never had to fight him before, and I don't know how start now. So I sit.

'I have my reasons, just believe that. I would never have kept you from my parents if I thought they had something good to give. To you and your mum. To our family.' He doesn't look at me as he says this, his eyes scanning the pictures above the sofa. There's one of Mum, vest top stretched tight over a belly round as a beach ball. She poses in front of their ancient Beetle after its final journey to the scrapyard, just days before I was born. The photograph is faded, bleached by the time that's passed.

'That's no real answer,' I say. 'It's barely even an explanation.' Also, not a hint of an apology. I've always rated Dad for admitting to his mistakes, while most adults I know pretend they're beyond them.

'They're bad parents. You weren't even born and I knew I didn't want you anywhere near them. Still don't, if I'm being honest. And I'm trying very hard to be honest.'

'You're not doing a very good job,' I point out.

'I'm out of practice. I haven't talked about them in years.'

Which brings me to the biggest question of all. 'What was so bad that you pretended they were dead?'

'It was easier that way. I planned never to see them again,

so they might as well have been.' His words are cold and practical, like he's making a grocery list rather than cutting his parents out of his life. And out of mine.

'So, it was easy lying to me?'

'No, not easy, but necessary. Your mum told me it was a stupid idea, but I was doing it to protect you.'

'And to protect yourself!'

'Yes, for good reasons.'

'Which you won't tell me!'

'Luca!' he shouts, finally. I'm relieved to hear his voice crack with real emotion. 'I apologise for lying to you. I know you're hurt and that's the last thing I want. But I'm not sorry for keeping you from my parents. Because I'd rather lie than give them a chance to hurt you!'

'Dad, why won't you just say—' but he won't let me finish.

'I don't need to lay out my childhood trauma in front of you! My parents shouldn't have been parents, simple as that. The only reason they had a child was to complete their set of status symbols, alongside the villa, the Bentley and the Schiaparelli dresses. But nobody wants to hear that sob story, and I certainly don't owe it to you or anyone!'

That shuts me up. Because he's right. If it hurts him to talk or even think about the past, who am I to dig around old wounds?

'There's one thing you need to understand about my parents,' Dad says, voice empty. 'They are utterly and categorically selfish. Their kindness is never that, because kindness comes without expectations. And my parents don't give without taking. I would know.'

Dad deflates on his chair like a popped balloon. If I had spared him a look these past few days, a proper look, the bags under his eyes would have told me that he hasn't been sleeping. That this falling-out is costing him as much as me.

I'm not a complete pushover; of course he's hurt me. But the anger I felt earlier is fading. I don't want the split between us to run deeper, so I stop myself asking about his parents again. But there's no way I'm able to move past it completely.

I grab our plates and get up but turn around before I reach the kitchen. 'I'm going to their barbecue on Sunday,' I announce.

'No, you're not.'

I expected that answer, so I calmly stack the dishes into the dishwasher. 'You do whatever you want, but you can't stop me.' Now that I have grandparents, I'm not going to waste my chance to get to know them. The fact that they're basically celebrities only makes me more curious. And a little intimidated. But I'm not telling Dad that.

'You're not going on your own,' he says flatly. The chestnut waves of his hair stand up in all directions.

A petty part of me is satisfied to see him so riled up. I kick the door of the dishwasher shut. 'Why? Scared of what else I'd find out?'

'Scared, yes, but only because you'd be walking into a lion's den, and you, my friend, are a defenceless puppy.'

'Hey, you're the one making me go alone, even though you know how to stand up to them.'

'Well, I don't, do I? If I'd known that, I wouldn't have had to run so far away from them.'

Point taken. But, 'They're here now, so there's nowhere to run. Also, don't you think there's a possibility that they've changed in the last seventeen years?'

A grin splits his face, one that makes him look rather manic.

'There's a lot of things I believe to be possible, like the existence of the ghoul in the supplies cupboard or Avril Lavigne dying and being replaced by a doppelganger, but my parents changing isn't one of them. If anything, they get more vicious with age.'

'You can't just decide for me, Dad.'

He's never set bans or given me ultimatums. His strategy was always to tell me his thoughts and then he'd leave me to make my own mistakes. Like that one time when I was nine and refused to wear an ugly pair of sandals to Simo's birthday picnic and I stepped on not just one but two furious bees. Or when I thought we should offer beetroot chocolate cake in the cafe, despite Dad's attempts to tell me people hate that vegetable, even if the cake tastes like heaven. He'd always let me have a go at proving him wrong.

'I'm older than you were when you decided to leave home. So let me decide to get to know my grandparents. And if they're as bad as you say they are, we don't have to see them again.'

Dad stares at me with wide blue eyes several shades darker than mine. 'I'll have to close the cafe.'

'No, you don't. You have staff to run it. We're only going for a meal, not a holiday. They can cope for a couple of hours.'

Dad groans like a toddler forced to eat something that isn't beige. 'Fine, we'll go. On one condition.' I raise my eyebrows, curious to hear him out. 'We stop fighting. I hate that we're not speaking, and when we are, that we're shouting.'

'I hate it too,' I admit. 'But I can't stop myself from feeling things, Dad.'

He gets up and bridges the distance between the dining table and the kitchen. 'I know that,' he says, and places his hands on my shoulders. They're firm and tanned and smell of the coffee he pours all day. I wish I had hands like his.

'I'm not asking you to get over it all immediately. But you know me well. Better than anyone in my life, except maybe your mum. I want you safe and I want you happy. And I think, so far, I've done a pretty good job of it. Grant me a little trust, OK?'

Trust is exactly the problem here. I can't give him what he's broken. I say nothing, which he must take as a yes. He gives me a hug and I hug him back, instantly feeling better.

'Thanks for cooking,' he says. 'It was good. Way better than that veggie bolognaise you made once.'

'I was twelve, Dad.'

'And I'm complimenting your progress, so let me.'

'You're a thirty-three-year-old man who can't bake for shit, so what should I say?' The man might have taught me to cook, but as soon as eggs, sugar and flour come into play, he's hopeless.

'Say that you will please do a morning shift at the cafe tomorrow?'

'Yes,' I grumble, but I'm glad that he asked.

'And promise you'll stop ignoring your mum's calls? The only reason she kept shtum about is because I asked her to. She doesn't deserve any of the blame, and she misses you.'

I'm not sure I fully agree, after all she went along with his lie, but I'd hate to be put in her position. Just the idea of having to lie to Dad because Simo asked me to gives me a stomach-ache. I nod and promise to ring her.

He heads back out to finish closing up the cafe, but halts in the hallway.

'So are we watching something later, or what?'

I check my phone to see if Simo's messaged. He's sent a selfie holding different snacks – crinkle crisps and cheese twists – and a question mark. My heart halts, then tumbles. That's the effect he has on me, a reaction so physical my body basically gives out. Even though the picture is blurry, the veins on the back of his hands have me weak, but it's the tip of his tongue pressed against his top lip that almost sends me to my knees. He immediately followed up to say he got the crisps *and* the twists. How I exist next to this human every day and keep my cool, I don't know.

Dad clears his throat, and I blink several times before I remember his question.

'It's between *The Favourite* and *Cruel Intentions*,' I answer.

'Which is gayer?' he asks.

Fact is, they're gay in different ways, but hopefully not so gay as to make it awkward watching it with Simo. One has cut-throat lesbians fighting for power in amazing clothes, the other has chaotic bisexuals fighting for power in amazing clothes, plus a gay blackmailing side plot. Now that I think about it, *The Favourite* is the safer choice.

'Wait, *Cruel Intentions* is the one with Ryan Phillippe's bum, right? I want that one,' Dad says, and walks out before I get the chance to argue.

CHAPTER 12 – SIMO

Luca's breath brushes the fine hair on my neck. His forehead is against the base of my skull, lips inches from my skin. He is fast asleep. My mind is in a dreamlike state that allows me not to think about Luca's proximity, about his hands folded over my shoulder blades. I float in the comfort of his touch and the knowledge that he seeks mine, even when he's unaware of doing so.

Irritation rises in my chest and unravels the blanket of obliviousness I've wrapped myself in. My body anticipates the buzz of Luca's phone before I do. The alarm is aggressive enough in broad daylight, but now it splits the room's drowsy silence like an axe. I reach out and quash the loathsome sound before it has a chance to build. It makes no difference; Luca would sleep through it regardless. The alarm only serves to wake me so I can wake him.

I nudge him with my shoulder, not that anything comes of it. The back of my T-shirt is trapped beneath Luca's unconscious body. I wear it, not because I get cold, but because Luca sleeps without one, and I need a safety layer between us. His nose nuzzles my arm, and it takes extreme effort to pry myself away and create the distance required for two boys sharing one bed and absolutely no romantic feelings.

I inhale. Luca smells drowsy, of sweat and sleep. My chest expands as I take several more breaths, until I realise what I'm doing. He looks so peaceful that I don't have it in me to use any of my more brutal methods. I tickle the spot where his jaw meets his neck and feel the softest stubble beneath my fingertips. He scrunches his brow, but I don't stop until he groans, eyelids twitching, and swats my hand away.

'Simo, no,' he mumbles, and something flutters in my ribcage, knowing that his day starts with my name on his lips.

'Luca, yes,' I reply, and take his pillow away when he attempts to bury his head beneath it.

When he's finally up and has gone to lend a hand in the cafe, I seek and find the pocket of warmth where his body was and doze for another hour.

'Before you leave, could you do me a favour?' Maz asks when I enter the cafe, where the morning bustle is in full swing. A queue of bright-eyed customers clogs the space between door and counter, and Luca dances around them, balancing dirty plates. 'Could you deliver a coffee to her majesty Miss M? I've not had a bathroom break in hours and if I pour another drink, I might have an accident I'll never live down.'

I grin and nod.

'My saviour, my hero,' Maz shouts as he hands me the cup and runs for his life.

Two floors up, I knock, and a regal voice commands me to enter. I've been here before, but always with Luca. When we were little we'd visit when Maz refused us sweets, so we'd turn to Miss M, with her stash of cookie tins always ready for us.

'Simo Lorca,' she says when I deliver the drink, 'my, you've grown even prettier than when I last saw you. You've got the eyes of Scheherazade and her lashes too. The girls at school must love and loathe you.' I almost blush at the flattery. 'Now don't just simper there like a docile English rose, sit and chat with this old woman.'

She slurps the coffee and smacks her lips in delight. 'But maybe you don't care for these girls. Maybe you're far too preoccupied with someone else, hmm?'

There's zero chance I'm having this conversation. 'Sorry, Miss M, I have to—'

But before I can finish my excuse, she ploughs on. 'Tell me, have you discovered who pulled that noticeboard trick on you and Luca?'

I try to keep my face composed, because I'm not in the habit of giving old ladies the evil eye, even when they're prying into things that are none of their business.

'We haven't, no,' I snap.

'Hmm, it would be easier to narrow down the suspects if we knew whether they were motivated by good intentions or malevolence,' she ponders, and takes another sip.

'Good intentions?' I snort, and jump up, desperate to end our chat. She grabs my wrist before I make it any further.

'Simo, darling boy, a word of advice. If you truly want to know how someone feels about you, take a petal from the bloom of an apple tree and hide it beneath their pillow. If they smell of it the next day, they reciprocate your desire.'

'Right,' I reply, because that's all I can come up with in the face of such bollocks.

She pats my cheek and finally lets go. 'Cherry blossom works too.'

'Have a wonderful Saturday, Miss M,' I say, and escape as quickly as my legs allow.

At the bottom of the stairs, I run into Luca, who's got a kitchen towel over one shoulder and a smudge of something on his cheek. I fight the urge to brush it off.

'You look spooked,' he says.

'I'm not.'

'Did you get stuck in the supplies closet again?'

'I'm not spooked.'

'You can admit it, you know.'

'Just drop it, OK?' It comes out harsher than intended.

He takes a step back. 'Fine,' he says, but I can tell he's hurt. I should apologise, but that would require an explanation, and I barely understand the source of my irritation.

'I'm gonna go for a run,' I say. I'm almost at the back door when I turn around, unable to leave him like this. 'Are we going to the harvest festival tomorrow? Betsy will be selling her pumpkin-pie ice cream.'

In the dark of the hallway, Luca's features blur into shadow. 'I don't think I can. I've got that lunch with, well, you know.'

'Ah, the grandparents,' I say. Luca squirms at the word, like it's a stiff shirt he's not used to wearing. I feel for him – I'm still getting used to being a cousin, nephew, grandson. Then again, my father never tried to hide his family; they were just too far to reach.

‘If you go, could you save me some?’ Luca asks, sounding hopeful.

‘Pumpkin-pie ice cream?’

‘Please, I’ll hate myself for missing out.’

‘I’ll try,’ I say, and by that I mean I will, because it’s Luca.

On the walk home, I study the lawns and gardens I pass, unsure what it is I’m looking for. Only when I reach the apple tree that stands guard on the corner of my street, I realise that Miss M successfully snuck her way into my head. Rotting fruit is scattered across the grass verge, but it’s early autumn, so heck knows where I’d get hold of blossoms. Not that I have a need for them.

I quicken my step and seconds later I cross our front yard, hundreds of daisies nodding their hellos. After a quick change, I head back out in my running gear. I pick up speed and allow the soles of my shoes to slap the concrete. It’s the outlet I need, a steady rhythm I can follow while sorting the mess in my head, the knots in my chest. I take the back route, a gravel path that circles Lombard, often used by hikers making their way across the hills from the nearest city to our shore. Tall beeches rustle in the breeze, and the berries of the rowan trees glow like rubies whenever the sun pierces the clouds.

They remind me of the pomegranate trees of Granada, the fruit hanging heavy and low, daring passers-by to pluck them. Which we did, plenty of times, because Luca loves eating the seeds, his lips and fingers stained red from the juice. There’s a pull in my chest, a sweet pain that hasn’t left me since I said goodbye to my tío at the airport. If I give in to it, follow the pain to its source, I’ll find myself back there, that much I know. What do you call homesickness for a place that's not your home?

Even if I returned, I wouldn't recognise the place, not without Luca. Imagining myself in Granada without him makes me feel unbalanced. It's the last place where he and I were just boys, just friends. Now I don't know what we are. And I don't know if I want us to be just that – just friends.

I reach the end of the gravel path and skirt the town's back streets, the little cottages and parks, until I cross the main street and find myself on the promenade. I've drawn a semicircle around Lombard, never straying far from its heart – the cafe, with Luca in it. Knowing he's there should fill me with calm, but lately doubt gnaws at me.

Since the day we met over ten years ago, he's been my centre of gravity. I never considered this to be a bad thing, because that's how it was with Hamza. I have always been wary of my parents; they're solitary creatures, unable to let others in. Hamza, though, was everything they were not – open and affectionate – so I naturally gravitated towards him. He was the best big brother a boy could have. When he was gone, I only found my feet again with Luca. I wrapped my life around him. Frankly, it's the only way I knew how to survive.

I can't lose Luca. And I'm slowly waking up to the reality that this might be a problem. Hamza's death, sudden and brutal, ripped a hole in my side that Luca stitched up. I needed him to save me, and save me he did, even if he didn't know it at the time. Ten years later, I live and breathe, but I can't be ripped apart twice over.

All my life I have existed as part of someone else, so

much so that I can't imagine being on my own, and neither can anyone else, it appears. For a long time, my parents couldn't look at me without being reminded of the son they'd lost. There was no Simo without Hamza, a unit so tight it couldn't exist without its other half. They got better at hiding it, but occasionally when Mum stares at me, deep in thought, I see a glimpse of the old pain. Even now, running past the familiar faces of this town, their eyes scan the air around me, searching for someone that isn't there, searching for Luca.

Paul's kiosk comes into view, signalling the end of my route, but my head is still brimming, thoughts running wilder than my pounding heart. I know how to drown them out. Without stopping, I make a break for the beach. Sand flies, fills my shoes, so I throw them off and run on, run until my feet hit water, until the waves beat my thighs, swallow my hips. I dive and fill my ears with the ever-roaring sea.

The first blow is a shock, but a welcome one. The drop in temperature means I'm surrounded by cold. It brings clarity, and what follows is a soft lifting by the waves. The salt holds my body and soothes my joints. I'm on my back, staring into blinding clouds. When all I see is sky, and all I feel is ocean, my mind finally relents. It takes but a few minutes before the cold seeps into me, driving me out of the water. I feel lighter, as if the sea caught some of my heavier thoughts and bore them away. My feet carry me back towards where I dropped my shoes, leaving a wet trail as the saltwater pours off my body and soaks into the sand. I peel the wet T-shirt off and wring it out, then shake the sea out of my hair. Instead of my shoes, I find a figure sitting cross-legged in the spot where I left them. A book rests open on her bare legs, and she looks up at me with a smile caught somewhere between amusement and disbelief.

'Is it a new thing, some sort of fitness craze where people go swimming fully clothed? Because it looks silly.' Mairi shuts the book, and I recognise the cover of a Bernardine Evaristo novel.

I plonk myself next to her, not minding that I'll be caked in sand and will get told off by Mum later.

'Not a trend. Just a good way to cool off after a run.'

'Good, cos I was worried. You ran past me with this look on your face, like you planned to drown yourself. You didn't, did you?'

'Nothing of the sort.'

'Phew. Honestly, I can barely keep myself above water, so I wouldn't have been able to save you.'

'Noted,' I say. Mairi and I don't tend to speak much outside of school, but I'm enjoying the banter. I do wonder what's happened to my shoes though.

'I saved these from a dog who thought it was a funny-looking ball,' Mairi says, and produces them from behind her back.

'Might have something to do with the smell,' I say, taking them from her. 'Sorry you had to guard them. And thanks.'

'Any time.' She gets up. 'I have brothers, so I've smelt far worse.' She brushes the sand from her long legs and a braid falls into her eyes.

I want to tell her about my brother, and the impulse is so new that I almost give in to it, but I bite my tongue. I don't know where it came from. I don't even talk to Luca about him. In the beginning I didn't bring him up because I missed him too much to speak his name, and now I'm not sure how to break that habit. But something about Mairi makes me want to open up. She understands what it's like to grow up with brothers, so she might understand missing them.

'Hey, you coming to the festival tomorrow?' she asks, pulling me out of my thoughts.

'Not sure. I know Luca isn't,' I reply.

'I wasn't asking about him,' she says, and twists the stray braid back into the knot. 'You should come. It might even be fun hanging out with us.'

'OK, thanks, I will,' I say, without overthinking it. I squash the little seed of guilt – it's not like I'm doing something behind Luca's back. If I'm worried about getting lost in someone else, I need to learn to stand on my own feet. And maybe that will finally put the rumours about us to rest.

'See you there, Simo,' Mairi says. She sends me this look, and for a second it feels like she's checking me out. I realise that my T-shirt is still in my hand and I'm only wearing a pair of wet shorts. But then she turns and stalks up the beach. I shake my head, certain that I was imagining things.

I recognise that look because Luca wears it too. It's not like it means anything. I think I would know.

AUTUMN

CHAPTER 13 – LUCA

'We're going to be late.'

My dad is a punctual man. He does things correctly and enjoys a certain order. But today he's in no rush at all. He collects stray crumbs, polishes glasses that are entirely spotless and tinkers with the cash register, which occasionally opens on a whim and causes bruises and dropped plates. It has been acting up for months, but apparently Dad has decided that now is the time to fix it.

'It's just a ten-minute drive,' he says, inspecting the depths of the till.

'Which means we're running a good five minutes behind.'

That gets his attention. He gives the till a nudge and it shuts with a renewed ease.

'Perfect,' he announces, and shoots me a grin. I'm not sure if he means the cash desk or the fact that we're late.

The streets are still wet from this morning's shower, and it takes us a while to get out of town, with the ongoing festival. People are clogging the sidewalks and horse-drawn carriages block the roads. Dad smiles and occasionally waves to townsfolk like a princess in a parade. It's only when we reach the country road that he spots the bouquet by my feet and drops the smile.

'What are they for?' he asks.

'I don't know, Dad. When I walked into Betsy's flower shop this morning, I thought to myself, why not feed the sheep some expensive chrysanthemums?'

'You got my parents a gift? That's very thoughtful, but don't expect any thanks. She finds flowers garish. Common, is the word she uses, if I remember correctly. At least the sheep would appreciate them.'

'You're making that up,' I say, apprehension making my voice hitch.

He snorts. 'Anna Brandenburg needs no embellishment.'

We turn on to a driveway enclosed on both sides by tall trees and dense hedges. For the first time in my life, the brambles are trimmed, and the ivy that used to rule this wood is nowhere to be seen. Everything glistens, even though the sun hasn't yet managed to break through.

Dad stops the car on the circular driveway, and that's when it sinks in. After seventeen years of believing them dead, I'm going to meet my grandparents. Officially. Over food and drinks, like the oddest of first dates. If Graham Brandenburg is anything like the steely man I looked up online, I doubt I'm ready to face him. The flowers I bought suddenly feel silly.

Dad and I are glued to our seats. We take in the tremendous azalea bushes that surround the drive. In its centre, a moss-covered dryad gazes up towards the manor's towering roof. I don't know when a manor becomes a castle, but I can see turrets and stained-glass windows and red ivy eating up the walls. All that's missing are gargoyles, so maybe that's where it fails to fulfil the castle requirements.

I open the door, but Dad stops me.

'Just … think of what I said. They are—'

'Utterly and categorically selfish. I remember, Dad.'

I want to call him overdramatic, but since we've reached a truce, I hold back. We walk up to the double doors beneath a stone arch. At its peak a small creature is carved into the stone, but I'm struggling to make out the details.

'It's a mermaid,' a voice says, and both Dad and I jump. We turn, and there she stands, wearing a crimson waistcoat over a white blouse, the sleeves left unbuttoned. Her casual elegance exudes wealth. 'Rather tacky, if you ask me, but the building is listed, as I am constantly reminded. Follow me?'

She disappears behind the house, and we do as we're told. When I turn the corner, a wide lawn stretches out in front of me, and beyond it, the sea. We reach a stone patio that overlooks the tennis court and a huge garden, twice the size of Lombard's town square.

'I still have to acclimatise to this weather. One moment it's the Genesis flood and the next you're at risk of heatstroke. But I set my mind on an al fresco lunch, and I tend to get what I want.' She spreads her arms towards a set of chairs dotted around a beautifully set table. The tablecloth is blindingly white and flutters in the sea breeze.

'Show-off,' Dad says under his breath.

Anna arches a plucked eyebrow. I notice that her forehead barely moves. 'Don't mumble, darling. It's bad manners. As is showing up late.'

Dad opens his mouth, undoubtedly to repeat what he

just said, but before he gets the chance, she approaches me with a dazzling smile. 'Flowers! For me? How thoughtful.' Though there's an air of performance to her every move, her reaction seems genuine. 'They are gorgeous!'

'Thanks,' I reply. 'Dad chose them for you.'

'Oh no, I can't take any credit,' he says forcefully.

Anna gives us a long look that I can't read. 'I'll ask Susie to find a vase for the dining table,' she says.

'Susie?' I ask, puzzled.

'The maid,' Dad explains with a judgemental undertone.

'My PA,' Anna corrects him.

'That's what I said,' he counters.

Susie arrives on the patio, interrupting their bickering. Everything about her says 'neat', from the kitten heels to the nondescript haircut.

'Susie, meet my son and grandson, Matthew and Luca. Might as well get acquainted since we'll be seeing them frequently from now on.'

'We will?' Dad remarks, but if Anna hears him, she shows no reaction.

'Tell my husband the boys have arrived, yes?'

Susie nods politely, first to us, then to Anna, and disappears into the depths of the manor with the bouquet in her arms.

'Sit, sit,' Anna urges, and takes the chair at the head of the table. 'Graham will be with us in a moment. No doubt he's micromanaging the chef about the correct temperature at which to grill a tomahawk.'

'I don't see a barbecue,' Dad says, and grabs the seat furthest from her.

'Please, I don't want such a monstrosity on my patio. It's in the kitchen, where it belongs.'

I grab the chair between them, facing the ocean, glad to sit down, dizzy as I feel. I don't know if it's whiplash from their relentless back and forth, or the unreal situation I find myself in; having lunch in the shadow of a castle owned by my estranged and very posh grandparents. I've decided it's a castle, despite the absence of gargoyles.

Anna's presence doesn't help. She is as striking as the first time I saw her, maybe more so, now that the shock has worn off. Nowadays the Brandenburgs lead a reclusive life, shunning the media and rarely making public appearances. The mystery around Anna makes her even more captivating. I'm not saying she exudes warmth, but there's something magnetic about her.

She meets my gaze and I try not to blush.

'Luca, it's wonderful to have you here,' she says with a sincere-sounding joy. 'I should have led with that. It's not every day that you get to meet your grandson. I …' She halts, shaking her head. 'Your grandfather should be here for this. I'll fetch him myself.'

Seconds later, she too is swallowed up by the manor, leaving only a whiff of citrus perfume in the salty air.

I turn to Dad. 'Can you not?'

'What?' he says defensively.

'You're prickly.'

'Am not.'

'Like a hedgehog with goosebumps. You take offence at every word she says and insult her whenever you can. I'm nervous enough as it is, and you're not helping.'

He breathes out loudly through his nose. 'Fine. But she's just as bad!'

'Maybe, but you're not fourteen!' I hiss.

Anna returns and as she crosses the patio, the grace in her step is unparalleled.

'Any second now,' she claims, and plucks a bottle from a cooler. 'Wine, anyone?' She fills our glasses before we get a chance to protest. As she sinks back into her chair, blonde hair swinging, her face lights up. 'There he is!'

I turn my head, setting eyes on my grandfather for the first time. Once again I'm reminded how much he looks like Dad. They share the same facial features and a wavy shock of hair, though Graham's is silver where Dad's is a deep brown. Next to them I'm the odd one out, which stings more than it should.

'Could it be, my own grandson?' he exclaims, and stops right in front of me, bypassing Dad without a glance. His blue eyes gleam, set off by a green polo shirt so dark it almost matches his black chinos and loafers. Insecurity sweeps over me. I don't have the slightest idea what to do, how to act. My body gets up of its own accord, but that's as far as I get. Do I shake his hand, do I hug him? How do you greet the grandfather you've never met?

'Let me look at you,' he says and takes both my hands in his with a self-assured grip. In my mind he was ten feet tall, but Anna, with her long legs and the neck of a swan, towers over him, over all of us. Graham might be shorter than me by a couple inches, but with his air of confidence, he feels like a giant.

He takes a step back and scans me from head to toe. I

spent hours panicking over what to wear, but in the end I opted for my favourite high-waisted trousers, a faded blue vest, and the pearl on a chain from Simo, which I remove only to sleep. If I couldn't impress them, at least I'd feel at home in my clothes.

'A true Brandenburg, if ever I've seen one,' Graham decides.

'It's great to meet you,' I manage, my voice sounding way too high-pitched in my ears.

'And you,' he says almost conspiratorially, pulling me close again. He still holds my hand as he turns to Dad.

'Matthew,' he states, and his voice is a noticeable few degrees cooler. 'It's been a long time.'

Dad watches us, his father and his son, with a detached expression. He made no effort to dress up, and I count at least two coffee stains on his T-shirt. His jaw shifts, and I know he's fuming. 'It has,' he agrees, but leaves it at that.

Graham marches to the seat across from me, not without planting a kiss on his wife's head. Something in me melts at this tender moment, and once again I'm glad to fall back into my chair.

'How nice to have all my boys gathered around me,' Anna says, and I think I hear her voice waver. 'A rare occurrence.'

'Yes,' Dad replies, 'which makes me wonder—'

But I don't find out what he wonders, because a flock of kitchen staff streams out on to the patio. They create an artwork of the dining table, placing an assortment of foods in front of us that can only be described as a feast. Chilli-and-honey-coated halloumi, steaks twice the size of my palms, roasted mini potatoes drowning in herb and garlic butter, salmon crowned with lemons and coconut flakes, and a platter of charred watermelon, pear and fig. As a final touch, Susie puts the flowers in a delicate blown-glass vase, and as quickly as the staff appeared, they're gone again. My eyes almost pop out of my head, but nobody else seems impressed.

'Eat!' Anna orders. I'm the only one who follows her invitation. Graham picks at his salmon with little enthusiasm, Anna only slices the tiny potatoes in half, and Dad is too busy scowling.

Having Graham Brandenburg sit across from me is intense. Not only does he exude confidence, he's extremely handsome. It's a weird thing to note about your grandfather, but the man is basically a stranger, and I'm not trying to be self-congratulatory. If there's a Brandenburg gene that gives you flawless skin and the power to squash someone with a single look, it passed me over.

I'm relieved I finally have something to focus on that isn't my grandparents or their bougie home. Personally, I don't understand people who don't eat food when it's offered and, most importantly, free. I dig in, steering clear of the meat and fish, and take a generous helping of everything else. I have no qualms when it comes to food – why hold back when you can just … not?

'So, Luca, tell me – you go to school still, don't you?' Graham asks.

'Don't worry, Father, unlike your son, Luca is not a dropout.'

'Nobody was asking you, Matthew,' Anna chides him.

'Yes,' I reply to stifle whatever comeback Dad was

preparing, 'I do. I've got two more years.'

'And how are your grades?' Graham wants to know.

'Ignore him,' Anna says. 'Who cares about grades? What subjects do you take?'

I don't actually mind, especially because it seems like a fairly safe topic for this hot-headed table. 'I'm doing design and technology, photography, English and business studies. And my grades are fine. I could be better at business and English, but I'm only taking them so I share classes with Simo.'

'Simo is your friend?' Anna inquires, and the heart on the pet-shop window flashes across my mind.

'My best friend, since we were kids.' As I say the words, I'm reminded that, despite everything, this is who we really are, at our core. Best friends, for ten years. Some words on a noticeboard shouldn't be able to destroy that. And yet –

'We ought to meet him then, considering he's so important to you.'

'That would be nice,' I agree, and smother the ripple of worry. Simo's opinion matters more than anyone's. And I want to know what he makes of them, cos I'm still undecided.

'And what are your plans after school? Any career goals?' Graham follows up.

'Uni or college, I think, and then maybe work in film and TV. I'm not entirely sure yet.'

'You're an actor?'

'Oh no, nobody wants to see me act. When I was six, my class put on a play of *The Rainbow Fish*, and my starfish was so bad they created a new role specially for me, so I spent several weeks unsuccessfully pretending to be seagrass.' Anna looks puzzled and Graham mildly amused. 'Anyway, I want to be behind the scenes. Or try my hand at becoming a pastry chef. I've not made up my mind.'

'You bake!' Anna exclaims.

'It runs in the family,' Graham says, sounding pleased. I wouldn't voice the thought, but I struggle to see him in an apron, elbow-deep in dough.

'I'm no professional. It's only a hobby, something I enjoy.'

'He's being humble. People regularly storm our cafe for his cakes,' Dad says.

'The cafe,' Graham scoffs, and Dad cocks his head.

'Just say it, Father.'

'Say what?'

'Whatever it is that makes you say "cafe" in that tone.'

'Matthew ...' Anna warns.

Graham shrugs. 'You lack drive and ambition. Always have done.'

'Graham!' Anna scolds.

'Don't start, Anna, I know you agree,' Graham retorts. 'The boy serves tea in a dilapidated diner when he could've run a global enterprise.'

I barely hide a flinch, but Dad only grins, halfway between amusement and annoyance.

'I own that dilapidated diner, thank you very much.'

'Yes, and you'll be paying it off for the rest of your life.'

'I shouldn't be surprised that you've been digging through my private affairs.'

'And what a delight it was to discover that you even

erased our family name from your life,' Graham says, striking with the precision of a scorpion.

'You did what?' Anna hisses.

For once, Dad has the decency to look guilty. 'Brandenburg would have pulled too much attention, so when Luca was born, Poppy and I decided it was best to take her name.'

That's when the meaning sinks in. I never questioned my surname, why would I? It's only normal that I share my parents' name. But Mum and Dad aren't married, never have been. If things had panned out differently, I wouldn't be Luca Dean, I'd be Luca Brandenburg. I have no idea what to make of that.

Graham looks at Dad with disdain. 'You hate us so much that you struck us from your family tree.'

'I did what I thought was best for Poppy and Luca. And I don't regret it.'

The last part he directs at me. It's all I need to hear. This surreal situation is enough to take in as it is. I will need time to mull it over, but I have seventeen years of evidence that he's a good dad – recent hiccups aside – regardless of surname.

'And I don't hate you,' Dad adds in a voice just above a whisper. Neither Anna nor Graham reacts. Their faces stay blank and rigid.

'Would you like to come see it?' I throw in, not even trying to be subtle about changing the topic. Someone needs to defuse the situation, and no one else seems willing.

'The cafe?' Anna asks, confounded.

'It's our life. It's where I grew up. And Dad's an amazing cook. Maybe you'd like to visit it – properly, I mean. We could have lunch there sometime.'

Dad laughs but it's more of a bark. 'Luca, that's very nice, but you've heard what my parents make of diners. The grease, the sugar.' He pauses. 'The commoners.'

So much for defusing.

'I agree with Luca, it's a nice idea,' Anna replies with a voice like honey. 'We'd love to take you up on your offer.'

For a second, it seems as if that's taken the wind out of Dad's sails, but he swiftly tries a different strategy. 'What are you doing here?' he asks.

'Straight for the jugular, I see,' Graham retorts.

'As is the Brandenburg way.'

'We want to know our grandson. And reunite with you. Is that so wrong?' Anna replies.

'Why now?' Dad presses.

'Well, after your disappearing act, it took a while to find you.'

'I'm sure it didn't take you seventeen years, Mother.'

'Don't call me that, I'm no crone.'

'You're right, Matthew. We've known of your whereabouts for a while,' Graham admits. 'But you made it decidedly clear that you wished no contact.'

'And yet, you're *decidedly* here.'

Silence stretches as Dad waits for their answer. Unsure what to say or do – and curious what the answer is going to be – I take a sip of the wine and barely manage not to spit it back out. That's bathwater in a bottle. It takes all my willpower to swallow. I pluck a fig from the platter to get rid of the awful taste.

'We've decided to take a step back from the business,'

Anna offers eventually. 'Find somewhere to settle, enjoy the peace and quiet.'

'To put it plainly, we're retiring,' Graham adds.

Dad is not convinced. 'You're lying.'

'I'm growing tired of fighting you, Matthew. There is no hidden motive or grand scheme. After three decades of running the company, it's only natural to desire a change of pace,' Graham says.

'And that's entirely unrelated to you picking at your salmon while you ignore the slab of steak that cost more than my monthly energy bill? And what about the wine? Neither of you has touched your glass.'

They exchange a quick glance, and Anna juts her chin out.

'Your father had a health scare, not too long ago. It has required us to rethink our lifestyle.'

'What kind of health scare?' I ask tentatively.

Graham watches me and his gaze softens. 'Nothing to worry about. A minor stroke.'

Dad hasn't dropped his attitude, but he is biting his tongue for once.

'Your grandfather has recovered well,' Anna explains, addressing me, 'but there's no guarantee that it won't happen again. It puts things into perspective. We'll be taking things slower from now on. Less work, less travel.'

'Less alcohol and red meat,' Graham scoffs, and it's clear what he thinks of that.

'More time spent with family,' Anna adds, sounding hopeful, 'which means you. If you'll have us.'

I feel three pairs of eyes on me. It's a lot, not going to lie. I'm still digesting that I have grandparents. Though we share

DNA, I don't know these people. It's obvious that there's history between them and my dad, and not the good kind. With so much ego around this table, such big personalities vying for space, I'm having a hard time staying upright in my seat. But what I'm sure of, despite the fact that I've known him for less than an hour, is that I don't want to lose my grandfather. I've only just found him.

'I'd like that,' I say. Anna rewards me with a smile so bright it requires its own warning sign, and Graham seems to grow in his chair, tension ebbing from his body. Could it be that they're … relieved? Maybe I'm not the only one who's intimidated by this out-of-body experience of a family lunch.

I catch Dad's gaze. I almost expect him to be mad at my decision, but he only tilts his head in acceptance.

'Marvellous,' Anna exclaims, still beaming. 'Shall we set a date for lunch at the cafe, then? And we haven't even mentioned the Christmas Gala!'

'Not so fast,' Dad says, making her smile flicker. 'Lombard is our home, not yours.' Graham makes to speak but Dad holds up a hand to cut him off. 'I'm not saying this to spite you, but because it's true. You hate peace and quiet. You'll get bored. You always do.' His eyes harden, from hurt or disappointment, I can't tell. 'Luca is your grandson, and I'm done taking that away from you. But he's my son first. If you want to get to know him, then only by my rules. You will have to commit. No excuses, no games, no lies, no bribery, no tricks or schemes or last-minute cancellations and absolutely no make-up gifts to try to distract from any of your mistakes. For once, you'll have to be responsible and show up.'

Have to admit it, my dad's a sassy one.

'Why, we feel flattered,' Graham deadpans.

'Yes, I'm a regular Lady Macbeth,' Anna adds.

I see where he gets it from.

'You have your chance and I'd hate to see you blow it,' Dad says, which prompts a snort from Graham. 'I mean it. You mess up, and it's Luca who gets hurt. So don't.'

'Does Luca get a say in this?' Graham asks.

'Of course he does. I can't and won't stop him. He's a good judge of character, as you'll soon find out.'

As much as I appreciate the endorsement, I'm growing tired of being talked about like I'm not listening to every word they say.

To my relief and joy, the kitchen staff are back, and this time they have cake. Not *a* cake, as in one, but cakes, as in Black Forest gateau, almond tarts, apple pie and a meringue masterpiece that resembles a peacock taking flight. Modesty clearly isn't a word that Brandenburgs use lightly, or ever. Even Dad is too busy eating to complain, which makes the rest of lunch a civil affair – not counting the moment that Graham criticises Dad for the coffee stains on his shirt, prompting Dad to drop his fork and eat with his fingers. The man is a werewolf, and his parents are the full moon, depriving him of both sanity and manners. It's only when we're on the road back home that he becomes his old self again. He's quiet, but he keeps giving me the side-eye.

I have this odd feeling, like I've been sucked into a parallel universe only to be spat back out again an hour later. Returning to familiar ground feels off, because Lombard is still its usual self, but I'm not sure I can say the same about me. Still, once I spot the lighthouse that watches over the squat rooftops of my hometown, it's a little easier to breathe again.

'What?' I ask, unnerved by Dad's looks.

'Would you have liked to be born a Brandenburg?' he asks. It throws me off, because of course I have been asking myself this, but I didn't realise he'd clocked me.

'I don't know, Dad,' I admit. Would I have liked my life as a Brandenburg as much as I like my life as a Dean? It's possible, but then, Dad hated carrying the name.

'Would you ever change it? You could, you know? I did.' He says this quickly, stumbling over the words, and I realise he's scared of my answer.

'I never had a reason to dislike my surname, Dad. Still don't. And I like sharing a name with Mum. It connects us, even when she's away, if that makes sense.'

'It does,' he says.

'I'm not going to change my name, whatever happens,' I tell him.

He takes my hand, interweaving his fingers with mine. We sit like this until we reach the sign welcoming us into Lombard, and then a little longer still.

CHAPTER 14 – SIMO

'I smell cheese toasties,' Joni says from behind the library counter. She taps her fingers on the wooden top, scanning us with obvious disapproval.

Food and water, the two things you'd be least likely to find in a library, banned for good reason. And we brought both inside. Three minutes ago we were waiting by the kiosk as Paul gave the toasties the perfect crisp. The sky was blue and held only a flock of innocent clouds. Two minutes ago, as we started walking down the promenade, warm parcels in our hands, the sun was swallowed up by clouds that inflated to tremendous balloons, turning an angry shade of slate. Before we could react, the flood gates opened and drenched us in seconds. The library was closest, as usual offering shelter to those in desperate need. That is, if its guardian allowed us in. Luckily for us, Joni has always been susceptible to bribery.

Luca weighs the tightly wrapped parcel in his hand and slides it over the counter, prompting a crooked grin. Joni's thick-rimmed glasses and the halo of salt-and-pepper hair might lend her an angelic air, but that exterior hides a devious mind and a sharp tongue.

‘Now we’re talking,’ she says, and her nostrils flare as she soaks in the scent of hot sauce and melted cheese. ‘Off you go, boys, but if I find a single greasy thumbprint on any of my books, I’ll turn your innards into porridge.’

We scramble up the staircase, with Orlando, Joni’s sheepdog, on our heels. He wags his tail and sniffs the air, but we’ve already lost one sandwich, and I’m not sharing mine with a dog. We sprawl across a pair of benches while Orlando finds a comfy spot beneath us. The library is one big space divided into two floors. The upper level is a gallery along the outer walls, leaving a wide square in the centre that looks down on the maze of bookshelves on the ground floor.

I fold the toastie out of the paper and hand a still-steaming triangle to Luca. My mouth burns from the hot cheese, but it tastes too good to slow down. I watch Luca demolish his half in less than thirty seconds. He licks the leftover grease from his fingers. For someone so conscious of his appearance, he has poor eating habits. I should be revolted, but I can’t tear my eyes away as he sucks on each finger. What’s a normal amount to be thinking about another boy’s lips? Is there such a thing?

He catches my gaze.

‘You’re disgusting,’ I lie.

‘So are you. Swallow before you speak, please and thank you.’

Attending the festival without him had felt odd. The pumpkin-pie ice cream only tasted half as good, and yet I also had fun. Mairi is so easy to get along with that I’m annoyed I didn’t realise it sooner. Beneath a friendly but reserved outer layer hides a whip-smart nerd. I was mercilessly mocked for stumbling into a hay bale and dropping my ice cream, but in turn I got to make fun of her obsession with vampire novels. She might deny crushing on *Twilight* characters, but her cheeks glowed suspiciously when Taylor Lautner was mentioned. It was nice, at least until our duo expanded. I'm still holding a grudge against Louise, and as for the fourth person of our party …

'Curtains asked about you,' I say. I regret it instantly, but at the same time I want to see Luca's reaction.

His eyebrows lift in confusion. 'As in … Jacob?'

I can't help but think that he sounds pleased.

'Him with the silly curtains, yes,' I say.

'What's silly about them?'

'They're too long. He constantly blows them out of his face. It gets on my nerves.'

Luca watches me with a look I can't interpret. He plays with the pearl pendant around his neck. The black vest he wears hugs his torso, especially the darker patches still wet from the rain. A few drops cling to his collarbones, forming twin puddles in the soft dips at his throat skin.

'Why don't you like Jacob?'

'I never said that,' I reply.

I had been more bothered to be reminded that I couldn't be apart from Luca without someone noting his absence. We're not conjoined twins. It's a stupid thing to feel annoyed about. Before the noticeboard, I was proud to be part of something that extended beyond myself. Ever since that rude awakening I've been questioning our bond, though I'd rather forget the message ever happened and go back to how things were before. At least then I knew where we stood. Now I'm stumbling in the dark, trying to find the light switch.

'I like him,' Luca says, as if to challenge me. 'He's in my photography class, and he's good. I've seen his portraits.'

He sounds like a show-off. 'Something about him doesn't sit right with me. Just a feeling.'

Luca opens his mouth, but whatever he wants to say, it doesn't come out. Instead, he changes course.

'My grandparents want to meet you.'

'The scary famous ones?' Just the idea has me nervous. I've never met anyone more famous than Anton the town mascot.

'They're not famous. Just …'

'Filthy rich?' I suggest.

Luca snorts but doesn't disagree.

'Does that mean I get to see their house?' I could live with meeting them if I get a tour of the manor in return.

'They're coming for lunch at the cafe on Sunday. It'll be more relaxed that way, if we're on home turf. As long as Dad keeps his head screwed on.'

I raise an eyebrow at him. 'More relaxed? It'll be a spectacle. Half the town will "drop by" for a coffee to ogle the rich couple who bought Hidden House.' Luca suddenly looks worried. 'I'm kidding – it won't be that bad.'

He groans and sinks on to the bench, his theatrics prompting a yap from Orlando. 'You're not – it'll be the event of the year. They'll watch us from the street like zoo animals. Or a Broadway show starring Meryl Streep.'

'Is it too late to rearrange things?'

Luca sits up with an expression like he's nursing a toothache. 'I could barely get Dad to agree in the first place. I mean, he'd be so happy to cancel, he'd likely throw a party to celebrate getting out of it. He's so weird around them, always snapping and lashing out.'

'And how do they react?'

'They snap right back. Where Dad's aggressive, they're passive aggressive.'

'Sounds like there's a lot of baggage,' I say, and am reminded of my own parents. Though we might handle conflict differently, it's always there, simmering. I feel for Maz. From what Luca has said, he didn't have the easiest childhood, and being confronted with his past must bring back its demons.

'Too much baggage to unpack,' Luca says, 'but I guess them reaching out is their way of making up for it. So, I want lunch to go ahead. Please come? Maybe they'll behave if you're around.'

It's not like I'd refuse him. 'I'll come.'

Overcome with relief, he falls back on to the bench and places his head on my thighs. 'Thank ya,' he says, and grins up at me. I don't even mind that the rain clinging to his hair is sinking into the fabric of my jeans.

'You can pay me back in muffins,' I reply.

'As many as you can eat and then some,' he promises.

'And you can show me pictures of the manor,' I say.

'I don't have any. I didn't even see inside.'

'You didn't find an excuse to sneak in? Not even to go to the bathroom?'

'I was too nervous to pee. Besides, I couldn't leave

them alone with Dad. Any interaction between Maz and his parents requires a referee. Or a bodyguard. Or three bodyguards.'

I can't hold back a snort. 'Yeah, I know the feeling.'

Luca's face grows serious. I feel too exposed to hold his gaze, so now it's my turn to fidget with his pendant. My parents are being odd – odder than usual. They've been whispering, scheming, and not knowing what they're up to makes me nervous.

'You can stay at mine if you want, you know that,' Luca says.

I want to accept. It's almost impossible not to, with him gazing up at me, true sympathy in his cornflower eyes. But this – us, cosying up in a public space – won't help quash the rumours.

I pretend to have an itch on my calf, forcing him up and away from me. How is it that girls can be as close as they like without anyone thinking they're together, but when two boys show a semblance of care for each other they end up being shipped by an entire town?

'I think I'd better go home.' If I sit in the lounge and read or write in my notebook it at least makes it impossible for my parents to continue their plotting.

'Who knew family could be so complicated?' Luca says, and stares across the gallery.

I knew, I want to say. I don't remember a time when my family wasn't complicated, even before the chasm left in Hamza's wake. Mum cut her parents out of her life long before I was born, something to do with her falling pregnant before there was a ring on her hand, and – to add insult to injury – marrying a (lapsed) Catholic. Dad has lived far away from his siblings for too long to maintain true closeness. That unease, the feeling of being incomplete, has always had a seat at our dinner table.

Luca grew up in a bubble. Though the circumstances might have been unusual, his parents sheltered him from harm for a solid seventeen years. His mum might be far away, but all he has to do is say the word, and Poppy would be back in a heartbeat. It's only now that he's being forced to navigate the waters of fraught family dynamics. There's an ugly part of me that feels a grim satisfaction at the bursting of the bubble, though it makes me dislike myself more.

'I have to ask Joni for those English books,' says Luca, thankfully interrupting my moment of self-loathing.

'I thought you weren't going to "invest in hard copies".'

We're five weeks into the term and not once has Luca made the effort to bring his own copy of *Twelfth Night*. Instead he shares mine, which I don't mind, so long as he doesn't moan about not being able to read my notes in the margins.

'I'm not. But, as Mrs Leppla reminds me every lesson, I can't always depend on you to provide everything I'm too lazy to obtain myself. Which is plain wrong, but I'm gonna borrow that next book just to shut her up.' He heads for the stairs, swiftly followed by Orlando, but stops on the landing. 'What was it called again? *Lottie*?'

I sigh. '*Emma*.'

'Gotcha.'

Luca and Orlando disappear to the ground floor, and I make a stroll around the gallery. Up here, Joni shelves romance, horror and true crime. I've long stopped questioning her system. The horror section holds celebrity memoirs and a total of five YA novels about teen pregnancy. I can tell that she went all out in the romance section, where V.E. Schwab's *Vicious* shares the space with George R.R. Martin's history of the Targaryens. And on a true-crime shelf, I spot a brick of a book on Yazidi persecution next to a novella by Adania Shibli that I've been meaning to read. Joni never misses an opportunity to radicalise her readers.

My gaze snags on a copy of *Giovanni's Room*. It's not Joni's twisted sense of humour that makes me halt, but the small carving in the spot where the book's spine meets the wood of the shelf. Two letters surrounded by a heart.

The library loses focus and the heart fills my vision. Splinters graze my skin as I touch the carving, trace its outline, a fresh scar in the wood. My mind remains blank, but my body is in turmoil. Heat surfaces in a fever rush. I itch all over, but I could scratch every inch of me and I know it wouldn't stop.

I go for the letters, dig in deep. Wood chips pierce the flesh beneath my nails. I don't relent, not until the varnish comes off, until there's a frayed wound in the wood where the letters used to be. When every trace of them is gone, the heat recedes, leaving a sheen of sweat on my forehead. My surroundings come back into focus. The space no longer feels like a sanctuary; it's too open. When I look over my shoulder, I'm the only one around. Low chatter reaches my ears, and I remember Joni and Luca on the floor below. Did Joni do this? I can't imagine her going around carving hearts in her bookshelves. Something tells me she hasn't even seen the vandalisation, or she'd be fuming. First the noticeboard, now this. I have no proof that the two are connected, but deep down I feel certain they must be.

I'm starting to feel sick, and it's not the toastie that's making my stomach churn. The air in here is stale; it smells of grease and wet dog. My legs carry me down and straight out of the library. Cold air hits my skin, followed by stray raindrops or sea spray. The clouds remain dense and heavy, preparing for the next downpour. It only takes Luca seconds to catch up.

'Hey, what was that about?'

I shake my head, unable to explain the carving and the state I'm in. He grabs my wrist, forcing me to a stop.

'You're bleeding,' he says, and lifts my hand to inspect it. His eyes widen as he takes in the ragged skin, the torn nails. 'Fuck, Simo, what did you do?'

I shake him off, but his grip lingers. 'I need to get home.'

'First we need to get that looked at,' Luca protests, but I'm already walking away.

'Simo!' he shouts, and the mix of hurt and anger in his voice stops me.

I turn to see his slender figure against an iron sky, puzzlement shadowing his eyes. He clutches a couple of books and looks as vulnerable as I feel. I want to close the distance, let him take my hand. But there are people on the beach and windows looking out towards us. I truly hate that this friendship isn't mine any more. It's been taken out of my hands and turned into someone else's idea of us. Between gross gestures in school hallways or the constant vomit-inducing shipping, I can't decide what's worse. Luca approaches, but the discomfort must show on my face, because he doesn't try to touch me again. I still don't move, caught between the urge to back away and the desire to pull him close.

'Let me at least clean it up before you go home, OK?' Luca's voice is gentle, but it finds a gap in the coil of anger and disgust wrapped tightly around my chest.

I feel myself nodding. Luca musters a smile that fails to hide his concern. He walks ahead, arms wrapped tightly around his torso, like he's trying to hold himself together.

I remain a step behind him. My fingers throb, and I think of the carved heart and the many outside forces trying to push themselves between me and my best friend. It doesn't matter how hard I try to shut them out, they keep coming back, and I'm getting tired. Tired of fighting them.

CHAPTER 15 – LUCA

The book lands on the table with a thud. The only reason it stays dry is because Jacob grabs his iced latte before it spills. He has good hair and good reflexes. In my defence, I didn't mean to drop it as bluntly as I did, but 300 pages of portrait photography weighs heavy, especially when the book is the size of a toddler.

'Sorry,' I say, embarrassed. The cafe is busy as ever, and it's only fifteen minutes until my grandparents will walk through the door with the chipped paint and sit down on our wonky chairs to share a lunch with me and Dad. The image is so strange it refuses to form in my head.

'It's all right,' Jacob says, setting the coffee down at a safe distance from the book. 'I'm just grateful you're letting me borrow this. It'll help with my project.'

I feel a few inches taller, proud to own a book worth lending. Not that it contains a lot of words, but that's kind of the point; it's a collection of rediscovered photographs of gay couples dating back to the 1850s. Simo has never shown an interest in it, and I've never tried to show him. It's a nice change, being able to share this with someone who isn't Dad, but someone my age.

‘What’s the project?’

‘I want to create a series about queer small-town life. Take portraits of people from Lombard, capture their story.’

I snort, and immediately feel bad when Jacob shifts awkwardly on his chair. ‘Sorry, I don’t mean it that way. I think it’s an amazing idea. In fact, I love it.’ I might be overcompensating, but as I say the words, I realise that I do love it.

‘But?’ Jacob asks, looking as if he might not want to hear the answer.

‘I’ve lived here my whole life, and my dad and I are literally the only gay people here.’ It never bothered me, because Dad was, *is*, the person I look up to most, shocking family revelations aside. But saying it out loud leaves me with a hollow feeling inside.

‘Just because your dad’s the only gay person you know, doesn’t mean he’s the only other queer person in town. Sometimes we can get so used to a place and the people in it that we forget to look past the obvious. We think we know everything and everyone and stop asking questions.’

‘I admit that’s deep,’ I say, ‘but you’re going to struggle finding anyone.’

Jacob doesn’t seem discouraged. ‘I’m new here, I come with a pair of fresh eyes. I’ll show you a new side of Lombard.’

His tone is confident without being cocky. I take him in, really look at him, maybe for the first time. He has a wide nose, gently curved eyes and a square chin. He makes me feel curious and comfortable at once, because his gaze never strays from me. It’s nice to have someone’s undivided attention, especially when that someone has the lush hair of a nineties teen-movie star.

'You've lived here what, a couple of months? You've seen what there is. But go ahead, I'd love see Lombard in a new light.'

'You will,' he says. 'And hey, if you ever want a change of scenery, what about a trip to the city?'

'The city?'

'Yeah, you know, somewhere where the only place with good coffee isn't owned by your—'

'Dad,' I say, when he suddenly appears by our table and places a chocolate-chip muffin in front of Jacob. We officially ran out of them an hour ago, but I saved some for Simo and my grandparents.

'New kids get free muffins,' Dad declares.

'Since when?' I ask.

'My cafe, my rules. Also, this is a reminder that we're expecting high-ranking and highly self-important visitors any minute. And that you got us into this, so you will be entertaining them.' With that he's off.

'I should go,' Jacob says. He rises to his full height and somehow manages to balance the headstone-sized book, his iced coffee and the muffin. 'Thanks for the book.'

'Any time!'

'Also, it's not true that your dad's the only gay person you know. You have me now,' he says.

We lock eyes, and my heart does a little stumble. By the time it's found its rhythm again, Jacob is out the door. I sit and watch his silhouette disappear down the street before I remember I'm meant to be helping Dad.

I don't get the chance to demand an explanation for giving away my secret stash of muffins. The big table by the window holds nothing but a reserved sign, so I do my best to cover the wear and tear beneath place mats and bowls of hummus, salted nuts and cucumber sticks.

The moment I hang the coffee-stained apron in the hall, I hear Dad shouting my name through the entire cafe. He sounds strained and threatening, which can only mean one thing. As I re-enter, Dad points his parents to the window table. The room's chatter has mellowed to a low hum. Clearly my grandparents' arrival hasn't gone unnoticed, but people are polite enough to stare only when they think we're not looking.

When Dad spots me, relief floods his expression. 'Where were you?' he whispers with an accusatory tone. I was gone a full three seconds, tops.

'Handsome as ever,' Graham says as I turn to him. I know it's shallow, but I like hearing him say it. Relieved that they're taking the lead, I let myself be pulled into hugs, because I've still not found the manual on how to behave like a grandson.

'The place is much busier today,' Anna notes. 'Last time I came it was so dead I worried it might be a dud.'

'Thanks for the vote of confidence,' Dad says drily.

I'd rather not be reminded of the moment that I first met my grandmother and realised Dad had been lying about having dead parents. To keep my hands busy, I grab the jug of homemade lemonade and fill everyone's glasses.

'It's quaint,' Graham adds, assessing the room. From the way Dad's lips tighten, I can tell that 'quaint' isn't a compliment coming from the mouth of a Brandenburg.

'Yes, or dilapidated, as some might call it,' he retorts.

Admittedly, Anna and Graham's regal appearance clashes with the relaxed atmosphere of the cafe and most of its customers. Anna's velvet wrap-around dress is likely worth more than every other item in here combined, espresso machine included.

'Simo is gonna join us in a bit. He's got a family thing,' I announce before Graham gets the chance to shoot something back. Simo and I agreed that he'd give us a head start, let us settle and adjust, which now seems like a reckless idea. Fewer people means more chances for Dad and his parents to exchange poorly concealed insults.

'I'm glad he's able to make it. After missing out on so much of your life already, we can't wait to meet your friends.'

Dad, who is grinding his teeth so hard I can hear it from across the table, gets up and stomps to the kitchen. I hope he dunks his head in a bucket of ice or finds another way to release his frustration. When he returns, there's a fake smile plastered across his face. 'Forgot the salt and pepper,' he says, and sets it down in front of us.

'What's going on in the store across the street?' Graham nods to the corner shop.

'It looks like the scene of a crime,' Anna remarks, eyeing the graffitied and boarded-up windows suspiciously. A group of construction workers stands huddled around the entrance.

'There is no crime in Lombard, Mother.'

'Unless you count the time when a group of teenagers doused all of Sheila's sheep in orange dye after she refused to sell them a rusted revolver from her antiques shop,' I add. For weeks it looked like Sheila was breeding giant Cheetos.

'That's a charming anecdote, but it doesn't quite answer my question,' Graham says.

'We know as much as you do, Father. But if you truly can't get through lunch without finding out exactly who is moving into an empty shop unit you didn't even know existed until ten minutes ago, I'll gladly go over and ask the crew.'

'I'm touched,' Graham says with the compassion of an oyster.

'By Monday, I'm sure the noticeboard will tell us exactly what's going on,' I grumble.

'That's a twee little tradition that you have here.' Anna's 'twee' sounds a lot like Graham's 'quaint'. 'I heard that, for centuries, it used to be a way for fishermen to warn the town of oncoming storms.'

Graham frowns. 'I was told it's only that size because the carpenter who built it in the eighties misread the measurements. By the time they realised the mistake, it was already up.'

The conversation is derailed when a man in a varsity jacket joins the workers across the street, seemingly to give them instructions. As if he senses the attention, he turns and waves. He's good-looking, with dark buzzed hair and the shadow of a beard. A look at Dad awkwardly mirroring the gesture tells me he's made the same observation.

'If I'm not mistaken, this man seems to know you, Matthew,' Anna notes.

Dad clears his throat. 'That's Daniel. He's new in town.'

'*That's* Daniel?' I do a double take. Joni's son smiles at each of us before his eyes stray back to Dad and stay on him longer than totally necessary.

'So you know him but not what he's up to in a shop that's facing yours? What if he's planning to open a cafe? You ought to be better informed, Matthew, especially if it comes to potential competition,' Graham says.

'I'd best check on our food,' Dad mutters.

'I'll get it,' I say, and I'm up before he gets the chance to escape.

Dad and I almost got into an argument about what to serve his parents. He insisted they receive no special treatment and get what's on the menu like any other customer. I reminded him not to kill his own father with burgers and mac and cheese, so we settled for a salad, the soup of the day and sweet-potato wedges. Nowhere near as impressive as last week's barbecue, but Dad's cafe rarely has a free table for lunch on a Sunday for a reason; he has a knack for making even the most boring-sounding dishes into your new favourite meal.

'Speaking of friends …' Anna says, eating the soup without a word of criticism, 'do you have a girlfriend, Luca?'

'No,' I say, mouth still half-full. 'But I wouldn't, because I'm gay.'

'How about a boyfriend?' Graham swerves without batting an eyelid. Anna smiles sweetly. I'm impressed by how unimpressed they are. Not that I expected them to be homophobic. But I can't lie – they have something conservative about them in, like, a really, *really* rich way.

'No boyfriend either,' I say, glad Simo isn't present. I

don't feel awkward telling my grandparents about me, but the thought of Simo hearing it makes me squirm. I don't want to think about why that is.

'And is there someone you like?' Graham wants to know.

'Not at the minute,' I lie, Simo still on my mind. Simo is always on my mind.

'What about you, Matthew? Are you single?' Anna attacks.

'Yeah, are you single, Matthew?' I grin.

'Yes, happily,' Dad says brightly. 'And that's enough of that.'

'For how long?' Anna continues.

'Excuse me?'

'Have you been single for long?'

'That's really none of your—'

'Don't tell me you've not met anyone since Poppy?' Anna doubles down.

'I didn't say that.'

'You didn't deny it.'

'Fine. I've not met anyone since Poppy. Happy?'

'Why would that make me happy?'

'That's not entirely true,' I chime in. 'A few years back there was that g—'

'There wasn't.'

Now he's straight up lying. I very much remember the guy sleeping in Dad's bed. 'I've been meaning to ask, whatever happened with Hen—'

'That's enough.'

It only takes two words, but Dad's tone drops from chilly to frostbite. Every sound in the cafe ceases. Dad never raises his voice at me. His face is blotched, and I instantly realise two things: Dad's parents don't know he's gay, and he's terrified they'll find out.

The revelation strips me of feeling. The room remains frozen; a real-life version of that painting where four lonely people gather in a diner late at night.

My grandparents weren't bothered when I told them I'm gay, so what does Dad have to be scared of? And why do I keep finding out more and more things that he's been hiding? We're not talking chocolate bars sneakily stored behind the mugs we never use. He's hiding stuff that completely alters the Dad I know.

We might still be there, sat together yet strangely apart, if not for Simo. The bell above the door chimes and, with a gust of air, life returns to the cafe. I have never been more relieved to see him.

I latch on to his smile, to the familiarity of his freckled face. It gives me the strength I need to take this newly gained fact about Dad and file it away into a dark corner of my brain, at least for the moment.

'Anna, Graham,' I say, a wobble in my voice, 'this is my friend Simo.'

He stands next to my chair, and as he places a hand on my shoulder, I notice the tremor in my muscles. It ebbs away at his touch, the warmth of his fingers sinking into my skin. A look passes between us, so brief that it goes unnoticed, but that's all Simo needs to realise something is up. He jumps into action.

'It's really nice to meet you,' he addresses my grandparents, his voice working its charm.

Anna's eyes twinkle. She raises herself up and swallows Simo in an embrace before Graham pulls him into one of those manly handshake-hugs.

'The pleasure is all ours,' Anna declares with a voice like velvet. She looks enchanted.

I know the feeling. I know it well.

CHAPTER 16 – SIMO

October comes
claws at the skin
strips branches of their leaves
till only roots remain

Half-hidden from sight beneath Lorca's poetry collection is my notebook, sketches of daisies littering the pages. Words fill the spaces between the flowers, drawn in sharp black lines that make them look more like weeds with angry edges.

November nears
draws light from skies
the sun out of the sea
till only roots remain

Dad's daisies have reduced in number and colour. The few that are left in the garden have their heads hanging, slowly giving up on the hope of catching sunlight. I stare out at them a lot from my window on the first floor.

daisies grow
and daisies die
and daisies grow again
life decays
and people go
and only grief remains

Sat on my desk, I should be focusing on homework, but instead I leaf through the collection of Lorca's poems, my mind elsewhere. Elsewhere being Luca, who has disappeared into himself, like he too is hiding from the cold. Something happened at that family lunch, but he won't say what. I'm half convinced that I've done something to upset him, and the only thing that reassures me is the fact that today, like so many days, he sits huddled at the foot of my bed. Sometimes he asks me to read, but mostly he scrolls and keeps his thoughts to himself. He's starting to become an enigma, almost like Lorca's poems.

I fear I might have to disappoint Tío Andrés; the kinship he speaks of is lost in translation. Maybe it's the language barrier, and on top of that poetry isn't known for being straightforward and easy to interpret. But even when I find English versions, the meaning escapes me. There's a whole lot of symbolism, talk of the moon and all kinds of flowers, turned into riddles. I wish I could copy some of his verses into my notebook, give my head a break from being haunted by Spanish sonnets, but I can't do it with Luca present. It would be like handing him a key to my mind and letting him roam free.

What I need is a change of scenery. I've stared at the

flowers with their drooping heads for too long. I shut the book of poems away in the desk drawer, careful to hide the notebook beneath it.

'We should see what they're showing tonight,' I say into the silence.

Luca throws me one of those befuddled looks that tell me he was worlds away and hasn't caught up to reality. I hand him my phone. When he sees the picture of the noticeboard, he stills. I know he also feels the whiplash of the memory of that one message from a month ago, but this week's announcement is as innocent as they come:

JOIN THE LOMBARD FILM FESTIVAL!

'But they show the same stuff every year,' Luca protests.

To combat the antisocial attitude that creeps into town with the autumn weather, the council screens a film each night for a week, in the hopes of drawing us out of our homes. Lombard Film Festival isn't exactly Cannes, so they mostly replay old classics and whatever blockbuster has finally become affordable, months after it released in city cinemas.

'Do you have a better plan?' I ask. 'Or are we spending another night stuck inside on our phones?' He pouts, knowing I'm right. 'You like films. And for once you'll get to watch one on a screen that's bigger than the palm of your hand.'

'Fine,' Luca says, and hands back my phone. As it moves from his hand to mine, his gaze lingers on my fingers. They have healed since the incident in the library, but he hasn't forgotten, and neither have I. Sometimes I still feel a twinge of pain, and it serves as a reminder.

For a couple of weeks I contemplated the dried blood beneath my fingernails, tried to let it scab over and heal without reopening the wounds. By the time the crust fell off, revealing a layer of new pink skin, I'd come to a realisation. People keep telling me how I feel, and in trying to prove them wrong, I'm pushing away the person who least deserves it. I hurt myself, then tried to shift the pain on to him so I wouldn't have to bear it alone. All because of a heart carved into a bookshelf. Some letters on a noticeboard. As much as it pisses me off, this expectation that we'll turn into a couple sooner or later, I can't let it change who we are. Ever since, I've been trying to figure out how to remain the Simo he knows, whatever people think. No more pushing Luca away, that much is clear. But beyond that? I'm not sure.

We arrive at the town hall, our shoes damp, rain dripping on to the colourless rug. Even before we reach the auditorium, I fear the worst. There are kids everywhere, holding boxes of sweets or chasing each other through the hallway.

'Of course we picked the day they're showing a children's film,' Luca says, still pouting.

Careful not to trample any toddlers, we reach the

corkboard displaying the schedule. I barely register the film title – *Coco* – before my eyes snag on something else. Ice settles into my bones. I try to steer Luca towards the auditorium, but he turns rigid beneath my touch. He has seen what I see. His expression jumps from surprise to confusion and before morphing into a stiff blankness.

The flyer is a pale pink and almost blank, except for three little words: *Spread the love!* Across the bottom, a row of tear-off strips, each with the drawing of a heart enclosing our initials.

For several suspended breaths, neither of us moves. When my heart slams back into my chest, I reach out and tear the whole sheet off. Though I'm shaking on the inside, I meet Luca's eyes, fold the paper up as if it's nothing but a flea-market announcement and slide it into my pocket.

'Let's just enjoy the film, yeah?' I say, and force him ahead of me, into the auditorium.

What he can't see is how I press my thumbnail into the tender flesh that has only just healed, trying to remind myself that I won't let this break me.

We find seats at the very back, and for the next fifteen minutes I scan the room, to avoid looking at Luca. I spot Joni with a man I assume to be her son, but apart from a gaggle of parents and the town council, they're the only adults. A few rows ahead, Louise is chatting to Jacob. Mairi and her brothers are being ordered around by Councillor Justine, their mother, while Heloise observes the crowd with the gaze of a schoolmistress who despises kids. When the lights dim, I realise that just because the flyer was hung in the hallway, that doesn't mean that the person who put it up is in the room right now. Anyone can walk into the town hall, tack something up and leave again unnoticed.

'I just want you to know,' Luca whispers, 'the posters and hearts and all that, none of it matters. They can say what they want about us, but I only care about you. About us.'

Tension trickles out of my body, and the ache in my jaw tells me I've been grinding my teeth. I relax into the seat and, rather than suppressing the impulse, I cover his hand with mine, although just for a second. It might look like I'm reassuring him, when really I'm the one seeking comfort.

Two hours later, I arrive home, without Luca. It took me a good thirty minutes to get out of my head and focus on the screen. And even then, I struggled to keep up. I was expecting a silly animated adventure, not an exploration of death and grief. Despite the promise to keep my best friend close, Hamza is on my mind. I need time to myself, time to sit with my thoughts, without distractions.

My shoes are so sodden they make a squelching sound when I remove them. I feel just as drenched, weighed down by memories of my brother. I wonder what he would make of the noticeboard and the love hearts. And not for the first time, I wonder what he'd make of Luca. Not that I'll ever find out.

'Simo, come here for a moment.' Mum calls from the lounge.

'I've got homework,' I call back, and though it's an obvious excuse to get out of a conversation, there's a paper on Jane Austen waiting to be written.

She appears in the doorway and frowns at the dirt I've trailed in. 'It won't take long.'

'Mum, I really don't—'

'It's important, Simo. If you could join me and your dad in the lounge, we need to talk to you about something.'

She withdraws, and red warning lights go off in my head. She didn't comment on my trainers muddying the hall, and now she and Dad want to sit me down and talk? I stand on the landing, rendered immobile by a sense of foreboding. They never want to talk, so this can only be about one thing. Or one person.

'Simo?' Mum calls, leaving me no choice but to follow her into the lounge. As I enter and see my parents sat side by side on the sofa like a panel of judges, I want to turn and run. It looks as if they've finally had enough of the rumours, the gossip about me and Luca, and refuse to keep turning a blind eye. If that's what this is about, I don't have answers. I barely understand my own feelings, so how can I give them clarity?

'Don't look so stricken,' Dad says through his beard. 'Unless you've committed a crime, there's no need to worry.'

'O-OK,' I say.

Mum narrows her eyes at me. 'You haven't committed a crime, have you?'

'No!' I insist. 'Just tell me what this is about.'

Mum doesn't take her eyes off me, but she pats Dad's knee, prompting him to speak.

'We're going back to Granada. All of us, together.'

A wave of relief washes over me, followed by another, bigger rush of fear.

'I'm not moving,' I force out through gritted teeth. If this is their strategy to put an end to Luca's and my friendship, they can bite me. I won't let them uproot me and drop me several countries away from him.

'Moving?' Mum asks. 'Nobody's moving.'

'It's only for a couple of weeks, during the Christmas holidays. It's been so long since we've all gone together.'

I stare into Dad's wide, bushy face, his dark beard peppered with streaks of grey.

'We thought you'd like the idea. Did you not enjoy yourself there?' Mum speaks into my silence.

'No, I loved it. I – I'd love to go again.'

'Good,' Dad hums. 'Because it took a lot of convincing to get your mum on board. Hates flying.' He chuckles but stops when Mum sends him a stern look.

'So we're all going together?' I ask, trying to comprehend. We're not moving. Luca and I aren't being separated. In fact, this isn't about me at all. I finally allow myself to breathe.

We haven't been on a family holiday since before Hamza died, and I barely remember that time. Happy memories have a habit of spoiling when the person you share them with is gone. Remembering becomes painful, and so they fall into disuse and begin to fade.

'It'll be just you, your dad and me,' Mum explains. 'Luca won't be joining this time, but it's only two weeks. You'll survive the time apart.'

There it is again, that weird tone she uses when speaking about Luca. It's so subtle I'm never sure it's there. In another universe where I'm less of a coward, I'd challenge her on it. But when she leans back, signifying that I'm free to go, I'm so relieved to have escaped a confrontation that I decide it's wisest to bolt.

In my room, I sink on to the bed. My hand automatically glides beneath the pillow, finding only air where the notebook used to be. Two fear-induced seconds later, I remember its new location and retrieve it from the desk drawer, my heart beating hard with relief. I don't want to imagine the reaction if my parents opened the book, but something else is what's upsetting me, and I'm trying to figure out the source of my unease. I take the conversation with my parents apart, or, to be precise, what I thought the conversation was going to be.

As I turn the tattered pages, something becomes obvious: Luca is everywhere. He's lyrics from songs I listen to on repeat and quotes from children's books, copied out in my handwriting. He's fractured attempts at writing poetry, he's poems stolen from better writers. He's a splatter of apple blossoms covering a full spread. He's unmissable, on every page.

Being confronted with the possibility of losing Luca had me about ready to start a war, guns blazing. I can no longer ignore that my feelings for him, tangled as they are by ten years of friendship with few days spent apart, go beyond loyalty. They're not purely platonic, and perhaps they haven't been for a while. It's only taken so long for my brain to catch up with my heart. I try to sit with this admission and not think about its implications. What this means for us, I can't tell.

My eyes stray to my bookshelf and the novels stacked there. Thousands of pages on matters of love and all that makes us human, and yet there isn't one that will help me out of this situation. I get up and pull the photo album from the top shelf. It's at moments like these that I feel Hamza's absence the most. He was four years older, and in the eyes of little Simo, wiser by an eternity. The album starts predictably, with an ultrasound, followed by images of my tiny mum with a huge belly. My favourite picture is from my first day of school, not because I'm the centre of attention, but because Hamza looks so proud to be my big brother. The picture that hurts the most, the last one he ever appears in, was taken a few weeks after his tenth birthday. Hamza is outside, sat on the lawn of what must be the backyard of our old house. His face is turned away from the camera, and he closely examines something in the grass, a flower maybe, or a ladybird. There's no point in wondering what caught his attention, but I always do. The album ends on a cliffhanger, a loose thread that won't be resolved.

Maybe Hamza sucked just as much at feelings as me. But having him listen as I talked about Luca would have helped, even if he could offer little in terms of advice. Without thinking, I pull the photograph of us on my first school day from beneath the protective film. The album goes back on the shelf, but the picture remains propped up on my desk. Hamza doesn't deserve to be hidden away. Like the daisies in the front yard, he should be seen.

CHAPTER 17 – LUCA

Lombard might not have a cinema or more than one place with good coffee, but it does have a train station. Granted, the train to the city stops here a total of three times a day, if it bothers to show up at all, but the journey is gorgeous; rolling hills and golden wildflowers on volcanic rock. It's giving Hobbiton, but with shitter weather. You'd be able to see the sea if it wasn't for grey clouds above the hidden valleys.

After half an hour of me pointing out landmarks to Jacob – 'The pasture where Sheila keeps the lambs in the spring! The willow that Princess Diana once sneezed on, allegedly!' – I eventually run out of unremarkable things to show him, and we end up sitting in silence, smiling awkwardly at each other.

When we finally get off the train, we find ourselves surrounded by the towers and church spires of a medieval city, now a modern hub of activity. I'm glad that I brought a scarf because the cold of the city feels more vicious, catching you when you least expect it. Sea wind is more direct that way.

Braced against these unpredictable gusts, I follow Jacob

up a busy street that leads deeper into the old town. I try to look like I'm enjoying this, but my face is all scrunched up, shoulders raised to prevent the cold from sneaking beneath the folds of my scarf. Jacob seems amused rather than concerned.

Just when I'm about to ask how much longer this walk will be, like the inner toddler I've not yet left behind, Jacob opens a nondescript-looking door and I follow him inside, keen to escape the elements.

I'm welcomed by low ceilings and brightly coloured drapes, upholstered benches with more cushions than anyone needs and the scents of cinnamon and other spices.

'This is an Indian restaurant,' I state.

'Aren't you hungry?'

'Always,' I confirm.

'And I remember you telling me that you don't like coffee. The reviews say that their chai is amazing.'

I'm already in love. With this place, I mean.

We peel off our jackets and huddle in a corner. Once the steaming mugs arrive and I've taken a sip of the chai, smooth and glorious, I'm ready to stay forever.

'You approve?' Jacob asks.

'Wholeheartedly. I've always thought that chai spices would make the perfect ingredients for a Christmas cookie.'

'I wouldn't know. I've never made Christmas cookies before.'

'Well, let's fix that. I'll turn you into a baker in no time.'

'I look forward to it,' he laughs.

We fall quiet, and because I don't know what to say, I drink too fast and burn my tongue. This doesn't happen with Simo, whose presence I'm so used to. It's just lately that the silence between us has grown more demanding.

'How is the portrait project going?' I ask, remembering how to make conversation.

'Better than you'd expect,' Jacob says with a smile. I notice that he has dimples.

'Oh?'

'I've been meaning to ask,' he continues, 'would your dad be up for taking part in it?'

I feel my eyebrows travel upwards at the idea of Dad participating in a portrait series of queer Lombard.

'You don't look so sure,' Jacob observes.

'I'm not.'

'Dare I ask?'

'It's complicated.'

'You don't have to talk about it. But I'll listen, if you want to.'

'I want to,' I say and set down my mug. 'I'm not used to discussing my dad's sexuality with anyone but him. Or my own, actually.'

'I find your dad fascinating.' His French accent slips through, and his eyes kind of glow. 'I've not met a gay father before.'

'I don't know it any other way. He's never hidden this part of himself, which is why I never felt like I had to hide it either.'

Why is it that I can say these things to a boy I've only just met, but not to Simo, who's known me more than half my life? Telling Jacob stuff I've never told my best friend feels disloyal, but I'm not sure who I'm betraying here; him or myself.

'Makes me wish my parents were gay. It would have saved me a lot of anxiety,' Jacob says.

'Yeah, it's taken a while to understand that it's not that easy for everyone. And that not every place is as welcoming as Lombard. I think it has a lot to do with Mum and Dad being so young and alone when they came to town,' I explain. 'People embraced them and wanted to help out. That's why Mum was able to go to university, and Dad felt safe to be himself.'

'What's changed? Does he no longer feel safe?'

'I guess not. His parents have just moved to Lombard, around the same time as you. They don't exactly get along, which is why they haven't spoken since I was born. But now they're here and they don't know that their son's gay and he doesn't want them to find out. So, long story short: no, I don't think Dad would let you take his picture for your project.'

'That's OK,' Jacob says. 'The important thing is that people feel comfortable having their portrait included.'

'So you've found others?'

'Maybe. You'll have to wait till it's complete to find out,' Jacob says with the hint of a smirk. 'What about your mother, is she … ?'

'A lesbian?' I ask. 'No. She only ever mentions the guys she dates, anyway.'

'And how do a gay guy and a straight woman end up having a child together?'

I'm taken aback by his directness, but when he turns a cute shade of red and apologises, I brush his words away. 'It's fine. Most people give us curious looks, but no one ever asks, and it's not like it's a secret.'

I set the mug down and launch into a short version of the story that Dad used to tell me. 'Mum and Dad grew up together and were close from, like, toddlers. Dad calls it a trauma bond, because they both came from messy families. Their parents were neighbours, and Maz and Poppy stuck together all through school. Apparently, Mum started fancying Dad, and he hadn't yet figured out that he didn't fancy girls. He thought he had to give them a go and everything would fall into place – his words, not mine. Either way, things did fall into place, only not in the way they'd imagined. It took a few months until I made my presence known. And voilà, here I am.'

'Excellent use of French.' Jacob applauds.

'That's where my knowledge starts and ends.'

'That's what I'm here for. I can teach you,' he says, without taking his eyes off me.

'What about your parents?' I ask after a moment, unable to sit in silence.

Jacob pulls a face like his tea has suddenly turned bitter. 'They're not speaking. And I prefer it that way, because when they're forced to communicate, it gets ugly.'

'I know that feeling. Put my dad and my grandparents in a room and it'll soon go up in flames.'

The corner of Jacob's mouth twitches, but it doesn't turn into a smile. 'Do your parents still get along? Or do you need to follow them around with a fire extinguisher whenever they're together?'

'Nah, they're all right.' It's a bit of an understatement, because they're literally best friends, but it feels rude to be lauding my parents' brilliant relationship when Jacob clearly doesn't have that. 'They raised me together. But when you're sixteen, with a baby, and a baby daddy who's just come out as gay, you might have doubts about your future. Mum went to uni and later joined a research programme in New Zealand. She's still out there.'

'And you don't miss her?'

The truth is that sometimes I forget to miss her, because I'm so used to it just being Dad and me. I shrug. 'I love her, and I know she loves me. But Lombard is too small for her, and I don't want to leave.'

'Ever?'

Jacob's question makes me think. Dad and Simo are my favourite people. The cafe and the beach and the island are my favourite places. I can't imagine being happy anywhere else. But I don't want Jacob to think I'm boring, so I shrug again, and he doesn't press for an answer.

After the food – rich curries, some creamy with almonds and raisins, others hot enough to make me hiccup – we set out again and find a bookshop with a view of the citadel. Jacob is the bookish type and walks straight to the literary section. He reminds me of Simo; I think their tastes would align. In the meantime, I wander to a room with coffee-table books, for a simple reason: more pictures and less text. I flick through one on the history of film photography, but I don't take any of the images in.

My mind is stuck on the fact that Dad is hiding who he is from his parents, and I'm at least partly guilty of doing the same thing with Simo. Because we don't talk about gay things. At one point we apparently agreed to ignore several elephants in the room, and we've continued to do so ever since. Now we're here, incapable of talking openly, feeling silly.

Dad is the foundation I built myself on, proud to have this honest man as a father. But his image has taken a couple of big whacks recently. Yes, I get that he's scared of his parents' reaction, and I don't blame him – their parent–child relationship is Royal Family levels of messed up. But I can't just ignore it.

'Luca?' someone says, and I look up. Jacob is standing in front of me, a French book in each hand. 'You seemed far away. I said your name a few times.'

'Sorry,' I say, but he shakes his head and smiles.

'We should make our way to the train station or we'll be stuck here for the night.'

On the train back, I can't shake the feeling that I've not been fair to Jacob. I've barely asked him anything about himself. Instead, I've been stuck in my own head. He, on the other hand, has been attentive and charming. I must suck as a date.

If you can even call it that. I have zero dating experience. How am I meant to know the difference between hanging out and dating? I mean, yes, Jacob is attentive, and cute, and I like being around him. But I'm already struggling with my feelings for one boy; I don't need another to add to the confusion.

As I stare into the darkness that's fallen outside, I catch his eye in the reflection of us, two ghost boys mirrored in a train window.

'You know, all day I've been wanting to ask this, but I've

been too shy,' he begins, glancing from my mirror image to the real me sitting next to him. My heart sinks, like it does every time I have to fend off questions about my friendship with Simo.

'It's a little intimate, but … would you let me take your picture?'

'Oh,' I say, flattered and self-conscious. 'I guess, why not?'

'What do you mean, why not?' Dad retorts with trembling nostrils. 'I have no plans to expand my business. Need I remind you that I have a house to pay off?'

Graham swirls the ice cubes in his crystal glass, leaving Dad to fume in silence. 'You don't generate wealth by sitting on your pennies like a mother hen,' he says eventually.

I guess this is our routine now. Lunches turn into heated family matches: Brandenburg vs Dean. Whoever holds on to their composure the longest wins. I try not to take sides.

'Says the man who only barely scraped by when his business went bankrupt. Twice.'

Point for Dad though. We're having dessert, which is when they drop all efforts to make shallow but polite conversation and pull out the big guns.

'Don't pretend to know what you're talking about, Matthew,' Anna jumps in. 'You weren't even born when your father reinvented the family business. It took a tumble, but it paid off in the end.'

'Because you bailed him out,' Dad reminds her.

'And that's why you should never put all your eggs in one basket. If one investment fails, another will pay the difference.'

'A massive inheritance helps too,' Dad says with a snort.

'Oh, don't you judge. That money paid for your clothes, food and education,' Anna reprimands him. A point for her.

'You mean it paid for the staff and nannies that provided my clothes, food and education,' Dad says.

Graham bangs his glass down on the table. 'That's enough,' he says and presses a palm into his chest, as if to calm his heartbeat. 'I've had enough.'

I try to look anywhere but at my feuding relatives. We're now taking meals in the dining hall, which is as extra as it sounds. It has an ornate fireplace as tall as myself, and the walls are dark wood panelling with a floor to ceiling tapestry that shows humans frolicking in nature, and far too many peacocks.

Anna is the first to speak again. 'We won't be around next week. Your grandfather and I have to travel back to check on the business – only to ensure that everything is running as it should without us.'

'It won't be too stressful?' I ask, over Dad's audible sigh of relief. A glance at Graham tells me that he's still battling his temper. I've not forgotten about his stroke, and I'm starting to wonder whether moving closer to his son will have been beneficial for his blood pressure.

Anna's expression softens. 'We're only making sure that things are running smoothly in our absence. It's social calls, a soiree, that sort of thing.' Her expression brightens further. 'You could join us sometime. Escape the small-town life, see something taller than a lighthouse, go shopping in a supermarket that offers more than one brand of ketchup.'

'When was the last time you saw a supermarket from the

inside? Or had ketchup?' Dad asks incredulously. In fairness, I struggle to picture Anna with a shopping cart full of veg as she stops in front of a shelf to pick condiments.

She waves his questions away. 'You're missing the point. A boy can't remain on the street he grew up on all his life. If you ever want to see something new, your grandfather and I would love to make it happen. There's a charity ball in the new year that we could take you to. It'll be fun!'

The idea of going away with my grandparents is daunting. A lunch is one thing, a brief couple of hours in which I'm mostly busy eating amazing food. But spending an extended period of time with them? I wouldn't know what to expect. On the other hand, I'm intrigued to see my grandparents in their natural habitat. I wonder if they watch TV and fall asleep snoring. Plus, Anna isn't wrong. Before I went to Granada, I'd never left the country. Going away can be nice. It makes you appreciate home even more.

'I'd like that,' I say eventually.

Everyone's focus shifts to Dad, who is busy turning his chocolate soufflé into expressionist art. Or is pretending to be. When he looks up, he wears a poker face.

'What's the question?' he asks innocently.

'We're taking Luca to the charity ball in the new year,' Anna repeats.

'That's not really a que—'

'Can I go? Please?'

After several seconds of silence, he shrugs. 'I can't stop you.'

I should be hyped, but Dad's cool demeanour annoys me. Of course he could stop me. He's my dad.

Anna claps with delight. 'I'll make the arrangements.'

'It can't interfere with school,' Dad reminds her.

'That goes without saying,' she retorts.

'And I won't be able to come. Someone needs to look after the cafe.'

'The boy doesn't need a chaperone. And he has us,' Graham says.

Dad's expression makes it clear what he thinks of that. 'You should ask Simo if he wants to go.'

'I will,' I say. 'If it's all right that he comes along?'

Graham frowns and Anna hesitates, but only until she sees Dad's battle-ready expression and quickly reconsiders. 'Of course, darling.'

I'm excited and a little relieved. With Simo by my side, even the strangest place feels like a piece of home. It'll make things more balanced – my grandparents have each other and I'll have Simo.

Anna gets up. 'Let me find Susie – I'll get her to drop everything and start organising ASAP.'

'And I'll arrange a visit to your great-grandfather's bakery; you can see where the first Brandenburg loaf was made.'

They're out of the room before I get a chance to reply. I've never seen them this excited before, like kids on Christmas Day. I have to admit, it's cute.

Dad, on the other hand, looks sceptical. He might not trust his parents, but letting me go must mean he has enough confidence in me.

'Thanks, Dad,' I say.

His lips form a tight line. He pushes back the chair, clearly ready to go. 'Don't thank me yet. Wait till the trip is over.'

CHAPTER 18 – SIMO

'Ready?' Luca asks.

'Ready,' I reply automatically, because I know the routine well. Only, this time, I'm not sure I'm prepared. Luca falls back on to the sofa and stretches his long legs, but unlike all the other times when we've settled in for a film night, he is mushed up against me, his head resting on my arm. I suddenly find myself unable to move.

'I hate your weird policy, you know. We could've watched this weeks ago,' he complains over the title music.

'You've made that point often enough. It's not gonna change anything.'

There's nothing wrong with wanting to read the book before watching the film. I like to make up my own mind about the characters and their world, so I can complain about the bad job the director has done in bringing it all to life. And it's usually a very bad job.

'It's selfish,' Luca says, and shifts. For a second his weight is gone, but, to my relief, his cheek settles back against my biceps.

'Selfish?' I manage, gazing upon him from above.

He looks up and grins. 'Yeah, it makes it impossible for

me to watch it too, just because you're not quick enough to read the damn book by the time the film comes out.' He breaks eye contact to grab a handful of crinkle crips and offers it to me, even though I know he loves them more than I do, and he can be possessive when it comes to his favourite foods.

'I think it doesn't hurt you to be inconvenienced. Consider it a lesson in patience.'

'No talking over the film!' he says, because he knows I'm right.

We watch Anya Taylor-Joy flounce around the English countryside in frilly dresses and bonnets. What I'm not prepared for is seeing so much – any – naked man butt. I try not to tense or make any sudden moves, because of course I'm totally unbothered by this bare-buttock display. Luca plays it cool too, and I could be imagining that he's chewing on a single crisp until the actor is fully dressed again.

I've not decided whether I do or don't like Jane Austen. Her characters are tedious, but sometimes she drops a one-liner that hits you straight in the chest and leaves you devastated.

The creaking of the floorboards announces Maz before he steps into the room.

'Simo, it's nice to see your face,' he says, and drops a container on the kitchen island.

'And yours,' I reply. A palpable tension hangs in the air, so I add: 'I heard Joni's son is opening an Italian restaurant across from you.'

Maz's face darkens. He glances out the window towards

the restaurant in question. 'I heard the same thing. He'd better not steal my customers. I hope he's a shit cook.'

Luca makes a choking sound, as if he's trying not to laugh. Maz's eyes flick to him before he turns and pours himself a glass of water.

'There's some leftover mac and cheese if you boys are hungry,' he says, and points to the container. 'I'm gonna have a shower.'

Once I hear the bathroom door lock, I clear my throat. 'Is everything all right with you two?'

'What makes you say that?' Luca asks, and sits up.

I know I'm on thin ice, but it's obvious that something is going on. They're not fighting, but there's also none of their usual playful squabbling.

'Well, for example, on a normal night, Maz would watch the film with us. But he basically fled the room.'

'He did not flee the room,' Luca protests.

'And the coffee tastes different too.'

'You're making that up.'

'You don't drink it, so you wouldn't know. But I had a latte the other day, and it's not the same. Mairi agrees that it tastes off, and I overheard Mayor Pickering telling Betsy that he's considering going back to drinking instant.'

'Pickering can choke on his dirt water then. And I can't believe you're blaming me for this coffee conspiracy.'

'All I'm saying is that Maz isn't himself. And neither are you.'

Luca huffs. 'It's all to do with Dad's messed-up relationship with his parents. It's affecting everything.'

A crumb of information, finally.

'If I can do anything to help fix things …'

He studies me silently before saying, 'There's nothing to fix. We're still … adjusting to this new family dynamic.'

Deep down I'm aware that Luca and I aren't family, not in that rooted-in-your-DNA kind of way. Most of the time I'm fine with that. We're close in a way I lack words to describe, because neither brothers nor friends fully captures what we have. But other times, when I'm not so gently reminded that I'm an outsider, that there are gaps I can't fill, this ugly feeling creeps over me. A mix of loneliness and jealousy. No matter how hard I try to rationalise it away, a seed of it remains, buried but threatening to unfurl. Like now, when Luca's knee is touching my thigh but still I feel like I'm not enough for him to confide in.

'But,' Luca says, and taps my leg with his index finger, 'thank you. For offering.'

'I'm worried because, well, I won't be here for Christmas.'

The tapping stops. 'What?'

'And I won't be back for New Year's either.'

Frown lines cloud Luca's eyes. 'Where will you be?'

'In Granada. For two weeks. And I'd feel less bad about leaving if I knew you guys weren't … moping.'

When he doesn't move to say anything else, my index finger maps out a path on the sole of his foot, asking him for a reaction.

'OK then. I promise not to mope.'

'Good,' I say. I wasn't sure how to bring up that we'd be spending the entire holiday in different countries.

'Two weeks, huh?' Luca says.

'Yeah,' I reply, well aware of the fact that we've never

gone so long without seeing each other.

'Don't look so sad. You love it there; you'll have a great time.' He grabs several cushions, stacks them up against me and lies down by my side once more.

I guess this means he's not mad at me for bringing up his dad, or my Christmas plans. His head rests on my ribcage, and for a while I keep my arm on the backrest above him. Then it starts to fall asleep, so I have no choice but to use him as an armrest. I pretend to be more casual about it than I am. We've slept like this before, our bodies close, but it's different when we're both awake. Currently, I'm very conscious that the heat of his body is seeping into mine, driving up my temperature.

'Talking about holidays,' Luca says, more than halfway into the film, 'do you fancy a weekend trip away?'

'Away where?'

'To the capital.'

I takes me two seconds to travel from the early nineteenth century onscreen and land back in the present. 'Why would I want to go to the capital?'

'Because my grandparents invited us, and I want to go.'

I blink at him, slowly, to signify that he needs to bring better arguments. 'Because we'll be staying in their luxury town house. Because they'll let us borrow their chauffeur. Because they'll take us to a charity ball where we might bump into celebrities or royals.'

'Literally none of that is doing it for me.'

'Because,' he says, propping himself up on his elbow, 'we could sneak away to second-hand bookshops and find you stinky old books with stinky bookmarks and old messages hidden inside. Because the town house has a library and a pool.' Now he has my attention. 'And I want you there.'

I try to keep a straight face, but it's hard keeping a lid on the sunny feeling that's rushing through my body.

'Just because it would be less scary,' Luca adds, sounding defensive.

'Sure,' I say, unable to swallow my smile any longer.

'You don't find my grandparents scary?'

'They can be intimidating,' I admit.

'Which means you'll come.' It's a statement, not a question. He gets his way too easily.

'If my being there makes you less intimidated,' I say.

'It does,' he replies with sincerity.

'Can't wait to find stinky old books with you,' I grin.

'Can't wait to see you wear a tux for the ball,' he retorts.

'Don't ruin it,' I say and flick him on the temple. 'And focus on the film. You can't afford to miss things, lazy-ass reader that you are.'

He doesn't complain. He got what he wanted, after all. I guess we both did.

With Luca's head in my lap and my arm around him, we continue watching. I could stay like this forever; I'd watch a thousand films with him, even without reading the book first. Luca tenses, and I look up to see the priest make a fool of himself in front of polite society. Luca is prone to second-hand embarrassment. While I close my eyes at gory stuff, he shuts his and blocks his ears whenever the cringe factor rises.

'I thought you liked that actor,' I say.

'I do,' he says, sounding surprised, 'in roles where he's not a twat, anyway. But I didn't know you knew that.'

'I notice things,' I say.

Luca hits the pause button. 'What things?'

'You seem to like Jacob too.' The words are out, and I can't take them back.

'I like Jacob,' he confirms, hesitantly, like he's unsure of the ground we're treading on. 'But not in that way.'

'In what way?' I inquire.

Luca's face forms a silent question. *Are we actually doing this?* it asks. I lift an eyebrow, indicating that, yes, we are.

'I like him as a friend,' he replies, keeping his voice calm.

'So your date—'

'I never said it was a date.' And the calm is out the window.

'It didn't go well, then?'

'It went well, thanks, but it wasn't a date. Just friends hanging out,' he says. 'Like us.'

He looks at me as if he's expecting me to challenge him. But my heart is thundering in my ears and I'm trying to breathe like a normal human being, so all I manage is to echo his: 'Like us.' And though it's but two little words, they sting like nettles on my tongue.

'I'm allowed to have other friends,' Luca says.

'Obviously.'

'I mean, you have friends beside me, right?'

'Right.'

'And you and Mairi, you're friends, right?'

'Right.'

'And nothing else.'

'Just friends.'

'Great,' he says, like it's everything but.

'It is great, yeah,' I say in the same tone.

Jaw set, he turns back to the screen and hits the play button a little too aggressively. I cross my arms and stare ahead, until I realise that I'm mirroring his exact posture and drop my hands in my lap.

I don't know what to make of that conversation. It plays on a loop in my head, as I inspect every word from all possible angles, unable to follow the film until the very moment when Knightley faces Emma and says: '*If I loved you less, I might be able to talk about it more.*'

And though I knew the line was coming, it leaves me devastated.

WINTER

CHAPTER 19 – LUCA

NEW RESTAURANT, THE OLIVE, OPENING TONIGHT!

'It's no crime to check out the competition, right?' I ask.

'Right,' Mum agrees, her voice sounding tinny through the speaker of my phone. I watch as she ties her blonde hair into a ponytail, getting ready for another day of monitoring the sex lives of kiwi birds. I wish I found birds as interesting as she does, but I've never really understood the fascination. 'I mean, I love your dad, and I'd die for him, but I'd also gladly stab him in the back for free pizza. If he wants to mope and miss out on a piece of *la dolce vita*, that's on him,' she says, brandishing what looks like a bottle of sunscreen.

'Feels like I'm betraying him,' I admit. I'm standing in an alcove just a few steps away from the restaurant entrance and occasionally wave when someone spots me as they enter.

Mum halts, several white dots of sunscreen on her face. Seeing her up close is almost like looking in a mirror. When I was younger and Mum was still around, tourists would often be confused by our obvious resemblance, unsure whether we were mother and child or siblings with an unusual age gap. If I grew my hair out and put the right make-up on, we might even pass as sisters.

'That's because you're sweet and pure,' she says. 'But firstly, your dad is shockingly brick-headed, and secondly, you should never feel guilty for eating mozzarella balls. And I presume there'll be mozzarella balls.'

I step closer to the window and glance inside. 'You're not wrong. About the mozzarella balls *and* Dad's brick-head.'

'Wait, can you turn your camera and point out Daniel?' Mum asks.

'Um, why?'

'Maz insists he's "not that good-looking" and I can always tell when he's lying.'

'Yeah, no, I'm not doing that. I can't have two parents crushing on the same guy.'

'Wouldn't be the first time,' she mumbles and starts blending in the sunscreen.

'What?'

'Never mind, now stop stalling and go inside!'

'No, Mum, that's not fair!'

'There are bird droppings that are urgently waiting for me to collect them, so I gotta go! Love you! Eat tons of pizza for me!'

She blows me lots of kisses and ends the call, cutting off my protest. I shake my head, thinking – not for the first time – that my parents never really grew out of being teenagers.

When I step into the Olive, I can't shake the lingering sense of remorse. But I remind myself that Daniel personally invited us, so it would be rude not to show up, which makes me feel a tad better. Lombard's new and only Italian restaurant is about half the size of the cafe, but Daniel's turned it into a modern space, with exposed beams and upholstered furniture in mossy tones. I look around as if I don't already know that Simo hasn't arrived. I spent the last ten minutes staring down the street to see if he was approaching, growing nervous for no obvious reason, until Mum called and offered distraction.

The smell of garlic and sage in the air calms my nerves. I pinch a couple of cherry tomatoes and find a comfy bench in the far corner with a good view of the entrance. You'd never think this used to be a pet shop. Nowadays, the only animal around is Daniel's miniature dachshund, who's obsessed with cheese. She keeps getting up on her hind legs to glance at the charcuterie boards, then throws me a look with pleading eyes. I'm close to giving in and sneaking her a piece of Parmesan when Simo finally arrives.

He doesn't spot me immediately. While he scans the room, I scan him, from the dark curls that I can feel beneath my hand just by looking at him to the way the light flatters his skin. When he meets my eyes, recognition flashes across his features, followed by a smile that temporarily knocks my ability to breathe. I barely have the chance to wonder why it's getting harder to function like a normal human being around him before he appears before me.

'You smell nice,' I say before my mind catches up to my mouth. It might be the mood lighting, but I think he's blushing.

'It's a nice occasion, so I put aftershave on,' he says, and sits down next to me, his thigh brushing against mine. 'Do you like it?' he asks, sounding casual, but now I'm sure there's a flush beneath the last few freckles on his cheeks.

'I do. It suits you,' I admit. Simo always smells of summer and the lemony detergent his parents use for laundry. Now there's a new note, one that pleasantly tickles my nose. It makes me want to lean in. Fold myself into the crook of his neck, lips locked to his skin. Inhale deeply until his scent fills my chest.

My lungs are burning, and a cocktail of aromas hits my brain; citrus and cedarwood and other notes I can't name. But beneath it all: Simo. The sensation slams me back into the present. I almost let my intrusive thoughts win. I almost crossed an uncrossable line, in a room full of people. And the scariest bit is that a tiny part of me regrets not doing it.

Simo is too distracted by the sausage dog to notice anything. She's returned, ready to persuade someone else to pull off a cheese heist for her.

'You must be Olive,' he says, and picks her up. I force myself to look elsewhere, because Simo with a puppy on his lap might seriously melt my brain. I spot Louise weaving her way through the crowd carrying a tray of violently orange drinks. She's tamed her ringlets into a tight bun, which highlights the heart shape of her face.

'You three make a cute picture,' she says when she reaches us. I resist the impulse to shift away from Simo.

'Hey, Louise,' he says, ignoring the remark. 'You work here now?'

'Yup. And I'd offer you two of these –' she nods to the cocktails on her tray – 'but you're underage and I don't want to get fired on my first day.'

'Is Mairi around?' Simo asks, which throws me back to the conversation we had while watching *Emma*. He says that there's nothing between them, and I believe him. He's never expressed interested in anyone. Whenever I suspected that he had a crush on someone – a girl from school, an actress – I was too chicken to ask him. Maybe it's my fault that we don't talk about his crushes, because I don't talk about mine. But I can't tell him about my true feelings for him. I couldn't even admit it to myself until recently. And even now I try not to dwell on those feelings, which is getting harder and harder. They refuse to stay contained.

'I haven't seen her,' Louise replies, 'but I'm sure she'll be here soon. There's free pizza after all.' She smiles, her cheeks plump and rosy, and disappears back into the crowd.

'She could be the culprit,' Simo mutters, as if he's been reading my thoughts. 'That comment felt pointed.'

I've asked myself if Louise could be the person splashing our names all over town, but I have yet to come up with a reason why she'd want to. Why anyone would care. That's the weird part: the motive. Do they want to harm us or … or what?

'But also, she's not wrong,' he says, and turns to me. Olive has made herself comfortable on his legs, and her eyes are half shut in bliss while Simo rubs her back. 'We do make a pretty picture.' He holds my gaze, and if I didn't know better, I'd say he's flirting with me. That's when I know I'm well and truly fucked. My crush is so out of control it's making me see things. Heat creeps up my neck while I scramble for an appropriate reply.

Daniel saves me. He's dressed in black, from his tuxedo trousers to the loose dress shirt, complemented by his dark hair and beard. It's the easy-going laugh and the heartfelt way that he greets people that make him truly shine. He looks at ease in his new restaurant.

'Boys, I'm so glad you came. Looks like Olive has made you her disciples already.'

'We don't mind,' Simo replies, 'and thanks for inviting us. You've turned this into such a nice place.'

Look, I know we root for rough boys, bad boys, boys who act first and think later, but right now Simo's gentle voice and impeccable manners are having a real effect on me. And on Daniel too, who is beaming.

'I'm proud of what I've pulled off, but there's one thing that would make me even happier,' he says, turning to me. 'Are you sure you can't convince your dad to come?' He points over my shoulder. When I turn, I get a clear view of Dad mopping the floor of the cafe.

'I doubt it,' I say. Guilt creeps up on me, seeing Dad alone in the shop while half of Lombard is squeezing itself into Daniel's place just across the road. Staying away is his decision though, not mine.

'Please?' Daniel says, 'I don't want to antagonise him. Life is going to be easier if we can be friends. And you could look after Olive from time to time.'

There's no way I can refuse now. 'If you let me borrow

her, I'll have Dad over here in no time.'

'She's all yours,' he says. I lift her from Simo's lap and scoop her into my arms. She licks my chin to say hello.

'Be right back,' I tell them, and I'm out the door and across the street, giggling as she tickles my neck with her sniffs. I've barely set foot in the cafe when Dad stops me in my tracks.

'Don't you drop that. I just cleaned,' he warns.

'*That* is a dog, and her name is *Olive*,' I retort. 'And she's clean.'

'What do you need?' Dad asks, eyeing her suspiciously.

'Daniel wants you to come over.'

'Does he now?' he says, and wipes the already spotless counter.

'So will you come?'

'I'm busy tidying.'

'The place couldn't be tidier, Dad.'

'Some of the tables wobble. I was going to fix that.'

'How about this: I leave Olive with you, and you're forced to bring her back over unless you want her to mess up your squeaky-clean floor – or you join us now?'

With narrowed eyes, he stares out the window at the crowd of townsfolk mingling, snacking, sipping Aperol.

'Fine, let's go.' He throws down the towel and heads for the door.

'You're not going to change?' I ask.

'What's wrong with my clothes?'

'I can identify about twelve meals you've served today just from looking at your shirt.'

Even Olive is craning her surprisingly long neck to get a

better sniff. Dad grumbles but stomps upstairs and reappears five minutes later, still grumbling, but in a clean white tee and a fresh pair of denims. I think he even combed his hair, and –

'Did you put on *aftershave*?'

He ignores me, so of course I repeat the question, twice, until we reach the restaurant.

'I don't want to smell of cheese, do I?' he says, and disappears through the door before I can accuse him of trying to impress Daniel.

Olive wriggles in my arms, so I let her down and follow her inside, where I almost run straight into Dad's back. Ready to throw a complaint at his head, I notice just in time what's made him freeze in the middle of the restaurant.

'What are you doing here?' Dad's question, which sounds a lot like an accusation, is directed at none other than my grandparents, both of whom look intentionally overdressed.

'We live here,' Graham says drily.

'So?' Dad bristles.

'We're active members of town now.'

'And that means we take an interest in Lombard's economic growth,' Anna adds.

'That's funny, tell another one,' Dad retorts.

Graham puffs out his chest. 'Tell you what, I'd have run this guy out of town already if my business was at risk. Nothing a good smear campaign can't settle.'

'Not here, Graham,' Anna warns.

'My business isn't at risk,' Dad clarifies.

'Let's hope it stays that way,' Graham says, and moves on to check out the snacks.

'Stay away from the prosciutto, Graham,' Anna says, trailing behind.

Dad's eyes follow them, until he shakes himself like he's awakening from a nasty dream. 'Right, I've shown my face, and I can't be arsed with—'

'Maz, you made it!' Daniel appears through a gap in the crowd. I admit, he has an amazing smile, the sort that's blinding but you can't look away. 'I hope this means you're not planning to run me out of town?'

Dad lets out a low groan that only I hear. I decide to slink away and leave them to it. On my tiptoes, I peer over the sea of heads to try to find Simo. Panic sweeps over me when I catch a sliver of dark curls and golden skin peeking out from behind the backs of my grandparents. They've cornered him by the charcuterie boards. I've never seen Anna and Graham out in the wild and have no idea what they're capable of when left unsupervised. As quickly as I can, which is not quickly at all, I wind my way through the packed room. Simo spots me and pulls me through the huddle of bodies like a drowning man grabbing a life ring. In the other hand he holds a cream envelope.

'What's that?' I prompt, latching on to the first thing I see.

'We were telling your Simo about our Christmas Gala,' Anna explains. 'We wanted to make sure he got the invitation.'

My mind is stuck on the way she called him *my* Simo, so it takes a moment before I catch the meaning of her words.

'Your Christmas Gala?'

'You ought to inspect your mail more often. We sent

your invitation days ago,' Anna reprimands me. The look she throws me could almost be described as doting, so I don't think she's annoyed. 'We always throw a Christmas Gala. It's a tradition from decades before you saw the light of day. And of course we'd like this young man to come too.'

'Oh, I swear I read about those parties,' I say, and immediately wish I hadn't. It was in the days after my first falling-out with Dad, holed up in Simo's room, both of us scouring the internet for information about the Brandenburgs. Even the documentary mentioned the event.

Anna, if anything, looks flattered. 'They're iconic,' she says in that way of hers that shows a degree of self-belief I've never seen in anyone else.

'If Luca is coming, I'll be there,' Simo says. I notice that he hasn't let go of my arm.

'I'd hope so,' Graham says, 'Anna's been planning it since we moved here. You don't want to miss it.'

'Who else did you invite?' I ask casually. While people are keeping a respectful distance, it's obvious that we have an audience.

'It doesn't matter,' Dad says as he pops up beside me suddenly, 'we're not coming.' His tone is cheery and very, very fake.

'Matthew!' Graham warns.

'Dad!' I exclaim.

'I've not come to argue,' Dad says with a placatory smile. 'Just came for the olives.' He pops one in his mouth and disappears, cutting off a discussion that is so not over.

'Ignore him,' Anna says.

'Our son has always been a bit of a snob,' Graham adds.

'Used to lock himself in his room whenever we threw parties.'

I have no appropriate response, so I turn to Simo. He bites his lip, trying to hold in a laugh, which doesn't help. I quickly look away again, only to catch Anna observing our exchange. Her eyes land on Simo's hand, the one still wrapped around my arm.

'I've been thinking. I could pull some strings, get in touch with friends in the fashion industry and see if they'd let you both borrow a look for the night. Maybe a matching theme.'

'Um, I'm not sure … I don't think …' I stutter, failing to come up with a polite way of rebuffing the idea. I don't mind fancy outfits, but matching looks is a bit on the nose.

Simo clears his throat. 'Thank you, Mrs Brandenburg, but I don't want to cause you more stress planning the party. Besides, I don't need to give Luca more reason to outshine me. He constantly steals my clothes, and somehow they look better on him too.'

See? That's what I mean.

Manners make a boy's knees weak.

CHAPTER 20 – SIMO

'They sent a limousine,' Luca murmurs for the sixth or seventh time. Minutes ago, he opened the apartment door to a driver in suit and tie, who announced that the car was ready and waiting to take us to Hidden House.

The three of us are squished into the back seat of the car like overdressed chickens on a roosting bar. Maz's face is a mask devoid of emotion. Luca alternates between gliding his hands over the car's smooth leather interiors and stroking the ribbed corsage and flayed suit trousers of his off-white custom clothes. I struggle to take my eyes off him. Not because of the expensive clothes, but because he wears that wonderstruck expression of a toddler on Christmas morning. It's so fucking enchanting; I have to fight the urge to text my parents that I'm not flying to Granada with them tomorrow, I'm staying right here, with him.

The limousine isn't the only thing the Brandenburgs sent. A couple of weeks after they invited me, I found one of those oversized gift boxes on our front step, to the puzzlement of my parents. When I untied the silk bow and opened the box, my fingers trembling as my parents watched with wide eyes, I discovered several items tagged with a designer label, as per the dress code stated on the invitation: strictly white and gold formal attire. Despite my telling her she didn't have to, Luca's grandmother went out of her way to organise us outfits.

At first, Mum refused to let me even touch the clothes, demanding I return them immediately. Once I'd explained that I couldn't insult Luca's grandparents like that, she gave in, but only on condition that I do not eat or drink or touch anything that could stain, tear, burn or otherwise harm the outfit. In fact, I wasn't even to sweat into the clothes, so I could send them back after the party in the exact same state they arrived.

When the car comes to a halt and the driver opens the door, I check repeatedly that my ankle-length trench coat doesn't touch the ground. It's white with gold buttons and made from the softest material I've ever touched. I never want to take it off.

'Shit,' I say, when I look up and discover what's in front of me. Darkness has fallen but cutting through the ink-black night are six giant baubles, some as big as me. They seem to float in mid-air and emit a faint glow, forming an archway that beckons us deeper into the gardens of Hidden House. Faint piano music reaches my ears, and I'm half convinced that rather than dropping us off at the Brandenburg manor, the driver has brought us to a faerie realm.

I only snap out of my daze when Maz steps in front of us. He's in a sharp tailcoat over a snow-white shirt and waistcoat, plus bow tie. His parents also sent a gold watch and a top hat, which he is refusing to wear. Still, he looks impeccable.

'Before we go in, promise me two things,' he says in a serious tone. 'Stick together, and don't accept anything from anyone you don't know.'

Luca snorts. I can't disagree. Maz is acting like the White Witch from Narnia is about to appear behind the giant baubles and ensnare us with Turkish delight.

'You think I'm kidding now, but you didn't share a house with these ... people for sixteen years. I've seen things at their parties I'd rather forget. So just to be clear: if someone offers you drugs, you're going to refuse. In fact, you're coming straight to me and we're getting out of here. Have I made myself clear?'

In all the years I've known Maz, he's never sounded so much like my mother, stern and unyielding. I nod.

'Good. Let's do this,' he declares, but he doesn't move. In the end it's Luca who takes the first step. His hand finds mine and he pulls me forward. My only thought is that it feels right. Maz follows us through the archway and down a path marked by more floating baubles. They sway in a breeze, and I can only gawp at them, because surely this is an illusion.

Luca tugs me gently ahead, past a bar decked out with thousands of pearlescent holly berries, until we reach an open-air ballroom. I'm glad of Luca's hand in mine because gravity has lost its hold on me. My brain fails to compute what it sees. Spanning the entire space is a canopy of shimmering spheres that move like a single body, their languid up-and-down sway forming a single wave a few metres above our heads.

I don't know how long the three of us stare, mesmerised,

at the kinetic entity rippling in the air. We might stand there still, were it not for Anna Brandenburg. Clad in a scarlet suit, like a ruby in a sea of gold, she lifts her arms. It's the gesture of a magician orchestrating the stunt of the century.

'Shall we start the party?'

An hour later, I'm standing in a patch of dark night just beyond the dance floor. My gaze follows the couples who, guided by the live music and the dancing spheres above, sway to their own rhythm. Joni and Daniel attempt an imperfect but spirited mother–son waltz, and Louise, Jacob and Mairi twirl around each other while also indulging in the variety of snacks offered by waiters circling the ballroom. There are whispers that Adele is due to appear, which, at this point, wouldn't surprise me. I have seen what the Brandenburgs are capable of.

As the first guests trickled in, Anna and Graham whisked Luca and Maz away for a 'family thing'. Separated from Luca, I felt like Alice abandoned in Wonderland, a stranger in a world that defies the laws of logic. So I stepped out from under the rippling canopy and found myself on a normal lawn, surrounded by normal trees. The cold sea breeze stung my skin, but I welcomed its touch on my burning cheeks and the soothing sound of the waves lapping the shore.

I flex my hand. Though everything that I've just experienced feels unreal, Luca does not. I can still feel the ghost imprint of his fingers pressing against my skin. It makes me wonder what my parents would say, if they saw us like that, holding hands. Nothing, is the likely answer. In the same way they have said nothing about the gossip that's been doing the rounds for months. The coal, that tight knot of frustration, still burns in my gut, fed by the stubbornness with which they refuse to have conversations that matter. Not just about me and Luca. About Hamza too. No one has said his name in years.

In the past few weeks, I've woken up to the realisation that I don't want silence to define me the way it defines my parents. I don't want it to come between me and the people that matter to me. It's a thought that fills me with a kind of soaring sensation, like I'm standing at the edge of a cliff, and though I know I'm strapped into a security harness, the reality of the drop is as scary as it is liberating. If I jump, there is no turning back. The question is which I'll regret more: if I speak or keep my mouth shut.

What will happen if I say Hamza's name out loud in front of my parents?

What will happen if I ask Luca for a dance?

I picture myself and Luca on the dance floor, and for a couple of peaceful seconds a pleasant shiver rolls across my body, making my fingertips tingle with possibility. Then I remember everyone else, all the eyes on us, and the tingling turns into panic. The feeling tells me all I need to know.

The fantasy fades, leaving me standing alone on a cold December night. I step back into the light and the warmth of the heat lamps, seeking a drink that will remove the taste of fear from my tongue. I notice too late that I've run straight into a group of familiar faces.

'Wow, Simo, you look …' Mairi starts, but can't seem to settle on a word.

'Hot,' Louise finishes, a wide grin across her face. 'What

she means to say is, you look hot.' Mairi punches her in the arm, while heat blooms on my cheeks. 'I'm only stating facts,' Louise adds with a giggle that makes her curls bounce.

Jacob, who's been watching the exchange with an amused expression, catches my eye and nods a hello.

'You all look good too,' I reply, taking in Mairi's sequinned dress and Louise's miniskirt. And yes, even Jacob manages not to be outshone by them. Barely.

'Just good or … hot?' he asks with a raised eyebrow, then moves to dodge a punch from Mairi.

Suddenly, Jacob straightens, and awe softens the hard edges of his face. I brace myself for another of Anna's other-worldly surprises, but the second I turn, my eyes lock on to Luca. And something stirs. It's not the haunting spheres above, or the heads in the crowd as they turn. It's a well in my chest, a dark mirror lying still until the very moment when the moon is revealed and touches a fingertip to the water's surface. A single ripple, and the darkness fractures, revealing what lies at the bottom.

I see what they see: a beautiful boy, wearing beautiful clothes like a second skin, looking like a true Brandenburg. But unlike them, I would find Luca in any crowd. Strip him of the name and the expensive clothes and he'd remain the same to me. Strip me of sight and touch, and I'd sense him regardless.

He comes to a stop before me, and I almost look away, because maybe it's all too much, maybe it's best to stay drowned. It might be dark at the bottom of that well, but it's safe too. In the end, I have little say in the matter. Now I'm drowning in the blue of Luca's eyes.

We don't get the chance to speak, as Anna picks this moment to launch the event. There's a welcome speech from Graham, the band is introduced, the buffet opened, but the words don't reach my ears. As the night goes on, Luca's presence sets me afloat, and it takes a while for me to realise that I'm tipsy. I could do with a break, and not just to clear my head. Turns out champagne, once it's released its alcohol into your blood, rushes straight to the bladder.

I excuse myself and weave my way through the throng of people. Like a breeze that lifts the fine hairs on my neck, I can feel someone's gaze on me, but I don't need to turn to know it's Luca. The feeling doesn't fade, even as I walk away.

Once I've washed my hands, I don't head straight back to the party. A pint of water in my hand, I find myself in the shadow of the manor, just off the patio. Ahead of me, Clifford Island rises from the moonlit waves. To my left, music spills from beneath the canopy. Two shadows detach themselves from the crowd and hastily make their way across the midnight lawn. I tense, thinking they're headed in my direction, but they stop several feet away, caught in an argument.

'You can't stop us from giving him gifts, Matthew.'

I recognise Graham's voice and make myself smaller, hoping the darkness will keep me hidden even in my white outfit.

'I'm not trying to stop you from giving him gifts,' Maz replies. I can tell he's fuming. As much as I don't want to hear this, I'm scared to draw any attention to myself, so I daren't move a muscle, staying exactly where I am.

'Then I don't understand why you're throwing a fit,' Graham says haughtily.

'Because I'm his father, and you can't go over my head and bestow him with a bloody trust fund! I'm responsible for that kid, for his health, for his finances, and his future.'

'You ought to be more grateful then, because his future is safe now, thanks to us.'

Maz's next words almost come out as a hiss. 'His future is safe and has always been safe, thanks to me and Polly, his parents.'

'You're mad because you hate that we could be involved in his life in any way, big or small.'

'And you're trying to pay off your guilt!' Maz shouts.

'He's our grandson – we should be allowed to be generous with him!'

'Oh, *now* he's your grandson! That's quite the change of tone to when Polly was pregnant.'

'You love to lay the blame on us, but don't forget that it was you who ran away, and you who told us to stay away from Luca. We sent gifts every year for his birthday, which you returned unopened.'

'Nobody wants your unsolicited cheques! Not then and not now!'

'So what *do* you want, Matthew?' Graham asks, exasperated.

'One of two things: you either leave and never return, or you start to care. Like, really, truly care. But let's be honest, you're not able to act in anyone's best interest except your own. You didn't give two shits about raising your own son, and when you found out about Luca, you didn't want him either.'

'That was seventeen years ago. You can't still hold that against us.'

'You wanted to force Polly into having an abortion, tried to bribe her with money!'

The glass in my hand slips. I barely manage to keep it from falling. Water sloshes over my hand and on to my shoes. I swallow a curse and pray they didn't hear.

'Now you're making things up.' The dismissal in Graham's voice is cold and practised.

'You've always been good at lying to yourself,' Maz spits. 'Rather than admitting your mistakes, you bend the truth, no matter the cost.'

'Don't you tell me about truth, Matthew. You should be grateful that we're sticking with you after everything that our private investigator dug up. Lying to Luca about his dead grandparents is bad enough. What do you think will happen when he finds out that you and Polly were—'

'Don't you dare finish that sentence.'

Maz's warning squashes the argument. In the sudden quiet, the two men stare at each other. I hold my breath until Maz turns. His silhouette bleeds into the darkness and only Graham is left, standing alone on the patio. He makes a sound, the beginning of a moan that never makes it past the lips. He moves towards the house, but I don't move until I'm sure he's gone inside.

Thoughts in shambles, I chug what's the left of the water and stumble into the night. My feet carry me away from the manor and towards the noise of the party, but I slow down before I reach the circle of light, unsure if I'm collected enough to face anyone. But Luca finds me first, and the voice telling me to avoid him shuts up.

'I want to show you something,' he says, and steers me away from the canopy, deeper into the gardens of Hidden House.

I refuse to think about what I just overheard. I don't dwell on that conversation or let the meaning sink in. If I did, I'd have to tell Luca, so I gladly let him distract me.

Following a trail of glowing baubles, we forge our way through the trees. The music dwindles but doesn't die. Another sound begins to build; one that I'd recognise anywhere, having grown up by the sea: waves lapping at the shore, and beyond that the gentle roar of the ocean. A heartbeat later, we step into the small private cove.

At first, I think it's the moon that sets the pebbles alight, but it's more than that. Rock formations jut out of the water and inch up the small stretch of beach. Not an unusual sight, except for the fact that they're clear like ice and emanating a silver glow. If I didn't know better, I'd say Anna Brandenburg personally hired someone to carve stones from the moon and artfully rearrange them in her backyard. It's surreal.

'It's magical,' Luca whispers.

'It reminds me of the volcanic beaches in Iceland,' I whisper, 'where the tide carries chunks of ice from nearby glaciers and drops them on the beach. Boulder-sized diamonds on black sand.'

'There's no way that's real,' Luca says with wonder in his voice.

'I'll take you there one day,' I promise. 'But this comes pretty close.'

We stand shoulder to shoulder, marvelling at the sight before us. I feel Luca shiver beside me.

'Here, give me your hands,' I tell him. When he offers them up, I guide them beneath the layers of my coat. He raises both eyebrows, but when I pull him closer, he gives in. The weight of his embrace settles around my middle, but the question in his gaze remains.

'If you wanted a dance, you could've just asked,' he jokes.

I cross my arms behind his neck and begin to sway our bodies from side to side.

'I've been wanting to ask that all night,' I reply, more candidly than planned.

It dawns on me that I didn't think this through. With Luca's hands pressing into my lower back and our hips touching, I might be in over my head. The moment is very intimate and very real. Unable to hold his gaze, I stare at the pearl against his chest. A few seconds pass, then Luca lowers his forehead and leans it on mine.

'I've been wanting to ask you too.' His breath grazes my skin. Now I'm the one shivering, but not from the cold. Once again I'm reminded that it's one thing to be so close when we're asleep, but a whole different story with my every cell in my body wide awake.

'What was the family thing about?' I ask, grasping for a distraction. Anything to keep me from going into cardiac arrest.

'They gave us our Christmas presents. Or more like seventeen years' worth of Christmas presents. I can't even think about it. Makes me dizzy. I'll tell you another time.' I realise I'm staring at the shape of his lips as he speaks.

I close my eyes, as if that's going to save me now. I can't shut out his scent though, or his nose grazing mine.

'You know I'm leaving tomorrow,' I remind him.

'Don't ruin it,' he whispers, and tightens his embrace. We don't speak, only sway from side to side, to the faint melody trickling through the trees.

An ache awakes in my stomach that has nothing to do with hunger. It spreads to my chest and pushes against my ribs, wanting to break free. One thing is becoming painfully clear: Lying in darkness, hiding in the familiar shape of our friendship, is no longer an option. I miss him too much, and I haven't even left yet.

Later that night, I find myself on my bedroom floor, heart heavy and head buzzing, the notebook on my knees. The flight leaves in a few hours, but my mind is too loud to find sleep. I pour my thoughts on to the pages, and with each line breathing becomes easier. I nod off at one point, though the sky is still dark when Dad wakes me. The notebook lies open in my lap, and with dizzy eyes I reread the words, my midnight thoughts captured in black ink:

I have seen the moon a thousand times but
nothing
can describe the feeling of seeing it
reflected on water.
A beam of light as
beautiful as it is brittle
because it stretches

across skies and oceans
to reach you
and still it evades your touch.
Close but never close enough.

CHAPTER 21 – LUCA

I decided running was a good idea, then changed my mind four minutes later when I reached the noticeboard.

> **MERRY CHRISTMAS, LOMBARD!**

The only reason I run at all is because doing it with Simo makes it less painful. Without him, I don't see the point, especially in December, when the roads are slippery and the wind is evil.

I almost turn back, but then I spot something that doesn't fit the picture. Like every year, Mayor Pickering has decorated a Christmas tree in the middle of the square. This year, he's gone for a white and green theme, so the single red bauble among the stars and Grinch-coloured sugar canes sticks out like a drag queen at an IT conference.

I know before I even reach the tree that I'm meant to

see this bauble. It's red hot, the size of a small pumpkin and someone's glued rhinestones in the shape of an S and an L on the surface. If it wasn't so creepy, it could be cute. After months of gossip and messages like this one, the only reason I no longer react with panic is that the game has become tired.

I pluck the bauble from the tree and consider dropping it in a bin, but I can't stomach the idea of our initials being buried beneath used tissues and cigarette butts. I'm also not going to leave it out in the open. I've become used to the discomfort of being talked about, but that doesn't mean that I like it. And I don't want this to get back to Simo and ruin his time in Granada.

Back home, I hide the bauble at the back of my sock drawer. Then I spend a good half-hour in the shower, not because I broke a sweat, but to drive out the cold. It's Christmas Eve, but I've never felt less festive. Simo is away, which is weird enough, but on top of that, Dad's unusually irritable. That might have less to do with me than with his parents, who have flown off to spend the winter break in their villa in Mauritius. Yeah, that's a thing. When Dad found Simo and me on the beach and told us we were leaving, there was a look in his eyes that I'd never seen before. Like an animal cornered. He barely let us say goodbye to Anna and Graham.

I can't find the energy to be mad at him for being mad about the trust fund. It doesn't feel real, which might have something to do with the fact that I won't be able to access it till I'm twenty-five. It's enough to buy the house we live in twice over. Dad has been working hard for years to pay off that mortgage, and for his parents to hand his son such a ridiculous sum must be a slap in the face.

Lately, I've been scared that Dad is lonely. He speaks to Mum on the phone, but with the time difference, her busy schedule and Dad's aversion to texting, I worry that he doesn't have anyone to vent to.

I need our routine back: the film nights, and debating the acting skills to hotness ratio of the shirtless male lead on the TV screen. All of it would lead us to the conversations that mattered. I'd check in on him, he'd check in on me. And I really need him to check in on me, because I'm so confused that I can't focus on anything. Hence the attempt to take up running.

Once I'm dressed, I make my way downstairs, determined to drown my thoughts in chatter and a chai latte. I'm barely through the door when a soft black nose pokes my ankles.

'Olive!' I exclaim, and she turns into a furry whirlwind, tail and ears wagging. I quickly pick her up, because I've learned from experience that her bladder is sensitive to excitement. I see it as a showing of love and appreciation, but Dad might ban all dogs from the premises if she pees everywhere again.

He's by the coffee machine, eyeing us suspiciously.

'What? I've just come to help out,' I say.

Dad grunts. 'Wash your hands first.'

'I gave her a bath last night, you know,' Daniel says. He leans on the coffee bar, an espresso in front of him.

'It's true, she smells good,' I confirm with my nose buried in her soft fur.

'I don't care what you say. With those short legs, she's so

close to the ground, might as well be a hoover.'

'I'm gonna stop buying your coffee if you keep insulting my dog,' Daniel says. I set Olive back on the floor and obediently wash my hands.

'You've not paid for a single coffee since you started coming here,' Dad retorts.

'Because you refuse to let me. Or even to repay you with pizza.'

I perk up. Dad takes the drinks he was making to a couple by the window.

'He always walks away when he's losing an argument,' I tell Daniel, who hides a smirk behind a sip of espresso.

The afternoon passes in a blur, as the town celebrates Christmas Eve and the beginning of the holidays with mince pies and other sweet treats. When the last customers trickle out at around five, we decide to close early. I blast the Sugababes album that I know Dad likes, and the place is tidy and sparkling in less than an hour. Still, wiping down tables and counters isn't enough to keep Simo off my mind. When I don't pay attention, I'm back in his arms, on the beach, at midnight, goosebumps covering my entire body.

'What do you say – shall we get that pizza and watch *Carol*?' Dad asks. And because I never pass an opportunity to watch Cate Blanchett play a lesbian with a fantastic wardrobe, I say yes.

It takes Dad longer than seems necessary to pop in and out of Daniel's place, which leaves me alone on the sofa scrolling through the chat with Simo. Typically we don't text because we sit shoulder to shoulder. He's never had to learn proper response-time, which tests my patience. I don't want him glued to his phone when he should be spending time with his family, but honestly I feel like I might be going through withdrawal. Two days ago we were so damn close, and now I hear from him once or twice a day. If I don't get my daily dose of Simo, I suffer. Knowing that the number of texts a person sends you has no relation to how much they care for you is one thing, understanding it quite another.

It's true, I'm the problem, but it's not all my fault. When Simo pulled me close, it meant something, right? I didn't imagine the slow dance or the embrace. Then again, I wouldn't put it past my deluded brain to read far too much into the way he doesn't break eye contact recently, or the moments where he touches my arm, my thigh. It's so casual it could mean nothing.

I throw my phone to the other end of the couch and get up. Ten seconds later, I knock on Miss M's door and let myself into her top-floor flat. Her company is way better than the noise that my own thoughts make.

She doesn't lift her head from the newspaper she's reading, but raises a hand, heavy with the many rings she wears, and points to the pot of tea. Once I've refilled her cup, she folds up the paper.

'If you're hungry,' she says and grabs my wrists, frowning at my chewed fingernails, 'have a liquorice stick.'

'I hate liquorice,' I say, but I get her point.

She lifts her gaze to my face. Whatever she sees there makes her purse her lips.

'And if your head is too loud, have a schnapps.'

'That's wrong on so many levels,' I laugh, happy to be

here in her presence. That loud head is feeling so much quieter already.

She waves my arguments away with a wrinkled hand.

'You know, you and your father are cut from the same cloth. When you're in love, you are helpless. Like a toddler with a scalpel. Couldn't cut a straight line if held at gunpoint.'

'Who gave the toddler the scalpel? And who's holding it at gunpoint?' I ask, and then, processing her words, 'Wait, who said I'm in love?'

Miss M points to a spot outside the window, and I follow the line she draws with her finger. I can see the foothills of the mountain range that separates us from the city, and the park with the shell-shaped stage. But to see what Miss M means, I have to shuffle to her side of the table. And there, between the lighthouse and the Christmas tree on the town square, sits the noticeboard.

I fall back on to my chair. 'That's just rude,' I say. 'And why do you need me to send you pictures of the noticeboard every Monday when you can see it from here?'

'I can't, can I? My eyes are old and tired.'

I scowl, not sure I believe her.

She waves her hand again. 'Do you know how Lombard ended up with the noticeboard?'

I send her a confused look, then mumble something about Celtic calendars and fishermen.

'Humbug,' she notes. 'No, when those fine lords and ladies whose names nobody remembers first decided they needed a mansion by the sea, they planned to build it in the very spot where the town square is today. It was an important place for the common folk in the area. A copse of apple trees grew there, and they believed those trees to be sacred. The lords and ladies agreed to move further up the coast, but the copse soon became a secret meeting point for the young lordling and a farmer's daughter. The years passed, and the daughter kept waiting for the lordling to ask for her hand in marriage, but for fear of losing his reputation, and his inheritance, the lordling never did. One new-moon night, the farmer's daughter stopped coming to meet the lordling, and in his despair, he lost his footing in the darkness and tumbled from the path into the sea, where he drowned.'

I gasp. 'He *drowned*?'

Miss M shushes me. 'In his grief, the lord of Hidden House had the copse razed to the ground, threw all the apples in the sea, leaving only a single tree standing to remember his son by. The farmer's daughter visited the lonely apple tree every night until the day she died, and when she did, she took her last breath right beside it. By the morning, her body had disappeared and a second tree grew in its place. To this day, on pitch-black new-moon nights, people say that they see thousands and thousands of apples floating in the bay by the square.'

Miss M folds her hands, as if the story is finished. But that can't possibly be it.

'And then?' I ask.

'And then what?' she says.

'At which point did someone chop those last two trees down and plonk the noticeboard there instead?

'You're not understanding the point—'

'That's a horrible, awful story. Who came up with it

anyway? I'm no book nerd, but I know a plot hole when I see one, and this story is the Swiss cheese of plot holes. It makes no sense.'

Miss M tuts in disapproval, then sniffs the air. 'Do you smell that? I think someone's eating pizza.'

'Thanks, Miss M,' I say and place a kiss on her papery cheek, grateful for the distraction she offered. Grateful to have her in my life.

'Silly boy! Think about what I just told you. You might learn something!' she shouts as I dash out the door.

The smell of olive oil on warm bread fills the staircase, and I almost fall down the steps in my rush to get back to our flat.

'How's Miss M?' Dad asks when I enter the lounge.

'She told me to ask Simo for his hand in marriage unless I want to turn into an apple tree.' Dad nods, like he expected nothing less. 'Um, I know we eat a lot, but this –' I wave to the tower of boxes on the coffee table – 'will feed us for a week.'

'Tell that to Daniel. I asked for two margheritas, and I got pear and Gorgonzola, honey and chilli, Parmesan and rucola, a load of garlic bread, a bowl of pumpkin ravioli and half a tray of tiramisu, plus salad and a ton of olives.'

My eyes dart from him to the food and back again. 'If I can just throw this out there …'

'Don't,' Dad warns.

'… I'd say Daniel likes you.'

We've not exchanged banter like this in a minute, but Dad's lips twitch in a way that shows me he's OK.

'He just feels guilty for drinking all my coffee.'

'Or he likes you.'

'Eat and be quiet, child.' He holds up a fork and a bowl of ravioli, and because I'm happy to be bribed with pasta, I do as I'm told.

Two hours later, Cate Blanchett's performance as Carol, a mother who falls for a younger woman but is trapped in a straight marriage, has me crying into my dessert. Dad keeps dabbing his eyes with his sleeve.

'Carol's right, you know,' he says with a croaky voice.

'Huh?' I say, and wipe my nose with a tissue.

'What she says about being a parent. How she can't be a good mum if she lives against her own nature.'

'Dad, I literally just stopped crying.'

'No, listen.' He turns to me, his face serious. 'When you were born, I didn't just come out for myself. I came out for you. For my son, who should never be anyone but himself. How could I be a good example to you if I was scared of myself? As a teenager, I'd felt so much shame. My parents made it clear that a gay son wasn't going to be tolerated beneath their roof. They might have come a long way, but I'm having a hard time letting go of years of fear and mistrust. As you might have noticed. That's why, when I knew I was going to be a dad, I made a promise that you wouldn't have to feel shame for anything ever. And in that way, you freed me.'

'Dad,' I say, but that's all I get out before I have to reach for another tissue. I can see that he's struggling from the way he takes several long breaths before he continues.

'Poppy and I had a deal. Once you were born, we'd stop pretending. We weren't meant to be a couple, and we didn't want that to come between us being friends. We were so much better as friends. I didn't expect it, but I loved being a dad. I loved my little family of three, and I'd never been happier. For the first time I didn't pretend to be someone else. I had Poppy and I had you. That's all I needed.'

He reaches out and wipes my cheek with his thumb. For a few seconds, he keeps it there, before his expression clouds over. 'Leave it to my parents to destroy my little utopia. But it's not their fault, is it? Not entirely. I thought I'd changed since leaving them behind, but a minute in their presence and I fall into old habits. I don't like who I become around them. And once again, it was you who reminded me that I can't give up on myself, because that would mean giving up on you. And in this life, you're the best thing that's happened to me.'

He lifts an arm, and I don't hesitate. I snuggle close, and it's the best feeling in the world. He places his chin on my head and holds me until I run out of tears.

'Your mum also gave me a good talking to. Called me an anger muppet.'

'She never lectures me, you know.'

'That's because some of us are maybe more mature than others,' he mumbles into my hair. 'Hey, want to see something cool?'

'Yeah?'

I groan when he breaks the embrace and disappears into his room. He returns with an envelope in his hands.

'It was meant to be a Christmas gift, but I think now is a good time.'

He hands it over. Clueless as what to expect, I prise

it open. Out comes a single glossy sheet of paper. In the photograph, Dad looks back at me, in his usual white tee, leaning against the coffee counter in the shop. Despite the directness of his gaze into the camera, I sense his shyness. It's a great picture, one that captures his introverted but steady nature. But why would he give it to me?

'I let Jacob take my portrait,' he explains. 'For his series. He developed it and gave me a copy, and said I could show you. The exhibition will go up in the spring. I was thinking of inviting your grandparents.'

I'm a bit of a wreck after that revelation. I almost burst into tears again, but I don't want to get the portrait wet and I manage to pull myself together. We've had a rocky few weeks, Dad and I, but he always shows up for me.

'I kind of feel like I should throw you a coming-out party,' I say with sniff.

'If you do that –' Dad plants a kiss on my head – 'I will disown you.'

When I unlock the door to the cafe at 11 a.m., Jacob shuffles in, his face hidden by a scarf. He peels himself out of a coat and reveals a camera bag slung around his torso. Dad's portrait is done, but today it's my turn.

'Let's get you warmed up,' I tell a shivering Jacob and lead him to the kitchen. 'You might want to put your camera away, because this will get messy.'

As he sets it on a high shelf, his knitted jumper rides up and reveals a slice of milk-white skin. I avert my gaze and quickly pull ingredients from the cupboards.

'What are we making?' he asks. He should become an

audiobook narrator, with a voice so deep.

'Since you've never experienced the joy of tasting a jammy dodger, we'll start there and see where we get.'

When I found out that Jacob's never made Christmas cookies, I saw it as my duty to fix the gaping hole in his life experience. For the next couple of hours, we mix, whisk and knead; we cut stars and circles and fill the cafe with the scent of cinnamon, hot jam and icing sugar. By the time Jacob pulls the first batch from the oven, his cheeks are flushed with warmth. Sunlight filters through the window, making the sweat on Jacob's temples glisten. Particles of flour hang in the air.

'Wait, this is perfect,' Jacob says, and steps out of the kitchen to set up the camera. I stiffen, suddenly unsure what to do with myself.

'Is this what you always do on Christmas morning?' he asks, fiddling with the settings.

'Yeah, it's a tradition that started with my mum, and she made us keep it even after she left. She'd call, and we'd bake, together but on different continents. Only this year she's busy hatching kiwi chicks.' I try to keep the resentment out of my voice. I'm proud of her, I really am, but when I have to give up the few precious moments we get together because her work is more important, I can't help my feelings. 'What about you? Do you have any holiday traditions?' I ask, to distract myself.

Jacob shakes his head. 'We're not that kind of family. Dad believes Christmas is a capitalist stunt, Mum's side of the family is Jewish, but secular. Besides, they're getting a divorce.' I don't know if I should pry, but Jacob is already moving on. 'My ex's family always threw a huge Christmas party, but I was never invited. He was scared of their reaction if they found out he was gay.'

I want to ask more about this ex, want to know what it's like having a boyfriend. But Jacob's face is hidden behind the camera, and I get the feeling it's not his favourite subject.

'Remind me to take you to Fountainbridge next December. It's this small town only a short drive from here, with a month-long Christmas festival. It's bonkers but fun.'

'Bonkers,' Jacob repeats, and rises to his full height, a grin tugging at his dimples. 'I'd like that. Anyway, I think we have the picture.'

'Really?'

'It took a minute to make you forget about the camera, but we got there.'

'You're good at this. Getting people talking.'

He shrugs. 'Listening is easy. It's the talking part I struggle with.'

'Talking is a lot easier when you get to clean off cookie icing.'

He accepts a whisk covered in sugary cinnamon foam and hums approvingly, a sound from deep in his throat. I start washing up plates so I don't have to watch him lick it.

'My dad's divorcing my mum, because he's convinced that she cheated on him,' Jacob says after a couple minutes of comfortable silence. 'So to punish him, she took me and moved us back to her home town. That's why I'm here.'

'Ouch,' I say, and wonder if she did cheat, but knowing that I'm too nosey for my own good, I stay quiet.

Maybe Jacob can tell, because he shrugs and says, 'He's

right, she was having an affair. But he wasn't faithful either. They're both hypocrites.'

'They shouldn't be dragging you into this. You're their child, not a toy.' His mother took him away from his friends and family to hurt her husband, but he's the one paying the price. At least Dad did it to protect me, not because he wanted revenge.

'Thanks. It's good to be reminded.' A strand of hair falls into his eyes. When he blows it away, I think of the way Simo calls him Curtains. I don't know what it is between them, but I need to find a way to make them get along.

Dad appears behind Jacob and claps his hands. 'Boys, it's almost time to open the cafe and, frankly, the place is a mess.'

'Oh, sorry. We'll clear up and then I'll get out of your way,' Jacob says, flustered.

'Ignore him – he's just mad that he didn't get to lick the bowls clean,' I say. 'And you should stay. We don't even need the kitchen. People bring their own drinks and food to share. Another tradition, a little Christmas party of sorts. Stay, please?'

Jacob looks unsure, but when Dad stuffs a cookie in his own mouth, rolls his eyes in pleasure and says, 'Yesh, pleash shtay,' he nods, a smile spreading across his face.

CHAPTER 22 – SIMO

'What do you think?' I ask, looking at the heart painted on the planks of the open-air stage. With the first day of school behind us, I thought it wise to see for myself what everyone was whispering about in class.

Luca's head is tilted, a vein tracing his neck like a river of quartz in pale rock. My gaze keeps snagging on it, that exposed piece of skin with a single blue line disappearing beneath the collar of his coat, so much prettier than the crass pink shape on the peeling floorboards.

Like me, Luca is taking in the newest work of the anonymous shipper. I've seen this motif before, the heart and our initials, but never spread over several square feet.

'They're getting less subtle,' Luca replies. 'And it's wonky.'

'Yeah, they're no Banksy.' I'm surprised by the calm in my voice. The first time I saw our names on the noticeboard, I'd have been happy to dig myself a grave and disappear into it. It was scary because it was true. But even if the shock has worn off, I still hate the thought of proving them right. My feelings aren't public property.

'This has got way out of hand,' Luca mumbles.

'It has,' I agree, caught between relief and irritation,

between the urge to run from this place and the desire to pull Luca back into my arms, with his palms pressing into the small of my back. At least Luca and I can openly address the hearts now, even if my pulse spikes every time – and not in a nice way, like it did at the Brandenburgs' party. I swear there was something in the air that night.

This, however, couldn't be further from romance. Our initials scratched into wood with a key or a knife or sprayed across floorboards that people trample over without thinking.

'They're all different styles,' Luca notes. 'Posters, carvings, graffiti. Makes me think that it's not just one person.'

The truth sinks in – a cold drop on the back of my neck that makes my whole body feel clammy.

'We have a fan club,' I conclude, repulsion tainting my voice. Before the break, things were changing for the better. I was more relaxed around Luca, it felt as if he was more open with me. We've reached a new level of closeness, and I'd hate for this to come between us again.

With a look on his face like he's seen enough, Luca steps out into the rain. I expect him to head to the cafe, but to my surprise, he turns in the direction of my house.

'Everything OK at home?' I ask, hurrying after him.

Though I've tried my hardest to forget it, the conversation I overheard between Maz and Graham still haunts me. I wonder if Maz told Luca about any of it. And I wonder what it is exactly that the private investigator 'dug up'. They don't need another family secret to rock their relationship. I can't help feeling guilty about not telling Luca what I heard. But if he doesn't know about his grandparents trying to bribe Polly into having an abortion, then it's not up to me to reveal that. It would only cause him pain. If Maz decided to keep it quiet, so will I.

'Everything's OK,' Luca says, pulling me back into the moment. 'But there's something I want to give you.'

I don't know what that's supposed to mean, and by the time we take the steps up to my bedroom, anxiousness has spread through my body, making my fingers twitch. What is it that he can only give me in my room, away from anyone else?

Luca sits down at the end of my bed and rummages around in his backpack. His hair is damp, water trickles down his temples and stains his jumper. I grab a fresh towel from my wardrobe, but instead of going over and rubbing him dry, I stand there, wondering if that'd be weird.

'Stop hovering,' he says, and throws me a quizzical look.

'Stop dripping on my bed,' I say, and throw the towel at him.

I move from the edge of the room and sit swivelling on my desk chair.

'Here, your Christmas gift,' he says and holds out a rectangular object in glossy paper. I stop swivelling. While he dries his hair, I carefully unwrap it. The sound of the paper mixes with the rustling of the towel, and though we've spent so much time in this room together, it now feels too small and quiet. I'm aware of his body and my body and our breaths steaming up the window.

'Did you make this?' I ask, uncovering a picture frame with subtle wood carvings.

'I found it at Sheila's antiques shop, but I sanded it down

and gave it a new coat of paint. Thought that photo should have a proper home.' He nods to the picture on my desk.

I try not to buckle under the realisations that hit me. First, that Luca noticed the picture, second, that he created something to protect it, and third, that for the first time ever, we're talking about my brother.

'Thank you,' I say, not quite able to meet his eyes. I take the photograph and attempt to slide it into the frame, but my hands tremble so much I almost drop the glass. A second later, Luca wraps his hands around mine. He holds me, while I hold Hamza. Neither of us lets go.

We sit like this until my fingers stop trembling, until my breathing falls in line with his. He gently unclasps my grip, and I watch as he reassembles the frame. When light catches the skin on the back of his fingers, fine hairs appear and shimmer like the crest of a wave. They're barely visible and only cover the first bone on each of his fingers, a soft patch of grass in the valley between his knuckles. I wonder if I could feel them if I touched his fingers right there.

I'm mesmerised, until Luca hands me back the frame. When I place it on the desk, Hamza looks at us with smiling, crinkled eyes. I thought I'd be sad, seeing him stuck in the past like that, but instead his smile makes the heavier days a little lighter.

'I have something for you too,' I say, my voice raspier than usual. 'But first, promise you're not going to judge.'

'I don't judge,' he says.

'Not out loud. But you make a face.'

'I don't make a face!' he protests, and when I stay silent, he adds, 'Fine, I promise. But I'd never judge you.'

'Well, you haven't yet heard my dark family secret.'

'How dark can it be?'

'Hmm. Murder?' I take a book of postcards from my desk drawer, but rather than the typical images of the Alhambra castle, they show something else.

'How is a flamenco dress connected to murder?' Luca asks, staring at the cover.

'It's not the dress. It's what comes after.'

He keeps leafing through and finally reaches the section that shows colourful men's garments with intricate embroidery.

'These are stunning,' he says, and traces the artful stitching with a finger.

'They're my abuelo's clothes. He used to wear them for bullfights in the arena when he was young.'

'Your grandfather was a *matador*?'

'Yup. Tío Andrés said that my abuelo and his brothers used to kill bulls for money and fame. They stopped when one very angry bull returned the favour and violently ended the life of one of the brothers. Abuela threatened to divorce him if he kept putting himself in danger. And she's a devout Catholic.'

Luca stares at me with horror in his bright blue eyes.

'We are talking decades ago,' I clarify. 'Anyway, my family still has a collection of traditional costumes gathering dusk in the attic, but a few years back this photographer turned it into a postcard set that's sold in shops around the city.'

'That's so cool. The clothes, I mean, not the animal cruelty.'

'My cousins made me try this one on,' I say, and show

him a black *traje de luces* adorned with so many silver leaves it gives the effect of armour.

'Please tell me you have pictures.'

'Sorry, I don't,' I say, and feel my neck grow hot. The clothes are very form-fitting, leaving little to the imagination. I both do and don't want to see Luca's reaction to the pictures.

'Are you lying? You're lying. You know I have your cousins' socials. I'll just ask them.'

'I'm offering you a piece of my ancestry and that's how you repay me?'

He sulks for a few seconds, looking far too cuddlable with his bottom lip stuck out and his hair up in tufts, before he drops the attitude.

'All right. Thank you.'

The sincerity in his voice fills my chest with warmth, slows my frantic heart. I can think of nobody I want to share my history with but him. Unlike his grandparents, my abuelos can't be found online. In my family, stories are passed on as night-time tales and dinner talk, a gift from one generation to another. I want to let him in on the lore, whisper it like secrets into his ear.

As if my thoughts propel him closer, Luca places the postcard deck on the bed and gets up. His knee bumps mine when he stops in front of me, and I'm forced to tilt back my head in order to meet his gaze.

'Your hair is wet too, you know,' he says, voice low and gentle. He pulls the towel from his shoulders and lifts his hand, but if he intended to dry my hair, I'll never know. He halts at the sound of steps on the landing, and when his attention flicks to the open door, I feel a rush of irritation at its loss.

A silhouette appears in the frame, followed by a knock.

'Luca, I shouldn't be surprised,' Mum says, and I can't tell if she's being nice or passive aggressive. 'Did you have a good break?'

He takes a step back, creates a casual distance between us. Before I can stop myself, I wonder if Mum is scared that his homosexuality will rub off on me. It's not a new thought, but always a brutal one. I try to banish it from my mind, find something to distract me. My gaze settles on Hamza, and I take several steadying breaths.

'I did, thank you. How was yours?' Luca asks, ever polite.

'I'll never be a fan of flying, but Granada is beautiful,' she admits.

'Mum, look what Luca gave me for Christmas,' I interrupt. I don't know what it is exactly that prompts me to take the frame with Hamza's picture and hold it out to her. Her face hardens and she steps back, as if I was dangling a dead bug from my fingers.

'That's nice. Luca, are you staying for dinner?'

He hesitates. From the corner of my eye, I sense that he's asking me what to say, but my arm is still outstretched, my gaze on Mum.

'I … I think Dad's making lasagna. But thanks.'

She makes an odd grimace, a failed attempt at a smile, and flees the room.

A bitter feeling settles in my gut. I don't think I'll be able to sit across from her at dinner tonight. I wouldn't be able to swallow a single bite. She acted exactly like this when

Abuela summoned up the little English she knows to tell us that she keeps Hamza in her daily prayers. Mum instantly changed the topic, pretended she didn't hear.

'She acts like he never existed,' I mutter, and the bitterness in my gut begins to simmer. *That's nice*, she said. How cold can a person be?

'She's hurting,' Luca says so softly the words are barely there.

'We're all hurting.' The last thing I need is for Luca to defend my mother. I slam the picture back on to the desk. Immediately I feel guilty for mishandling Luca's gift, for mistreating Hamza.

'I should go,' Luca says after a minute of tense silence. He grabs his backpack and makes to leave. As I watch him cross the room, something in me buckles with a violence I haven't felt before.

For the past two weeks, the whole time I was away, I held my breath at every boy I came across, quietly hoping for Luca. He was hundreds of miles away, more distance between us than ever before, yet I saw him in the curve of a neck, the fall of a step, in strangers passing by. I saw him in my nights too, in the moonlight that fell through the shutters, wishing it was his fingers drawing lines on my skin instead.

'Luca,' I call out. He stops in the door but doesn't turn. 'Mind if I come?'

His shoulders relax.

'Course not.'

I leave without saying anything to my parents. Outside, I'm glad, for once, that night falls early. At least nobody will see us in the dark. I don't keep a forced distance, instead I let my body find its usual spot to his right, so my shoulder nudges against his. I catch his scent – a hint of coffee, a bite of sea salt – and inhale deeply. He's where I belong.

Luca's gaze is glued to the ground. In the faint light, the exposed skin of his neck glows white like the moon, the vein a dark shadow blooming beneath.

'So your dad's made lasagna?' I ask, to break the silence.

'Daniel, more like,' he replies. The way he says it makes me perk up.

'Is that, like, a regular thing?'

'We've definitely had a lot of Italian food lately,' Luca replies. 'I'm not complaining.'

Overcome by a sudden boldness, I place my hand right below the base of his skull and pull him into me without breaking our stride. His skin is cold, and I feel the ridges of his vertebrae press into my palm. We continue like this, heads close, hearts beating, all the way home.

SPRING

CHAPTER 23 – LUCA

Simo has beautiful hands, wide palms with strong fingers. He pulls at one end of the croissant, and it comes apart, buttery sweetness rising into the air. I never thought I'd envy a croissant, but I'd give a lot to switch places right now. His fingertips glisten with grease. He catches me looking just as a piece of flaky pastry disappears between his lips. As if he can hear my thoughts, his eyes flash golden in the ceiling lights of the bakery. I'd look away, but it's physically impossible.

'And? What say you?' Anna leans in. She's in one of her trademark suits, azure-coloured, that says business as well as extravagance. She clashes with the clean but tiny kitchen that Simo, Graham, Anna and I have squashed ourselves into. This is the place where my great-grandfather made and sold his loaves in the sixties. This is the first Brandenburg bakery.

'It's stunning,' I say, half a croissant in my own hands. It's still warm, but I can't say much about its taste because Simo is far too distracting.

Graham nods proudly. 'Our chefs are excellent. Much better than I was when I worked here, before we expanded.'

I look at him now, crisp and elegant, and can't imagine him as a young man, arms covered in flour, baking bread to support his family.

When we arrived late last night after a six-hour train journey, we spent the evening settling into our rooms at my grandparents' townhouse. That is, they gave us a room each, but we dropped our things in the first one without even checking the second. The bed alone is twice as big as mine back home. It would have been weird to sleep in separate beds when we've been sharing since we were seven.

This morning Anna and Graham are taking us around the capital. I've never been in a place so busy and so loud. Sure, at home you always hear the ocean, but being here feels like you're being shouted at from all sides. Everything flashes and screams for your attention. Following a visit of the culinary school that my grandparents founded, and a twelve-course lunch on the thirty-ninth floor of a skyscraper, we stopped by the humble kitchen where it all began.

'So, what do you want to do next? We could board Graham's sailing boat and go on a river cruise, or get a private tour of the Portrait Museum,' Anna offers.

I don't want to sound spoilt and ungrateful, but—

'Would it be OK if Simo and I checked out some bookstores? I know he has a whole route mapped out.'

Simo's cheeks flush. He looks angelic, dark curls out in full force and a glow in his eyes, like a kid that's been promised ice cream. No one could deny him a bookshelf-browsing session. I can't deny him anything.

'As long as you're home by six,' Anna says, with a hint of relief in her voice. Maybe she's just as glad as me at the prospect of a break. 'We need to ensure your tuxes fit before the ball.'

Outside the bakery, their limousine has barely disappeared around the corner before Simo pulls me into the labyrinth of the capital. He was quiet around my grandparents, more so than usual. He brightens up when we reach our first stop, a poetry apothecary that offers books for those seeking hope, comfort, heartbreak cures and other remedies.

'Thanks for the escape plan,' he says.

'I didn't know you needed one,' I laugh, expecting him to laugh too. But he doesn't. 'What is it?'

He shrugs, his fingers gliding over the spines of books on the shelves.

'Simo, tell me,' I say.

He glances up at the worry in my voice, then quickly looks away again. 'Maybe I'm making it up,' he starts, 'but I get the sense your grandparents don't like me that much.'

I don't know what I expected, but it's not that. 'What makes you think that? Of course they like you.' Anna and Graham have been nothing but charming. They're the type of hosts that go out of their way to please their guests.

Simo shakes his head. 'I shouldn't … Forget I said anything.'

'No, Simo—'

'Pick something,' he says.

'What?'

'Pick a book,' he repeats and motions to the shelves. I know he's trying to distract me, and it works, mostly because there's a flake of leftover croissant clinging to his jaw. I see myself drop it on my tongue and swallow. I squash the instinct and brush the crumb from his skin like a sane person. He watches me with gold-specked eyes, one eyebrow slanted in question.

'Seriously?' I ask.

'Come on. Poetry can be short and sweet.'

'Do I have to?'

'I want to buy you a book,' Simo says quietly, 'as a memento of this weekend.'

I melt away. I don't tell him that I don't need a memento to remember this, or him. But I nod and step closer. Simo tracks my movement, and his attention warms my neck. In the end I pick a book solely based on its title: *Clouds Cannot Cover Us*. Simo holds his palm out, and I want to take his hand again, like I did the night of the Christmas party. Instead, I hand over the book. He reads the title with a smile, and I feel like I made the right choice.

The charity ball is held in a converted gas holder. A red carpet leads into the domed building. Inside is a wide platform that easily holds a few hundred people, surrounded by water. As cameras flash and people pose for pictures, Anna introduces us to her friends, men and women in smart tuxes and glittering dresses with ageless faces that tell me they've been touched by a surgeon or two. I'm not being judgemental, simply stating facts.

'These are your boys, Anna?' a lady with earrings the size of chandeliers exclaims.

'My grandson, Luca,' Anna says with pride in her voice. Either she forgets to introduce Simo, or she purposely skips over him.

Simo is easily the most beautiful person here. I see the glances he gets, and it's not because he looks good in a tux, which of course he does. It's his gentle nature peeking through a layer of shyness. He's charmingly himself in a place where big personalities vie for space. Which is how I know that Anna didn't forget he's here.

'Luca, please let me introduce you to my granddaughter,' earring lady says. 'She's fallen for a Windsor, and I don't wish that receding hairline on my future generations.'

I grip Simo's arm. 'Don't let her marry me off to her daughter,' I whisper in his ear.

'I'm not letting anyone take you away from me,' he whispers back, and bites his bottom lip to hide a grin.

The entire evening, during speeches and performances, I try to concentrate, I really do. But I can only focus on him. I follow the pull, lean in and feel my pulse spike when his lips brush my ear as he tells a joke. It's impossible to withstand his charm when a laugh spills from his chest into the room, when he gets caught up in telling a story about his abuela, and his fingers dance through the air to embellish it.

I wish the only disappointment of the night was the dessert, a dollop of chocolate mousse so tiny it would fit on the tip of my thumb. My grandparents aren't rude exactly, but the temperature drops by a degree whenever they turn from me to Simo. It's so subtle I might have missed it if he hadn't brought it up at the bookshop.

'Hold that thought,' Graham interrupts him in the middle of a story, 'I see the chancellor of the exchequer. Must have a word with him about that new tax law.'

The further the evening goes, the more we drift away

from my grandparents, who are busy with shop talk. I try to make up for their behaviour by hunting down a whole tray of mini chocolate mousses and offering it to Simo.

As the night goes on, people loosen up, but Simo deflates. He keeps up the smile, but I can tell that he's out of his comfort zone.

'Hey, why don't we bounce?' I suggest.

'Bounce?'

'Find the driver and ask him to take us back.'

'Are you sure? I'm happy to stay longer if you want to.'

'I've seen everything there is to see here. What I haven't seen is the pool at the house.'

'The pool at the house,' he repeats, and there's a new spark in his eyes.

I crane my neck to find my grandparents and spot Anna working her charm on a group of silver-haired men. I don't know why she started giving Simo the cold shoulder, but I don't feel like speaking to her right now. We navigate through the drunken crowd, and I try not to trip over sparkling trains as I send her a text instead, telling her we're on our way home.

Half an hour later, the car stops in front of a modern brick building between two Victorian houses. This view of the house is deceptive: behind the low facade hides a mansion built around a square courtyard. Once inside, it's easy to forget the city and imagine yourself in a Tuscan villa.

On impulse, I grab the bottle of bubbles from the limo. We head straight for the basement, giggling and nearly tripping over each other as we descend the winding staircase.

'Whoa,' Simo says, and I bump into him when he stops

in an archway. I settle my chin on his shoulder and take in the scene. Light filtered from somewhere above gives the pool a sapphire tint. Frescoes adorn the walls, but the details are cloaked in shadow. It's like we've stumbled into a forgotten Roman cave. It takes Simo only seconds to rip his shoes and shirt off and jump in.

'Simo! Fuck! Your suit!'

He only laughs and dives under again.

I sit at the edge of the pool and am trying to get the shoes off when he breaks the surface and grabs my ankles. Water pours down his angular face, and mischief dances in his eyes.

'If you pull me in, I'm gonna kill you, and then my grandparents are going to kill me, and my dad is going to kill them.'

'So if you fear a family bloodbath, why don't you hurry up and join me?' he says and it sounds like a dare. He floats on his back as I strip to my briefs and vest. Next, I aim a water bomb at his head.

I hear a yelp as he ducks away beneath me, and a blink later I'm surrounded by a stream of bubbles. It's colder than I expected, but it clears my head. At least, until Simo tackles me and drags me to the deep end. We splash around the pool like two young retrievers that know no bounds. I earn a kick to the ribs and Simo's arms show red lines where I accidentally scratched him, but we're both laughing and gasping for breath.

Simo pulls me close again, but this time his grip is different. Gentler. Our thighs cross and I place my hands on his shoulders, as if to seek balance, when I'm establishing a fraction of distance to keep my brain from giving out.

'You look happy,' he says, his voice raw. Water streams from his hair, curls flattened against his temples like rivers of ink. Droplets glide down his face and gather on his chin, where they catch the light, glittering like diamonds, before they fall.

'I am happy.' Happy enough to drown, almost. I don't want to miss out on him. I'm in his arms, exactly where I want to be, but with so many things unsaid, I'd truly hate to go now. 'Are you happy, Simo?'

He takes his time to answer, leaving me to admire his lashes. They look as soft as the tip of an artist's paintbrush. I want to trace the curve of them.

'Happiest I've ever been. So is it fair to ask for more?'

'More happiness?' I ask, and earn a nod. 'Always.'

For once, my want is stronger than my fear, and I lift my hands to his face. With my thumbs, I trace the arcs of his eyebrows. They're the brows of a poet, flawless and sorrowful. His eyes flutter shut, so I graze the lids like they're butterfly wings, barely at all.

I get a sense of déjà vu. Something has been lifted, and I see clearly. It's almost like I've been here before, in a dream, but now we're both awake. Simo's hands have found their way beneath my vest, his palms burn into my skin. Blood rushes from my head to a different part of my body. I want him to pull me closer, but I'm suddenly so freaked out by the strength of my own desire that I dive out of his embrace and find the edge of the pool. Once I've calmed down enough that there are no giveaway signs, I lift myself out and grab the bottle of champagne. Before this goes any further, I need to set a few things straight. I deserve honesty, and so does he.

I let my legs dangle and loosen the cork. With a pop, it explodes, showering me in champagne. Simo is in fits and struggles to keep his head above water. He pulls himself to the edge, half giggling, half hiccupping. He grins up at me, and that alone is enough to make my pulse spike. A person should not be able to wield such power with nothing but a smile. I offer him the bottle so he'll stop beaming.

'How about a game?' he suggests. Without taking his eyes off me, he sets his lips to the mouth and takes a deep chug. I watch as he swallows, and it's like I've never seen an Adam's apple move before.

'I'm not doing dares, Simo.' My throat is dry, so I take a sip too.

He places his palms by my knees and raises himself out of the water. It runs down his torso in a hundred little streams and disappears into his trousers. They hang low on his hips; the fabric clings to him.

'Dares are boring. Truth requires more guts,' he whispers, inches from my face. Truth is what I'm most scared of because I want it so much. So I say yes.

'I'll start us off.' Simo pushes himself off and floats into the middle of the pool. His voice is clear and echoes around me. 'Those two weeks in Granada? I missed you every single day.'

My heart beats in my throat, but I can't let the moment pass, or I won't get the words out.

'I missed you too.'

There is so much bubbling to the surface, all coming

from the place where I shove the thoughts I can't face. But I'm reaching a boiling point, my secrets spilling out.

'The night of my grandparents' party, it felt like there was something between us that wasn't there before. Like if Dad hadn't made us leave … I don't know.'

'There was something between us,' he confirms.

'Do you think it's there still? Because …' I start, mustering all the confidence I have, 'because I know it's there for me.'

But I can only guess what's going on in him, and I'm sick of not knowing. If this is the moment that breaks us, I can't stop it. My gaze locks on to his. Even if I wanted to look away, I couldn't.

'For me too.'

These words are all I need to hear. I glide back into the water, and Simo doesn't move, only watches as I close the distance between us.

Fear runs through my veins. Not the kind of fear before a fall, or during, but the half-moment between, when the body reaches the tipping point and it's too late to change your mind. It's too late when I see the black of Simo's pupils swallow up the brown and only gold specks remain. It's too late when the heat of his breath hits my skin. My fear roars one last time and our bodies meet. His lips find mine. I've never felt so scared and so good at the same time.

Kissing, in my mind, is two people melting into each other, becoming one. But with no holds left, we collide. I'm hyperaware of where I end and he begins, every point of contact firing up my nerves. My teeth scrape against his skin, his fingers sink into my flesh. I want him so much, haven't learned how to curb my desire, and so it takes me under. As I pull him deeper into my embrace, Simo makes the smallest sound, caught between a sigh and a moan. It slips from the back of his throat, travels from his lips to mine and lands on my tongue: a drop of pleasure.

Locked in this kiss, we start to sink. I might be drowning, but with nothing but Simo on my mind and his breath in my mouth, I've never felt more alive.

We're close. Closer than ever.

We kiss for hours, kiss all night. It's like meeting Simo for the first time. I don't know him like this, have never known the feel of his lips. Every kiss is a surprise. He can be soft and demanding, his grip firm and light. When his nails dig into my ribs and the edge of a tooth scratches my lip, I want more. When I break the kiss, seal his mouth with my thumb, he bites it, his gaze burning with mischief and longing. It's a glorious feeling, knowing that he wants me as much as I want him, so I let it overwhelm me, let him overwhelm me. I remove my thumb, let him kiss me softly and roughly, and discover him all over again. I lose all sense of place, don't care about time. All we do is float and kiss.

I run so hot, it's only when Simo lifts his lips from mine that I realise my skin's like ice. We stumble out of the pool, unable to find our balance. Wet and disoriented, we slip and stumble against the half-empty champagne bottle. I barely hear it crash, because I'm busy kissing Simo. He lifts me up and carries me away, giggling and dripping, and I get a glimpse of a foaming puddle, glass shards glimmering in the half-light. It's immediately forgotten when he presses me against a wall and strips me of the soaking vest, his hands burning as they glide over my torso. We keep stumbling towards our room, into a hot shower, on to a king-size mattress. We've shared a bed so many times that our bodies fold into each other like it's the most natural thing. I fall asleep as soon as my head hits Simo's chest, his heartbeat lulling me into a dream.

When I wake up, the house is on fire. Bright light burns into my retinas, shouting pierces my eardrums.

'What do you think you're doing?' Anna stands at the end of the bed. Her nostrils flare, and I have never seen her so dishevelled. 'Where were you?' Her voice is reaching ear-splitting levels. No fire then, but maybe something worse. Simo sits up beside me, but I don't dare look at him.

'We wanted to try the pool,' I say, relieved to find that I'm at least wearing briefs.

'And try it you did, judging by the broken glass in it,' Graham grunts. He stands behind Anna looking just as furious. His head is so red, it looks fit to burst any second. They're still in the clothes from last night, mostly because it still is last night. The clock on the bedside table shows 1.33 a.m. My body begins to sweat from shame.

'I'm sorry – I'm sure I texted you.'

'No, you didn't!' Anna shrieks. 'You texted your father, who was asleep until we were forced to call him in a panic. I cannot believe you stood us up like that! After all we've done for you!'

Beneath the shame, something else starts to simmer. So that's why they're throwing a fit, because they thought they'd messed up and Dad was called to witness it? I try to keep the anger in check, try not to think about how they ignored Simo. It won't help me out of this mess.

'I really am sorry. It was an accident,' I say. Beneath the duvet, Simo finds my hand and squeezes it.

'Young man, this family has no tolerance for accidents. You risked your life! This isn't some lousy town at the arse end of nowhere where bored farmers dye cows and exchange news via a noticeboard like it's the sixteen hundreds! This is a city with real crime! Stabbings! Murders!'

There is a moment when it's OK to laugh at the image of Anna Brandenburg throwing her hands in the air and screaming about stabbings and murders, but this isn't it. I bite my tongue. Hard.

'We are sending you back on the first train. Best to pack your bags,' Graham commands with forced coolness.

They both turn their backs and go to stride out of the room, but not before I say my piece.

'So, I slip up once, and barely even that, and now you're mad that I didn't hang around so you could show me off to your friends, only to forget me when you got bored? How long did it take you to notice I was gone? It must have been hours!'

'We are not having this discussion, Matthew!' Graham roars, mistaking me for Dad in his anger, and slams the door shut. My heart beats so fast it hurts.

Two hands find my shoulders and begin to rub the muscles there. Simo kneads out the tension, and tears fall from my eyes, leaving marks on the duvet. I hate that they have the power to make me cry.

'Hey,' Simo murmurs, wrapping his arm around me, 'it's OK.'

'It's really not,' I say, and fall into him.

'But it's going to be.' He combs his fingers through my hair, and for a second I feel a little less miserable and small.

'How do you know?' I ask, because that was so ugly I can't imagine facing Anna and Graham again.

'Hmm, remember when our names landed on the infamous noticeboard from the sixteen hundreds? That felt like the end of me then, but I'm OK with it now. Because we're still here.'

The tears fall even harder after that. He's defending my grandparents and they don't deserve him. I don't deserve him. My conscience only grows heavier. Looks like I have truly made a mess of things.

Sleep is impossible, so we put on a sitcom in the empty hope of making ourselves feel better. We pack like we were told, and though the last thing I want is to run into anyone, I steal out of the room and hunt down our phones. We each have several missed calls from my grandparents, which makes my heart sink, and a string of texts from Dad, which kicks it even lower, until I spot his final text:

> Love you, speak tomorrow. Don't let them get you down.
> Dad xx

At four in the morning, there's a knock on the door and Susie announces that the car is ready to take us to the train station. Neither Anna nor Graham is there to see us off.

This early on a Sunday, we're the only people in the compartment. It's several hours until dawn creeps into the sky. Simo snoozes on my shoulder, but despite the fatigue, my mind is in tatters.

Reality has come crashing down on us. Gone is the pool, the cover of night, the glitz that gave everything a magical feel, that made the impossible possible. Though like Simo said, we're here, and we're together. We survived. If we can own up to our feelings and come out on the other side, nothing can break us. Guilt makes my stomach cramp, but now there is hope too.

'Simo?' I say and nudge him awake. 'I have another truth.'

'What is it?'

There's one last thing I was too afraid to say last night. I fear I might be sick, so if I don't get it out now, something else will appear.

'It was me. I put our names on the noticeboard.'

CHAPTER 24 – SIMO

'You did what?'

I must have misheard.

'I-I put our names on the town noticeboard.'

If the repetition wasn't enough, it's the panic written all over his face. He looks faint, with a green tinge around the nose. Meanwhile, my body is shutting down. It might be going into shock, while my mind is still catching up. I can't even speak. 'Or at least I submitted them to the webpage. I didn't think they'd make it up there. I was as shocked as you.'

'I doubt that.'

He shrinks back, like I've punched him. He has no right to look this hurt. All I've endured these past few months, the sickly-sweet comments, the probing questions into the most private parts of myself from people I've never even talked to, all because of Luca? I've been choking on my own fear – of being found out, of losing what I love – this entire time, because of him?

'How could you?' I say, but my voice breaks on the last word, bursting into a sob. I swallow it back, because I can't let him see me like this. I've never let myself be so vulnerable with anyone, and he goes and exploits that trust.

'Simo …' he starts and reaches out, but I jump back.

'Do you know how sick that is? Creating those posters, the hearts all over town, and as if that's not enough, you put on this whole big act and pretend you had no idea?' As I say it out loud, the scope of his betrayal hits me. I think I might pass out.

'No! That wasn't me!' he shouts with terror in his eyes. 'That first message on the noticeboard, yes, but the posters and hearts and baubles, that wasn't me!'

'As if I'm going to believe you!' I shout back, 'As if it matters now!'

'Simo, I had no idea it would snowball like that! By the time the message was up, it was too late to take it back, but the rest of it is nothing to do with me!'

'Of course it is; without you, none of it would have happened!'

'But I needed *something* to happen!'

'What the fuck does that mean?'

He's breathing hard and holding back tears, which is good, because I can barely stand to look at him. He doesn't deserve self-pity.

'Why did you do it?' I press him.

It takes him several attempts to get the words out, but when they fall, his voice is clear.

'Because I've been in love with you for as long as I can remember.'

I shut my eyes. Here are the words I've longed to hear, delivered as a final blow. I focus on the fabric of the seat beneath my palms, the rattle of the train, because I don't want to feel anything.

'I can't do this.' I get up and grab my bag. 'Don't follow me,' I say without looking at him. 'Don't call me. I don't want to speak to you.'

The floor jolts beneath my feet as I walk away, or maybe I'm the one shaking, barely able to keep it together. I lurch ahead, into the next carriage and the one after that. When there's nowhere else to go, I drop into an empty seat. I can't break down yet, so I hollow myself out, don't allow any emotions. I barely breathe until the train pulls in at Lombard. I do my best to ignore the dozens of hearts smeared on the wall of the bike shed by the platform. When I finally get home and close the door to my room, I bury my head in a pillow and scream until my throat is raw.

I do what I always do when I can't listen to my own thoughts. I escape into someone else's mind. I get through two books in the first night, despite the sleep deprivation. I need to stay distracted, otherwise I'll have to face all that's broken within me, and I'm not prepared for the hurt. I can't think about Luca's confession, because that means thinking about the night in the pool, and those memories combined will tear me apart. I drift off early in the morning, from the lines of a sad French novel directly into fitful sleep.

For two days, I only leave my room to pee or steal into the kitchen when my parents are out. I must look as shit as I feel, because Mum accepts my excuse to skip school without a fight. They don't ask questions, and for once I'm glad that they leave me to wallow.

Still, fiction can only keep thoughts of Luca at bay for so long. He's more powerful. He sneaks up on me when I turn a page, and suddenly I'm back in the water, his legs around my hips. He stares back at me from the poems in my notebook, when I open it out of habit. He's in my dreams, pressing his lips against mine, and I wake with a racing heart and sweat-soaked sheets. I didn't know you could miss someone, hate someone and want them at the same time.

Luca is inescapable, even in the refuge of my room. I've taken the corkboard off the wall and stashed it behind the wardrobe, because I can't stand looking at pictures of us; memories tainted by his lies. There's a drawer with Luca-items, socks and other stuff collected over time. Now it's empty for the first time in years, the contents dumped in the kitchen bin. It didn't feel as good as I hoped. If anything, the empty drawer adds to the misery. What remains is the frame with Hamza's picture, because I can't bring myself to remove it.

I'm in a timeless state, because I refuse to move on. I lock myself in this room, because I can't face the future. Moving on would mean grieving, would mean rethinking every aspect of my life without Luca, and I wasn't lying when I said that I don't know how to cope without him. Feelings aside, he's so integral to who I am as a person that I'd have to change myself in every way. On top of everything, an identity crisis is brewing, and I'm resisting it for as long as I can.

Here's the most ironic thing: I feared admitting my feelings for Luca would end us, but he pulled the trigger all by himself. We were going to be fine. Now, thanks to him, we're nothing at all.

⋆ ⋆ ⋆

My parents last until day three, before Dad tells me to shower and join them for dinner. Sick of myself and the gloom of my room, I'm almost relieved to sit down at the dining table.

Dad dishes up, and I eat with a hunger I didn't know I had. Except for the clink of cutlery on china, the room is quiet, though I can sense that they keep throwing each other looks. Having two painfully non-confrontational parents means neither of them wants to speak first. I eat quickly and hope to escape the table unscathed, but when she lets out a frustrated huff, I know Mum's lost the silent battle.

'Simo, are you and Luca … together?'

I freeze. Adrenaline jump-starts my flight instinct, setting my body on high alert. From zero to escape mode in under a second.

'I'm sorry, what?' I manage.

'Are you boys a couple? Are you …' She wrinkles her brow, grasping for the right word.

'Dating,' Dad offers.

'Dating. Are you dating?'

'Wha— What makes you say that?' I ask, to buy time. For years, they tiptoed around the topic of Luca's sexuality and our relationship. Now, with a single question, they're toppling our well-established dynamic. Half of me wants to run, freaked out that what I've always feared is finally happening. The other half remains glued to the chair. The moment has arrived, for better or worse.

'It's hard to not notice,' Dad says almost apologetically. 'With everything that's going on.'

It's a weird way to describe my emotional breakdown, but I don't exactly want to linger on the specifics. Though Mum is spending more time looking at her plate than at me, and Dad wears a worried expression, it's not the nasty reaction I dreaded. Yet. My parents have always treated anything outside the norm as something they don't want to touch with a stick, and I don't expect a sudden change in attitude.

'So?' Mum says when I remain silent. 'Are you dating?'

'I don't know,' I say, cold sweat running down my spine.

'What do you mean? How can you not know?'

Seriously, out of all the moments to bring it up, this is the one they pick? The timing is abysmal. If they know that Luca and I aren't talking, why ask?

'I mean,' I begin, and try to breathe evenly while also attempting to translate my tangled emotions, 'I mean we're not a couple, and we're not dating, and we're not together, but maybe … there recently was a moment.'

Saying it makes me feel sick, and not just because I'm finally admitting something I've been keeping from them for years. I'm so painfully aware of the fact that there was one night with Luca where everything fell into place, only for it to crumble within a matter of hours.

'That's good, no?' Dad asks with genuine sincerity. I only stare at him, confused at which bit he means. 'I mean, we like Luca, right?' he follows up, looking from Mum to me and back again.

'Of course, we like Luca,' Mum says matter-of-factly.

They're starting to piss me off. Why are they so goddamn nonchalant?

'Well, I don't,' I say and slam my cutlery on the table. It earns me a reprimanding eyebrow lift from Mum, but I currently don't give a shit.

'I'm confused. I thought you had a moment?' she asks.

'No, I'm confused! Why are you acting so chill?'

'How would you like us to act?'

It's the tone she uses – like she's speaking at a parents' evening – that drives me up a wall. Angry tears threaten to flood my eyes.

'You hate all that! That Luca is gay and that I could be gay too!'

Dad reaches across the table. I flinch back, but he takes my hand and doesn't let go, even when I pull away. Instead, he wraps both his hands around mine and forces me to face him.

'Simo, listen to me. We could never hate you. Never, you hear me? You're the most precious thing we have.'

We stare at each other, and I could be wrong, because my sight is all blurry, but I think Dad's crying too.

Mum pulls out the chair next to mine and hands me a tissue. 'What makes you think all that?'

I take several calming breaths, because I can barely form a sentence in the state that I'm in. I'm only a boy with limited room for big emotions. I can't deal with so much at once.

'You get … funny when you're around Maz or Luca. Cagey. Like their presence makes you uncomfortable.' They look surprised, but neither of them says anything, so I go on. 'Sometimes when you talk about Luca, you use this weird tone, as if he's beneath you. And you warned me away from "those" bars last summer.'

Mum wrings her hands, while Dad wears a shameful expression.

'I only wanted you to be careful. I never thought … I didn't think.'

'Maybe we've not been very good or understanding. But we do love you, Simo. Very much,' Mum says quietly. 'Being a parent is hard enough, you know. Nobody teaches you how to raise a child that isn't …'

'Straight?' I offer through gritted teeth.

'Yes, that. It's no excuse. But I guess we weren't sure how you really feel and didn't know how to ask.'

'A "How do you really feel?" would have done the trick,' I say, and I can't help that I sound bitter.

'Well, now we know,' Mum says. I think that's as much an apology as I will get from her.

'And, so we know for next time, what was so wrong with the question about you and Luca?' Dad asks. My heart, which has just stopped pounding, is twitching in my chest.

'It wasn't such a bad question. I wasn't prepared for it, is all.'

'OK, that's good,' Dad says, and pats my hand, looking more self-assured already. 'But I'm still confused on the matter of what's going on between the two of you.'

Might as well tell them now. 'He's the one who put our names on the noticeboard.'

Dad nods. 'Yes, and?'

How are they not getting this? 'He's a coward.'

'So, he confessed his love for you for all of Lombard to see, and he's a coward?'

'He never owned up to it!'

'But I thought he just did?' Mum asks.

'Months later!'

'I'm not entirely sure I see the problem. Does he want to be with you?' she doubles down.

'I – yes. I think so anyway.'

'And do you want to be with him?'

'I thought I did. Now I don't know.'

'Well,' she says and seems to ponder her next words, 'if it helps, I think he's good for you. And you for him.'

I want to get angry again, because it's a little late for the endorsement, but I'm running out of energy. I wind my hand out of Dad's grip and get up.

'I've got a headache,' I say truthfully. Crying does that to you. 'I'm gonna take a nap.'

'Simo, you can come to us any time, OK? I want you to know that,' Dad says before I can leave the room.

'And you're going back to school tomorrow,' Mum adds.

'Safa!'

'What? He can't hide forever.'

Obviously, I don't stand a chance at sleep, because my sleep pattern is fucked, and I'm far too riled up. That exchange with my parents was not on my bingo card. I thought we'd ignore the elephant in the room forever, until the day when they'd get my wedding invitation – if I decided to go down that route, anyway.

It went … better than expected and, simultaneously, it was one of the most uncomfortable moments of my life. I never want to repeat it.

The one good thing that came from it? I know that they

care. Most of the time, it feels like I'm a duty, a box to tick at the end of the day, right after 'mark tests' and 'weed the garden'. And on bad days, where my most self-destructive thoughts scream the loudest, I suspected that the only reason they kept going is because they'd already lost one son, and they somehow had to keep the leftover one alive.

But to know that I'm wanted, it's something I've been longing to hear.

The same is true for Luca. Though when he told me on the train that he loved me, I blocked my ears and ran. But I already have a headache and don't want to dehydrate my body any further. Which means back to the books, and back to Lorca, so I don't have to think about anything else.

I've reached a section that rings differently to the rest of his work. *Sonetos del amor oscuro* – Sonnets of a Dark Love – draw on the same distressing images of weeping moons and pooling blood that I've encountered before. At first, I can't put my finger on why it's these poems that speak to me, with their disorienting pull between violence and tenderness. It dawns on me slowly, as I comb over the lines and collect pieces of evidence. The poet – Lorca – addresses his lover and pleads to be loved in return. But this lover isn't just anyone; the lover is a man.

A quick search on my laptop confirms what I already know. Lorca was gay. The country's favourite poet and playwright was a man who wrote poems to other men because he loved them.

I guess Tío Andrés was right. Federico García Lorca and I speak the same language, just not in the way I expected.

Tú nunca entenderás lo que te quiero
porque duermes en mí y estás dormido.

I find myself in the simplicity of these lines, and that's not all. Though I want to escape him, Luca is there too. He's the breath on my cheek when he sleeps next to me and the beat of my heart when he dreams on my chest. Lorca was meant to distract me from Luca, but all he does is pull me back to him. He forces me to remember the moments when I was at peace; endless days reading and studying on the sofa, the hundreds of nights with my arms wrapped around his chest. That was real, wasn't it?

I hate myself for missing him. I miss his casual touch and the muffins he bakes because he knows how much I like them. His confession was a shock, but now that that's wearing off, the longing is returning.

I throw Lorca off the bed, feeling like he's complicit in the betrayal. The books, too, aren't serving their purpose; the escapism is turning into life lessons. Though it's late, I steal down the stairs. Huddled in a winter coat, I leave the house. If even poetry fails me, maybe darkness will swallow me up.

CHAPTER 25 – LUCA

I've been drowning myself in chai lattes. It means I've been buzzing from the sugar intake, rushing through the cafe, serving and collecting dishes at double my usual speed. It also means that every time someone starts asking about the charity ball, I'm off again before they can finish the question. Our display bar is bursting with cakes and muffins, because I stay up till late and bake until I'm exhausted. The beetroot cake is back, and this time I'm forcing it on customers whether they want it or not. People don't know what's good for them. I've also been spending more time with Mum, not even talking, just kind of hanging out on the phone. She takes me with her on hikes, occasionally points out insects or landmarks, and lends me company while I bake.

'You're making me redundant,' Dad said on the second day, 'and not just me, all the other staff too.'

I kind of had to tell him what happened when he picked me up from the train station, with Simo running off in one direction and me being a whole snotty mess.

'Have to admit, I'm kind of proud of you,' he said, once I'd collected myself enough to tell the whole story.

'Huh?' I said.

'I mean, first of all, I applaud anyone who pisses off my parents. It is my life's mission to inconvenience the Brandenburgs, and I stand in solidarity with all those who join the cause. So, well done, son.' I only stared at him, my sense of humour absent after single-handedly laying waste to mine and Simo's friendship. 'But to get back to the point, you took a risk. Because you love someone. Do I think the method was flawed? Duh. Do I understand what it's like to act on impulses when personal feelings are involved and subsequently bury your head in the sand rather than owning up to the mess you made? I am the master of burying one's head in the sand. Did it explode in your face when you pulled your head back out? Sure. Did it pay off in the end? Who can say?'

'Who can say? I can say!' I sniffed.

'Don't count your eggs before they're laid.'

'Yeah, that's not how the saying goes. And the eggs are laid and smashed, thanks.'

I've not heard from my grandparents since. Not that I can blame them for what happened after the ball, but that doesn't excuse their behaviour towards Simo.

'Oh, babes, they did that with my friends all the time,' Dad said when I told him about the ball. 'They think he's not good enough for you. It's kind of sweet, in an extremely twisted way.'

If anyone's not good enough, it's me. I don't deserve Simo. Mostly, I followed his warning not to contact him. I sent a text when he didn't show up at school on Monday, but the message didn't go through. Either I'm blocked or his phone is off. I really hope his phone is off.

'I still remember the day my first boyfriend ended things with me,' Miss M tells me, when I take a piece of beetroot cake up to her flat. Mind you, I've not asked for her opinion, but as usual she decides to share it anyway. Must be the misery written all over my face. 'Striking resemblance to Freddie Mercury, that one. I knew how to pick them! But I wasn't going to let him get away with it. Do you know what I did? Found myself another man. A strapping lad, with hair like a young Björn Ulvaeus!'

'Who?'

'ABBA! He's the first "B". Or the second one. Doesn't matter. What matters is, Freddie came running back with his tail between his legs, begging at my door!'

'Freddie Mercury?'

She tuts. 'You're not listening.'

'Sorry, Miss M. But Simo … he's not my boyfriend. I know it's what everyone wants. And I guess I did too,' I admit, my voice almost giving out. 'Pretty sure that I've ruined our friendship too.'

I can feel her watching me, but I can't bring myself to meet her eyes. Seconds pass, then a hand brushes my cheek, the metal of her rings cool against my skin.

'Darling, of course you haven't,' she says, and I don't know where she gets the confidence from. She drops her hand and slides the cake towards me. 'Now be a good boy and take this back where it came from, yes? I'm not eating that.'

It's almost ten by the time I enter the flat that night. I'm at the kitchen sink, scrubbing dough from beneath my nails, when the house phone rings, which either means the caller is old or a teacher. Or, I realise as I pick up, it's an emergency.

'Luca?' a voice asks, and it takes me two seconds to place it. I was right about the teacher bit.

'Safa?' I say, and immediately regret it. I tend to avoid calling her anything, because 'Mrs Lorca' feels weird after knowing her for so long, but her first name implies a closeness we don't share.

'Luca, is Simo with you?'

'No, he isn't,' I say, my throat constricted.

'Do you know where he is?' She sounds panicked. 'He isn't home and he left his phone behind.'

'I really don't know, I'm sorry. Did he go running?'

'In this weather?' Her voice jumps to uncomfortable heights. A quick look outside tells me that the world has been swallowed by fog. 'I hope not. Oh god, what if he did?' I hear quick footsteps and the creaking and banging of several closet doors.

'His running shoes are here,' she says, sounding relieved. 'Are you sure he's not with you?'

It's an odd question to ask. I'm pretty sure he hasn't snuck into the flat to hide beneath my bed, though I'd welcome it if he did.

'I can go look for him?' I tend to have a good sense of where he could be.

'I'm not sure that would be safe,' she says, and I think I can hear actual fear in her voice.

'It's no problem. I could find my way around this town blindfolded.'

'Would you? But please be careful. And call me!'

'I will,' I assure her.

'Be careful!' she repeats, before I hang up.

Dad is snoring softly in his bedroom, so I send him a text as I make my way out. For a while, I linger in the doorway, trying to decide where to go. The fog is a wall; I can't even make out the flower shop, and the light of the street lamps is struggling to reach me. It's so thick that it soaks up every sound. Usually I'd be able to hear the ocean from here, and any cars on the junction. I take a few steps and it's like walking into a void.

Everything is closed, so Simo won't be at Sheila's or the library. The stage is out of the question, as something tells me that he'd rather not stare at a giant heart with our initials in it, and Clifford Island is cut off by the tide. But sad people are drawn to the sea, and if Simo is anything like me, and I hope he still is, he'll be on the beach.

When my shoes slide over sand, I know I've reached the promenade. Even from here I can't make out the sound of waves.

I should be worried, but I'm as eerily calm as the fog around me. If something had happened to Simo, I would know. You can't unravel a connection so deep in a matter of days. It's impossible to ever get Simo out of my system, because he's been with me at almost every important step of my life. It's a calming thought, but I still feel heavy, grieving what I likely destroyed.

A walk along the waist-high wall that separates the beach from the promenade leaves me empty-handed. There's no point in shouting, so I step on to the sand. I go barefoot, because even though it might be cold, there are few things I hate more than sand in my shoes.

The bank where the ocean laps against the shore leads me down the beach again. My instinct tells me that I'm getting closer. Heat gathers in my chest, like a magnet finding its opposing pole. But when I reach the point where I think he is, there's only vapour milling shapelessly around me. Maybe I have lost it, the bond I considered unbreakable.

'You looking for me?'

I jump and almost land on my arse in the water. But when I follow the voice a few steps away from the shore, there he is, sitting cross-legged on the sand. His feet are bare too, and he's only wearing running shorts. I try not to stare at the exposed skin, reminding myself that this is the worst time to thirst over his thighs.

'How did you see me when I couldn't see you?'

I can't see his eyes, because he stubbornly keeps his gaze on the sand, but his hair is tousled and there's a shadow of stubble on his cheeks. Neck bent and shoulders hunched, he looks angry and vulnerable at once.

'I didn't. But I could hear the sand crunching beneath your feet.'

'So you knew it was me?'

He looks up at me with an unreadable expression. 'I knew.' Despite the hardness in them, I've missed his brown eyes and the flecks of gold in them.

I swallow in a useless attempt to get rid of the shame at the back of my throat. 'I'm not stalking you.'

'OK,' he says. Neither his voice nor his expression gives away any emotion.

'Your mum called, looking for you. She sounded upset.'

A flash of guilt crosses his face. 'She hates the fog. She's scared of it.'

'I find it kind of soothing. Almost like snow. Everything is muffled.'

Silence unfolds. We stay frozen for so long that I begin to wonder if time has simply stopped, until Simo speaks up again.

'You say that, but … the day Hamza died, he was riding his bike home from a friend. It was only a few doors down. He was wearing a helmet, and his lights were on. But in the fog the car still caught him. He didn't stand a chance.'

My knees buckle beneath me. I glide into the sand, and though I want to reach out, I stop myself.

'I had no idea. I shouldn't have said.'

He shrugs. 'It's not like I ever told you.'

I pull out my phone and frantically type out a message.

'What are you doing?' he asks.

'Texting your mum that I found you. And that we're back at mine, so she stops worrying.'

'So you're lying.'

'Yes, I'm lying,' I challenge him. 'Sometimes, when the truth is too explosive, you have to lie.'

Simo snorts. 'You and I both know that's bullshit.'

'Oh, so let me ask you this: in all the years we've known each other, you've never pretended? Never acted against your feelings? Never kept the truth far away from yourself because admitting it would've hurt too much?' He stares at me with cool disdain. 'Fine, just me then.'

The vein on his forehead pulses, 'No, not just you,' he

admits, 'but, Luca, there's a difference between not acting on your feelings and lying about your actions.'

I know he's right, and I have too much respect for him to point out that I never said I didn't do it. Omissions are lies in a different coat. 'That was the worst part. That I thought we were on the same page, when all this time you were putting on an act.'

I shake my head. 'It was never an act, Simo. When I realised what I'd done, I was so damn scared. I was angry at myself. I was ashamed. I just couldn't say that out loud. Like so many things.' The truth is that I'm still angry, still ashamed. A little less scared though, because the worst has come to pass.

'So why did you?' he asks.

'Huh?'

'What made you do it? Something must have changed.'

I think back to the morning when I typed out the message on my phone and submitted it to the council webpage. 'We'd both just turned seventeen. You were asleep next to me, and watching you like that made me feel happy. And safe. In that moment, I let myself feel how I'd secretly always felt about you. It was such a strong impulse that I couldn't keep it to myself.'

'I was right there. You could've told me.'

'That's easy to say, now that I've missed the chance. And who knows – if I had woken you up, I might still not have been able to tell you. So I chose a more anonymous way.'

'You didn't think to, I don't know, write a letter instead? Set up a fake profile and send me a DM?'

'It needed to be something drastic that I couldn't take

back. Something to force us into action.'

'It sure did.'

'I regret pressuring you. Pushing you so far out of your comfort zone that it hurt.'

He tilts his head, as if he's considering my words. 'I don't regret it.' I stare at him, confused. 'I hated the attention, don't get me wrong. But you're right, it forced me out of my comfort zone. It woke me up.' He meets my gaze and holds it. 'You woke me up.'

I can't tear my eyes away. Something begins to break through the messy feelings I've had since our falling-out. I don't dare to hope, but the way he looks at me has changed. The hardness has shifted into something softer.

'Simo, have you … picked up *The Current* lately?' I ask, because whatever is happening, he needs to have the full picture. And there's more than enough pictures of us in the town newspaper.

'*The Current?*' he repeats, and I can tell he's not following.

'It's all over social media too. Have you looked at your phone at all?' He shakes his head. 'Tuned into Lombard FM? Watched the regional news?' Still nothing. 'Then I think you should know—'

'I don't care. I don't care what they have to say. Come here.'

A tingling sensation travels up my spine. 'What?'

'I said, come here.'

I shuffle forward on my knees, but before I can fall back into a sitting position, his hands wrap around my neck and pull me forward. His grip is far from gentle. I struggle for balance, until my hands find his thighs, and the next moment, his lips are on mine. His hot breath fills my mouth and burns in my lungs. We don't break the kiss, not even to come up for air. He pulls me down, down on top of him. With my entire weight on him, he still tears at me. I've never known a kiss could hurt this good. Something breaks in me, wracks my bones, covers all of me in shivers. It's longing, built up over years, then doubled in the past three days, tripled under his touch, and, finally, released.

He winds his fingers through my hair, grabs shocks of it in his fists, as I sink mine in the soft flesh of his thighs, let them wander over burning skin. I might be crying, or maybe he is. All I can think, with our bodies pressed into the sand, and the fog erasing everything but us, is that Simo feels truer than anything I've ever known. He feels like home.

CHAPTER 26 – SIMO

When I wake in Luca's bed I don't know what time it is. The light that filters through the blinds grazes his parted lips and tells me that the day started without us. I slept like Snow White in her glass casket; I might as well have been dead. Considering this is the first decent sleep I've had this week, I'm not surprised. And judging by Luca's snores – the lightest snores known to mankind, more like a string of contented sighs – he hadn't fared differently.

His hair is endearingly unkempt; it sticks to his temples and stands up in all directions. I comb my fingers through it, because I don't have to resist any more. I smush my nose in the crook of his neck, the softest, safest place in the world. He hums, a sound that vibrates in his chest and wraps his arms around my torso.

'It tickles,' he whispers, when I cover the spot below his ear in kisses. 'Don't stop.'

It's exhilarating that I can do this now; scoop him up and kiss him without inhibition. I was stupid not to try it sooner.

Hunger eventually drives us out of bed. I drift into the lounge wearing one of Luca's hoodies and stop when I spot

Maz seated at the table. He's served up food. I smell fried mushrooms and eggs and fresh toast. Luca is beside me, barefoot and befuddled.

Maz is looking mighty smug. 'Aw, good morning, boys. Though strictly speaking it hasn't been morning for hours. How nice of you to finally join me.'

'You're not being weird at all,' Luca says, and drops into a chair. I follow his example.

'Well, I have the pleasure of informing you that not only have you missed an entire day of school, you also missed a short but delightful visit from your grandparents, who graciously let me know that they're "not angry, just disappointed". They also bestowed some parental advice on me, namely that if I'd raised you better, you'd have known not to bring champagne bottles near a pool.'

'So you're being a pain now, because you had to deal with them on your own?'

'Correct.'

'Thanks.'

'Anything for my son and his best friend. Boyfriend? Or are we so modern that we decry any form of labelling?'

I feel my neck going red, though something in me stirs at the sound of the word boyfriend. Luca's face shows a range of emotions, panicked at first, then pissed.

'Not quite. I find some labels incredibly helpful, such as "deranged parent" and "none of your business".'

'But the masses want to know! And now that the storm clouds have passed, I want to share all the newspaper clips I've saved for the occasion. In fact, I've already shared them with Poppy, but I thought you might want a look too.'

Luca groans and sends me a rueful look. 'I'm really sorry.'

'I'm not.' Maz grins and slaps a stack of newspapers on the table. 'Here we go: "The Most Dashing May Couple Yet", front page in the local newspaper. Look, it comes with a picture of you on the red carpet entering the charity ball, not that you can miss it, considering it takes up the entire page. A day later, the school newspaper drops a think piece on the use of charity balls – "Brandenburg Boys: Budding Activists or PR Props?" Another picture, of you and Simo leaving the ball, holding hands too! And my favourite: "DeLorca Represents: from the Humble Streets of Lombard to the Red Carpet". A bit of a mouthful, but they coined your official shipping label.'

I run my eyes over the articles in front of me. Now I get what Dad meant by 'everything that's going on'. A message on the noticeboard is one thing, but the news coverage is so blatant that I can see how it left my parents no choice but to intervene.

Luca is suspiciously still. He bites his lip and avoids my gaze, until I link my pinkie finger with his.

'DeLorca,' I say. 'I expected worse.'

The renewed attention makes me queasy, I won't deny it. But the fear that I experienced on that first day of school has reduced to a faint echo, now that my parents are on board, now that Luca and I are on the same page. I was afraid of their reaction, because their reaction is what matters.

'We look good,' Luca murmurs, and sends me a shy smile.

'We do,' I agree. I want to say that I don't care what anybody says, but that's not true. I do care that what ought to be mine isn't fully mine any more. And yes, Luca might have played a part in that, but he didn't write these headlines. Also, I'm not completely naive. When I showed up to the charity event with the Brandenburgs, it crossed my mind that people might pay attention. Especially the busybodies that make up most of Lombard's population. But I wasn't going to let that ruin time spent with Luca.

'Yes, you look so good that everyone is talking about you, and nobody is talking about my exhibition,' Maz says.

Luca is the face of disbelief. '*Your* exhibition?'

'OK, fine, Jacob's exhibition. But I'm in it.'

'I'm in it too. And it doesn't open till tomorrow, so.'

'Yes, but you're stealing all my thunder. Try to keep a low profile until it's over, yeah? Don't want another press ambush.'

'You're a pest.'

'Don't insult your dad when he's made you breakfast,' Maz says, and pushes back his chair. 'Now the pest must return to work. Without a trust fund, I simply can't afford to laze about all day.'

Luca snorts but obediently reaches for the bread basket and offers me the toast. Instead of leaving, Maz grins down at us.

'What?' Luca asks, frowning.

'You know, I'm really happy for you two. In case I've not said that.'

I can feel heat rising up my neck, but for once it's not shame making my ears burn. Maz's words feel like a big warm hug.

'Thanks, Dad.' Luca tries to hold back a smile, but it breaks out and lights up his face.

I want to lean in and kiss it from his lips, but I don't dare to do it in front of Maz.

He turns mock-serious and points a finger at us. 'I trust you to behave yourselves when I'm not looking. Keep it PG, yeah?'

'Says the man who got a girl pregnant at sixteen,' Luca retorts. He takes a criminally big bite of mushrooms on toast and doesn't see what I see. Maz's face slips. For an instant, his expression flickers, but it's back to normal before I can make anything of it.

'Don't try me, or I'll enforce an open-door policy,' he grumbles, and walks out.

Luca and I eat in silence. That is, we don't speak, only shovel food in our mouths, occasionally nicking it from each other's plate. It's almost exactly like before we kissed, only back then Luca wouldn't have wiped crumbs from the corner of my mouth and licked them from his fingertips. Something pensive steals into the look he sends me.

'What?' I ask, and receive a shake of the head in return. 'Come on, tell me.'

'Well ...' he says, and hesitates. 'It's about what Dad said.'

'The PG thing?'

'The decrying-any-form-of-labelling thing.'

'Ah. The best-friends-slash-boyfriends thing.'

'Yeah. That.' Luca looks awkward. He's kind of cute when he squirms, so I draw out the moment and wait till he can't take it any more. It takes two seconds until he cracks.

'Do you have any ... thoughts on it?'

'I mean, the being-boys part is true.'

Luca barely holds back an eye roll. 'Sure.'

'And we're friends.'

'Best friends, some would say.'

'So that part is also true,' I confirm, and nudge the scrambled eggs with my fork. When I look up, Luca pouts, and there might be smoke coming out of his ears. I can't tease him any longer, so I drop the fork, take the seat of his chair, and slide him close.

'The only thing that matters to me is that you trust me, and I trust you,' I say. 'That we tell each other the truth. That we care. And that we're good.' I wind my hands around the back of his knees and pull. He glides on to my lap, winds his fingers through my hair, makes my heart beat against my ribs. He gazes down at me, his eyes blue and earnest.

'And if that's what they call best friends,' I continue, 'so be it. But I also fancy you so damn much, and I think you maybe feel the same way. And if that's what they call boyfriends ...'

Luca leans in, almost touches his lips to mine, and stills, leaving a fraction of space. We hold out like that, and his breath dances across my skin, hits the tip of my tongue, mingles with mine.

'So be it,' I whisper, and he seals the kiss.

The exhibition is being held at the library. For the grand opening, Joni has stowed the movable bookshelves away, which creates an open space to mingle. I've saved myself a nook on the first-floor balcony, because I prefer observing to being observed. And Maz wasn't completely off; we are pulling attention.

Jacob's portraits of queer faces in Lombard are good, I

must admit. Not that I know anything about portraits or the technicalities that go into taking them. But from what I've seen, Jacob captured his subjects in a place of their choosing, like Maz in his cafe or Luca baking cookies, so they look at ease, despite the lens pointed at them. Which, to Jacob's credit, is no mean feat.

'I don't want to say much, because I'm not good at speeches, and I believe that photographs say more than words ever could,' he explained minutes ago, nervously pushing a strand of ginger hair out of his eyes. 'Photographs capture queerness without complicated terms. They show our facets but don't demand an explanation. I want to thank all of my subjects for letting me take your portraits. You shared your stories with me, and with the people of this town, and made us come together. It means a lot to me, especially as someone still new to this community. Thank you.'

To my surprise, Jacob's words ring true. In Luca's portrait, he's chaotic and golden, a boy who bakes. He's Luca the son, Luca the friend, Luca the boy who likes another boy. He's everything I can't explain. I believe poets do the same thing, using images to describe things that hold too much meaning to fit into everyday words.

From my vantage point, I watch people enter the library, timid at first, until Joni descends upon them with snacks and lemonade. Louise is down there, with her school reporter hat on, a camera around her neck and a notepad in her hands. Maz has his arm around Luca's shoulders and they're chatting with Daniel, while Olive chases Orlando around the room. In Daniel's portrait, Olive is dressed in a yellow and purple bandana and snoozes in his arms.

My attention snags on Mairi, who appears on the other side of the balcony. In her heels and with her braids piled atop her head, she has to duck to avoid the ceiling.

'Can I hide with you?' she asks. 'My mum just arrived, and as supportive as she is, I don't need a live reaction when she sees my portrait.'

I shuffle over to make space for her. 'It's a good picture though,' I say, thinking of Mairi in front of a wall graffiti that shows two figures locked in an embrace in a purple-tinted scene of paradise. 'I had no idea you did street art.'

'Lombard isn't exactly big enough to follow that passion without finding yourself on Pickering's naughty list. But it's a good creative outlet,' she explains. 'And thanks, anyway. I wasn't sure if I was ready, but I'm glad I chose to take part in the end. It's an important project. Not sure I would've figured out that I'm pansexual without it.' Her voice drops at those last words, as if she's still testing out how it feels to say them.

'I'm happy you did,' I say slowly, understanding that it must've cost her to share this with me, and aware that I can't return the compliment, not yet. Things with Luca are too new, and I don't want to think about how people in Lombard would react after everything that's happened since the summer.

My eyes find Luca again. He must have said something funny, because Maz is chortling away, until his gaze strays to the entrance and his laughter dies.

A couple steps into view, as always dressed head to toe in clothes that are completely out of place in a humble town like Lombard. Maz pulls Luca to his chest, a human shield to ward off his parents. Luca looks just as unsure but drops his guard when first Anna and then Graham give him a hug. Maz remains on edge, never letting go of Luca. He doesn't speak, only studies his parents as they study his portrait.

I know what's going through his mind. I'm familiar with that chest-crushing fear that your parents are about to see you for who you are and will think less of you for it.

Several seconds pass. I hold my breath all the while, then watch as Graham lifts his arm and covers Maz's hand with his, where Maz still grips Luca's shoulder. Graham gives a small squeeze before removing his hand again, and though the gesture may be small, I know Maz will remember it forever.

'You know, you played a part in why I agreed to do it,' Mairi says next to me. For a second, I'd forgotten she was there, and I blink at her in confusion. 'You and Luca kind of helped me open up to my mum,' she clarifies.

'What do you mean?' I ask, not sure I follow.

She plays with the beads in her hair while she chooses her words. 'I know that you two aren't really a thing, despite what the noticeboard said. But I still got caught up in the frenzy of it all, like most of Lombard. And it made me realise that maybe this town was more accepting than I gave it credit for.'

'Because people were shipping us?' I ask.

'Yeah, everyone was rooting for you. I wanted to show my support, so I sprayed a few hearts on the bike shed.' She smiles to herself, not realising that my mood is taking a tumble.

'Did you create any other … signs of support?' I ask. Something in my voice snags her attention, and when she sees my expression, the smile drops.

'I didn't, no. Though I know other students who did,' she says hurriedly. 'But I don't think they meant any harm.'

'Who else?' I follow her gaze downstairs, and at first I think she means Jacob, but it's the person he's talking to. 'Louise?'

'She drew a few hearts and made a bauble for the Christmas tree in the square. I thought it was cute.'

'It wasn't,' I say. 'What is wrong with people? Don't they have their own lives to worry about?'

There's a hint of guilt in Mairi's eyes, but she only shrugs. 'It gives them hope.'

'How?' I ask, trying to keep my voice from rising.

'Just take a look,' she says, and points to the people below. 'Visibility goes a long way. Seeing other people step into themselves gives you a sense that things are going to be OK. Especially if you can't fully be yourself, for whatever reason. It creates a safe space.'

'I'm a person, not a safe space.' I clench my hands around the bench to keep them from trembling.

'I know that. And I realise that things went a bit far.'

'A bit? While everyone was having a great time speculating about me and my feelings for Luca, I was panicking that our friendship would fall apart. It was shit.'

'I'm sorry, Simo,' she says, and I finally see understanding dawning on her face. 'If it helps, people only want the best for you and Luca.'

I have a few comebacks on the tip of my tongue – like if

they wanted what's best for us, they'd have stayed the fuck out of my relationship and projected their creepy fantasies on some fictional couple – but I'm not going to get into a fight with Mairi in the middle of her coming-out moment. I'd considered us friends. I excuse myself and find Luca among the crowd on the ground floor.

'Hey, I'm gonna go. I need a breather.' I want to take his hand, but my senses have gone into overdrive and the world feels too raw for touch.

'Oh, yeah. Let me just tell Dad—'

'No, you stay here. Celebrate. I need a moment for myself, to mull things over.'

'OK,' he says, and searches my face. He must sense my reservations, because he doesn't attempt to reach out. 'Call me though. If you want to hang out later.'

'I will,' I say, but I know that I'll get an early night. I crave the relief of letting my messy thoughts spill out into the notebook. The tenderness in Luca's eyes almost makes me change my mind, but I walk out of the library, glad to be breathing sea air.

When I get home, Dad is in the front yard, shifting pots around and adding new seeds to the flower beds. He once told me that some daisies need to be planted a year before they flower. I'm not sure I'd have the patience. I go into the kitchen, watch him brush dirt off the tiles outside. When he joins me a few minutes later, I've finished off three Nutella sandwiches. Hamza loved Nutella. Each birthday, he'd ask for a jar, and despite Mum's disapproval, she gave in every time.

'Don't let your mum see that,' Dad warns, and I dutifully

hide the spread at the back of the cupboard. He washes his hands and makes himself a coffee.

'Dad, why don't we remember Hamza?'

I almost expect him to flinch at the mention of my brother's name, but he only blinks slowly.

'What makes you say that?'

'There are no pictures of him in the house. And you guys don't talk about him, ever. If I bring him up, Mum changes the topic.'

Dad takes a sip of coffee before he replies. 'Your mum, she's a very private person. She keeps things close to her heart. Doesn't like to be vulnerable. A bit like you, you know? But she remembers him, every day. It's impossible not to.'

'So that's why we don't have pictures of him?'

'No, that's my decision. I don't like pictures. They freeze people in time. And Hamza – Hamza is free.' He looks out of the window as he speaks, but then his gaze lands on me. 'But if you want, if pictures are how you want to remember him, you can pick some from your mum's albums and hang them up. She has a lot of them. Or you could do what I do.'

'Which is?'

'Do you remember what Hamza's favourite flower was?'

For a second, my mind is blank, and I'm terrified that I've started to forget my brother without realising. Then: 'Daisies. He loved daisies.'

'He did. So I make sure they don't ever stop blooming.'

CHAPTER 27 – LUCA

It's the last Sunday of spring and dolphins have been spotted in the waters off Clifford Island. Every year, their arrival brings the first wave of tourists to Lombard, and you'd think Dad would be happy about the uptick in business, but he only complains. *Are we all ignoring the sharp teeth? Dolphins are killers, not puppies*, he says, and yet I know he'd far rather be chasing dolphins than having lunch with his parents.

Whenever Anna invites us over, Dad plans a trip to a theme park or suggests finally following Mum to New Zealand, then calls me a killjoy when I turn him down. I tell him he doesn't need to come, but he does anyway, like he still doesn't trust his parents enough to leave them alone with me.

'I don't know how you can taste anything with all that Parmesan,' Anna comments.

Dad's buried his food beneath a mountain of cheese, and while I, too, am a Parmesan fan, he has taken things a bit far.

'Gotta stifle the truffle taste somehow,' Dad says, and pulls a face. 'And I despise asparagus, so I used the cheese to hide it and now I can pretend it's no longer there, see?'

'Our chef's Michelin stars are wasted on you,' Graham says, sounding resigned.

Dad looks pleased with himself.

'I have an announcement to make,' Anna begins. 'I spoke to that Jacob boy, the little photographer, and he's agreed to let me buy your portraits.'

The smile slides off Dad's face. 'You can't have our portraits.'

'Of course I can. They're good portraits, and I don't have any recent pictures of you.'

'You bullied a seventeen-year-old boy into selling his first exhibition?'

'Your mother did not bully anyone,' Graham intervenes. 'She simply made him an offer, a very generous one, and he accepted. For a young artist so early in his career, that's quite the feat, you know.'

Dad looks to me, as if he expects me to take his side, but I don't see the problem. I think it's sweet of her, and great for Jacob, but I know Dad won't want to hear that.

'The exhibition made me remember something about you, Matthew,' Anna starts.

'It did?' Dad raises an eyebrow.

'Before Luca, before you left, you and Polly, you were always around that handsome boy from down the street. What was his name?'

While I perk up, Dad goes still. A muscle in his jaw twitches.

'You mean the Harper boy,' Graham confirms. 'Nice family, good breeding.'

'Rollo Harper, yes! I don't know how I didn't see it then, but you were quite smitten with him, no?'

'Just because you no longer live under the misapprehension

that your son is straight, it does not mean you get to poke around my love life. I've told you, it's off limits.' Dad's voice wavers, and though he tries to keep his emotions contained, I can tell something has upset him.

'Where do you think you'll hang our portraits?' I ask, to try to take the heat off Dad.

We manage to keep things civil even during the dessert course, mostly because Dad seems too caught up in his thoughts to speak.

'Come on, boys. We have something else to show you,' Anna declares once our plates are cleared and she leads us into the entrance hall. Beneath an arched skylight with a chandelier stands a massive table made from marble. On it rests a velvet box that she opens with dramatic flair.

'We want you to have these.' Graham nods to the two sturdy metal keys in the box. 'They're for the house.'

Dad looks puzzled. 'I thought you used face recognition.'

'They're symbolic, Matthew!' Anna scolds, like that should be obvious.

'We're off to Mauritius for the next month, so you may come and go as you please. We've designated a room for you upstairs, Luca,' Graham explains.

'It's blue, the same colour as your eyes,' Anna adds proudly.

Dad pouts. 'He gets a room the colour of his eyes and I get a rusty key?'

'Did you want a room, Matthew?' Grahams asks with a voice like he's speaking to a toddler.

'No, thanks, Father,' Dad replies, honey-sweet, 'I just like to complain.'

⋆ ⋆ ⋆

May Day arrives, and despite school being closed for the holiday, I'm up early on my usual mission to report the week's noticeboard message to Miss M.

I woke early to beat the crowds, because I'm not showing my face in town today. I've come up with a plan. They can appoint us May Couple, but they can't stop nature.

Though things have quietened down in the past couple months, Simo and I are still keeping a low profile. Everything about our friendship had become so public that we decided not to tell anyone that we're boyfriends. It's not like much has changed, except that we make out now. Which, admittedly, is hard to resist, so we've come up with a system where we leave our respective classes at the same time and shut ourselves in an empty classroom or a cubicle of the boys' toilets. Anywhere private will do.

As much as I like being a boy of many (one) secrets, I find it hard to keep a lid on my feelings, now that I'm no longer hiding them from Simo. I'm not denying my part in the whole mess, but that's why I won't be the one to bring up a potential soft launch. This town is so truly starved for excitement that a day later we'd be a headline again.

The good news is that the shipping has stopped. Mostly. The rumours are still rumouring, only more quietly. I suspect that Mairi put an end to the love hearts all over town, once she realised the pressure it put on Simo. I can't say that I had a blast with it exactly. But if you make a mess, you can only complain about it quietly, in your own head.

Now that it's spring, Paul is back in his kiosk by the promenade. He salutes me as I walk past. It's 7.16 a.m., and I can hear the clatter of Heloise's trolley before I reach the square. When she spots me, she winks. I immediately fear the worst. Heloise is not a winker.

With slow steps and dread in my chest, I approach the noticeboard, but I don't need to get close before the words rise above me.

SIMO AND LUCA ARE
IN LOVE

'It wasn't me!' I say when Simo picks up on the first ring.

'Luca—'

'I did not submit our names for the noticeboard!'

'I kno—'

'I say we find the town council ASAP and wring them out until they tell us who it was!'

'Luca, it was me!'

'What?'

'It was me. I went to the town council. I asked them to put it up.'

I gawp up at the noticeboard. The panic melts away and is quickly replaced with so much adoration for the boy I love that it makes my knees wobble. I decide to give up on standing for the moment and land on my bum. 'For real?'

'I was tired of kissing you in a toilet,' he says, and I'm glad I'm already sitting down.

'Was a bit smelly,' I agree.

'But also, kind of hot.'

I'm not going to deny it. 'But what about the May Couple?'

'What about it?'

'I thought we didn't want to be part of that.'

'Yeah, I stand by that.'

'OK, phew. Good. So we're still meeting at ten?' I ask.

'We're meeting at ten.'

'Don't get caught. They won't let you get away otherwise. Not after the stunt you've just pulled.'

'Don't forget to send Miss M the pic,' he says with a smile and hangs up.

Three hours later, we lock up our bikes and cross the causeway. Clifford Island rises out of the mudflats in front of us, and I hope to reach it without slipping or getting my shoes muddy. Simo has brought the parasol and picnic blanket, I'm responsible for the snacks. The May Day celebrations start at midday with a parade through town, but unfortunately we're not going to make it. We will be cut off from the mainland all day. Gotta love the ocean for its tides.

We find our spot by the remains of the stone wall, and I watch Simo wedge the parasol into the ground. A couple days of sun and already the freckles are popping up on his nose. When we're set up, I hand out the muffins I made this morning. Simo takes a bite and reveals not one but three books he has brought.

'Scared you'll run out?' I laugh.

'I like to be prepared,' he says. 'If I don't feel like a novel, I'll read the memoir. And if I don't want non-fiction, I switch to poetry. And if you get bored, you can borrow one.'

I decide not to comment, because he's cute when he tries to turn me into a reader. But I won't get bored. Not with a view of the sea and Simo in front of it, lost in a book. The wind pulls at his hair and a curl falls into his eyes. His dark brows are slightly furrowed, and the vein draws a line across his forehead. It's the most beautiful picture. I'm so lost in him that it takes me a while to notice he's stopped reading. Though the book remains open, his gaze is blank.

I tap him with my toes. He looks up, and whatever world he was in is fading from his eyes.

'Where did you go?' I ask softly.

'I was wondering ...' he begins, but seems unsure how to continue. 'It's not a very nice thought.'

'Few thoughts are. But sometimes we have to let the bad ones out, to keep them from haunting us.'

He pulls on the threads of the picnic blanket. With his shoulders bent, he looks gloomy. 'Do you think we would've met if Hamza hadn't died?'

I'm glad Simo isn't looking at me, because for a moment my face slips. I keep my breath even, despite the wave of grief that comes out of nowhere. Grief for a boy I've never met. Grief for another that I couldn't bear to be without.

'I think so,' I say, after a while.

'You do?' he asks, looking up. I read surprise and sorrow in his light brown eyes.

'There are two things I'm sure of: you, and my dad. I'm not sure what else I believe in, but I know I'd find you anywhere in the world. So, yes. We would've found each other, if not at seven years old, then at uni or later in life.'

He nods but stays quiet. We watch the waves pull in and out.

'I'm glad we met at seven,' he says eventually.

'I am too.' And then, because it feels right: 'I would've loved to meet Hamza.' It's the first time I've said his name. With my heart beating hard, I watch a smile appear on Simo's lips.

'You would've fancied him so much.'

'I would not.'

'All the girls at school did. He had a stack of badly spelled love letters.'

'Maybe they did. But I would've fancied you.'

He drops the threads he was picking apart and rests his head in my lap. We spend most of the day like this, barely moving as the clouds speed across a blindingly blue sky. Neither of us checks our phone, because we have all we need right here. I almost forget that there's a party going on without us, until the wind carries tunes of a brass band across the stretch of water. Simo is dozing, until I tickle him awake with a blade of grass.

'Why'd you do it?' I ask him.

He snatches the leaf from my hand. 'I told you, I didn't want to hide us away any longer.'

'Yeah, but if that was all, you could've just kissed me in the cafeteria.'

'I don't know – it doesn't smell much better there than in the loos.' I pluck a fresh blade of grass and flick it at his nose, because if he isn't giving me an answer, I'm going to be annoying. He grabs my hand and holds it tight. 'I wanted to take back what's mine. Change the narrative to what I want it to be, not what others have twisted it into.'

'Despite the reaction that will surely follow.'

'We know the reaction already. But this time, I'm the one who caused it.'

'I get that,' I say. 'People kept telling me how I felt. About you, about boys in general. Like they could see inside my head, when they had no idea.'

'Is that part of why you did it?'

'No, when I did it, it was all feels and no thought. I had a fat crush and no self-control.'

'That's pretty cute.'

'You were there that Monday. It was not cute! I was terrified of what I'd done.'

'I was terrified too,' he says, and my gut twists from the shame that I scared him so. 'But it also woke me up. I'd suppressed my feelings for so long.'

'We were silly,' I say.

'We were afraid,' he corrects, 'and alone. It's still a little scary. I mean, I'm glad we're here and I don't have to face the consequences of my actions for another eight hours.'

'Hmm. I can steal us more time.'

'Oh?'

'If you want more alone time with me, far away from the consequences you speak of, I can make that happen.'

He leans in and begins to kiss me, only to stop again. 'I want you to make it happen.' Then his lips are back on mine. Between the flowers tickling my neck, the sky above, and Simo on my tongue, I forget everything else. I only come back to my senses when he props himself up. His head blocks out the sun, but as long as I get to look at him every day, I have no need for it any more.

'This, though, is the main reason why I put the message on the noticeboard,' he says a little breathless.

'What is?'

'You. I wanted to tell you that I love you.'

As the words fall from his lips, my world tips. My brain gives out for a second, and all the blood rushes from my head.

'Oh my god,' I groan, and press my fingertips against my eyelids, trying to keep everything from spinning.

'What?' Simo asks, suddenly panicked.

'I … nothing.'

'No, tell me! You can't act like you're having a stroke when I tell you I love you for the first time!

'I just – I just got an instant boner.'

Simo is silent for several beats, and I open one eye to check on him. He is grinning. 'You did?'

'Stop laughing, Simo, it's not funny!' It's not that I'm not used to this happening, it's kind of an unavoidable side-effect of kissing Simo. But this is different. It's so much more intense.

'I gave you a love boner.'

I open the other eye too. 'Don't call it that. Don't call it anything. We're just going to ignore it until it goes away.'

'But it's the most romantic thing I've ever heard.'

'Leave me alone.'

'As you wish,' he says, and sits up.

'No, don't go!' I say, and pull him on to me. His silent laugh reverberates in my chest. We lie like this for so long I can't tell if he's nodded off again.

'Simo?'

'Hmm?'

'Before all this, before my grandparents and the noticeboard, I had dreams about this.'

''Bout what?'

'About being in love with you. I mean, that part was real, but I was so afraid of the truth I didn't allow it when I was awake. But asleep, I was defenceless.'

He winds his arms tighter around my waist. 'And now? Are you still afraid?'

With my thumb I trace the arc of his eyebrow, then I sink my hand into the waves of his hair. It's warm and soft beneath my touch.

'No. Now it's just fact.'

CHAPTER 28 – SIMO'S NOTEBOOK

how to drink the moon

I kiss him
set my lips to his.
I drink him the way I drink moonlight
cup my hands
fill the mould with water
lift it to my mouth
take gulp after gulp of the silver light
that flits across the surface.
I drink until there's nothing left
I lick each finger
I
cup my hands
and fill the mould with water.

SUMMER

EPILOGUE

When the bell above the door announces my arrival at the cafe, Dad's head whips around. He looks guilty, like I caught him doing something illegal, but he's only sharing a coffee with Daniel.

'Hey, Luca,' Daniel says, his voice warm. I don't know what it is with that man, but he's always zen, like nothing in the world can stress him.

'Good date?' Dad asks, and waggles his eyebrows. I texted him last night that Simo and I would make use of the empty manor and avoid the May Day beach party. It would have felt rude not to put my grandparents' house key to use.

'I could ask you the same thing,' I retort.

'This is not …' Dad huffs and points from him to Daniel. 'We're not on a date.'

They look pretty cosy though, sat so close that their knees are definitely touching beneath the table. Also, they're the only people in the room. Total date vibes.

'You know, Maz,' Daniel says as he gets up, 'if you ever did want to go on a date, just say the word.' He strolls to the door where I'm still standing and turns back to Dad. 'You know where to find me.'

Dad watches him leave in a daze, until I clear my throat.

'Not another word,' he warns, his head the colour of a warning light.

I feel smug and don't try to hide it.

'You still haven't answered my question,' Dad points out.

'What?'

'Come on, did you do something dirty?' he asks with an evil glimmer in his eyes.

'Dad!'

'Did you or did you not sit on your grandmother's antique sofa in your street clothes? Please tell me you ate food without using side plates. Or cutlery!'

I sigh. 'We had breakfast in the library. We used side plates, but we were barefoot, if that makes you happy?'

'Your grandparents would hate that. So it makes me happy.'

What I don't tell Dad, because the memory is too raw, is how Simo kissed me awake, then told me he had an idea. Drowsy as I was, I let him lure me into the garden and all the way to the little private cove. But then I protested – just because it's May and the sun is out does not mean the sea is warm enough for skinny-dipping. In the end, though, Simo got what he wanted. And you kind of forget the sting of the cold ocean when you're making out in it with a boy you love.

I'm pulled from the daydream when a motor roars out on the street and a vintage Porsche pulls up in front of the cafe.

'What are they doing? They can't park here,' Dad says. He throws his towel on the counter, ready to put the driver in their place, when the car door opens, and a man gets out. He looks like the type of guy who holidays in Monaco and owns a racehorse; with a perma-tan and a spring in his step. In the sun, his polo shirt is blindingly white. He removes a pair of sunglasses to look at the sign above the shop, revealing a handsome face with sharp angles.

Dad freezes, and the sense of doom is instant. The look on his face is the same one he wore when Anna first stepped into the cafe. I don't like it. Whatever is happening, I want it not to.

I can't stop the chime of the bell or the stranger entering the cafe. He scans the empty tables before his gaze comes to rest on Dad. His eyes are a startling shade of blue.

'Maz,' he says with a deep voice, 'you're looking well.' He sounds polite, but I swear he's checking Dad out.

I turn to see Dad's reaction, and to my surprise, his eyes are shooting daggers.

Then the stranger notices me, and I might be imagining it, but his confidence flickers. 'And you must be Luca. Your grandparents have told me all about you.'

'Leave,' Dad says. 'Now. Get out!'

The stranger shows no sign that he heard Dad. He only stares at me, half-puzzled, half-smiling.

'And who are you?' I ask, when no one offers an explanation.

'I'm Rollo, and I guess I'm your dad's ex,' he says with nonchalance. 'But I'm also your mum's ex. And to you that makes me …'

'Nothing,' Dad growls. 'You are nothing to him.'

The man shrugs. 'Either that, or I'm your father.'

ACKNOWLEDGEMENTS

No words can express my gratitude to Ben. Thank you, Stella, Laura, Ash, Kathi, Matt, Chris and my incredibly supportive families. Big thanks to Gyamfia and Ellie for shaping this book. Thank you to the freelancers and teams at ANA & Bloomsbury, and everyone behind the scenes in Editorial, Design, Sales, M&P, Rights, Production and more: Sarah, Tim, Emily, Danielle, Jessica, Talya, Thy Bui and Melania. Thank you to my four-legged emotional support heroes Brontë, Olive and Bryan.

LONGING TO KNOW HOW SIMO AND LUCA'S STORY CONTINUES?

LOOK OUT FOR THE SEQUEL AND RETURN TO LOMBARD IN 2027!

ABOUT THE AUTHOR

Kai Spellmeier is a German author currently living in England. He has published several books in Germany, including YA novels and non-fiction, and he has been blogging about books on Instagram for many years. *Boy Friends* is his English language debut.